A CONFLICTED WOMAN

A CONFLICTED WOMAN

TB MARKINSON

Published by T. B. Markinson

Visit T. B. Markinson's official website at lesbianromancesbytbm.com for the latest news, book details, and other information.

Cover Design by Erin Dameron-Hill / EDHGraphics

Edited by Kelly Hashway and Jeri Walker

CHAPTER ONE

"*W*hat in the…? Did a Toys'R'Us explode in here?" I waded carefully through the pile of toys, party supplies, and who knew what else only to skirt the perimeter of the dining room, terrified I'd never make it out alive.

Sarah and Maddie glared at me from where they sat at the dining room table. Maddie had her hair in a makeshift bun on top of her head, while Sarah used her stylish workout sweatband to keep the hair off her face. Even with the air conditioning on, it was still sweltering. The dog days of summer were in full swing, and our ancient AC unit couldn't cope.

"You're here, finally. We need more of these." Sarah hoisted a party blower to her mouth and let loose, but it didn't inflate. "Two are broken."

I surveyed the table, which looked to be an assembly line of sorts. Ladybug wooden maracas, zoo coloring books, rubber ducks, glitter sticky hands, rainbow Slinkys, toy binoculars, bubbles, flashlight key chains, plastic ball puzzles, squishy balls with emojis on them, foam animal masks, and whistles on spiral bracelets. I knew it was useless to point out the blowers weren't needed given the whistles. In the corner of the room sat a helium tank for the balloons, which were not yet inflated. On the floor next to it were stacks of boxes containing *decorate your own* tea party sets. Overflowing shopping bags obscured the view of other whatnots.

Had Sarah lost her mind? Money wasn't a huge issue for us considering our sizable trust funds, but what would the guests think? And, if she planned to throw elaborate parties for every birthday, I cringed thinking about what their sixteenth would be like. Bentleys? Aston Martins? Spaceships? She'd mentioned recently it was weird not working and she missed the thrill of planning her classes, staff meetings, and coaching. Was this her way of filling the void? This, however, wasn't the time to bring up Sarah's over-the-top birthday plans for the twinkies. I took a deep breath.

"Okay, where are the party blowers?" I asked.

Maddie slanted her head and spoke slowly, "We're out. You have to make a run."

Peering through tiny neon orange binoculars, I asked, "What are you doing, anyway?"

"Are you glancing down my shirt?" Sarah asked, playfulness in her expression.

"Pul-lease, I can't see anything with these." Although, her spaghetti strapped tank allowed access from my viewpoint. I put the binoculars back on the table, leveling my eyes on Sarah and conveying she hadn't answered my question.

She blew stray hairs off her face, shaking her head. "Making gift bags for the twinks birthday."

"Why do the twins need so many? Last time I counted, there are only two of them and…" I started counting the bags on my fingers.

"Twelve of these." Maddie, our dear friend and honorary aunt of the twinks, hoisted a zoo-themed gift bag. "And we only have ten functioning blowers. See the problem?"

Sarah tugged on the front of her sweaty shirt, sighing for

the umpteenth time about the lack of air circulation in the older mini-mansion she'd insisted we purchase a handful of years ago.

"These are the bags for the kids who are coming tomorrow," Sarah filled in the blanks.

Maddie pressed her nose with an index finger and extended the other toward me. "That's right. You didn't have friends growing up, so you don't know birthday party etiquette."

I flipped Maddie the bird, although her comment wasn't all that far off the mark. Petries weren't known for their social skills.

She laughed.

Sarah gave Maddie a *play nice* look. "Please, Lizzie. Can you run to the store? The one in the mall so they'll be the same as these. Take a broken one so you can match it *exactly*." She pronounced the last word with emphasis, probably to let me know cheating wouldn't be the best course of action given the amount of effort she'd put into the party.

Secretly, I wished Prime Air's fleet of drones was fully operational, saving me from a trip to the mall, which was one of my versions of hell. From my personal experience, no good ever came from going to a mall. Suppressing the need to say any of this aloud, I tucked the blower into my shorts pocket. "Of course. Anything else while I'm out?"

"Wine. Lots and lots of wine," Maddie said.

Before exiting the room, I kissed the top of Sarah's head. "Dinner?"

Both Maddie and Sarah looked at each other as if I'd asked them if they needed oxygen to live. "Yes," they both said.

"Any special requests?" I fished my car keys from my pocket.

"Pizza. Extra cheesy and meaty," Maddie blurted. "I'll place the order. All you'll have to do is pick it up." She eyed me like she was determining if I was capable of performing this task without messing it up.

"Chinese," Sarah said. Without uttering the words, she tapped the screen on her iPad to place the order.

"Party blowers and pick up pizza and Chinese." I ticked each off with a finger.

"Wine, that's the most important," Maddie added, "after the party blowers, of course."

"Of course," I parroted, not willing to suggest the twinks couldn't care less about all the fuss.

* * *

IN THE STORE, I held the broken blower at eye level while I wandered the aisles looking for more just like it, except functioning. I'd never hear the end of it if I purchased more defective toys.

"Professor Petrie?"

I turned to face a student from last semester. "Oh, hi, Marjorie."

The young woman blushed. "Can I help you?"

"Do you work here?" I blurted, before taking in the toy store logo on her white polo. "Uh, stupid question."

"Didn't you always say in class there are no such things as stupid questions?" Her smile was infectious.

"I think in this case…" I pointed to her shirt, before the horror sunk in. Marjorie, a former student, had a rack befitting a porn-star whose nickname was Triple D.

Maybe she assessed my *deer in headlights*—clearly, not the best word given the situation—look and moved on to the matter at hand. "Oh, it's broken." She took the blower from my hand as if it was a baby bird in need of tender loving care. "The poor thing."

"Y-yeah," I stuttered. "I need replacements for gift bags."

"Are you having a birthday party?" The beginnings of a

blush appeared on her cheeks, and she shifted on her feet. "My turn to ask a stupid question."

Feeling even more uncomfortable in my own skin than normal, which I chalked up to the stress of starting a new semester soon, I ignored the last statement. "Yes, not mine, though. For the twinkies—twins. I have two one-year-olds. That's hard to say in one go." Feeling like an ass for saying *two* after twins, I forced a smile, which I hoped conveyed I needed help. Serious help.

"Let's go find them in the party favors aisle." Her bemused eyes skimmed all the LEGO boxes.

I tailed her, with my head down, wondering how I could salvage my pride. Here I was, a history professor who was clearly an inept toy store shopper.

Marjorie's eyes zeroed in on a bag of blowers. "Here ya go. Anything else?"

My eyes glazed over, and I fumbled around in my brain for words, any words. Not able to speak, I shrugged.

Her expression claimed she thought I was adorable in a helpless way. "How about these?" She held up a packet of temporary tattoos and SpongeBob playing cards.

"Cool. I need twelve, I think." I laughed, shuffling in my flip-flops. "I'm sorry. My wife usually takes care of these things."

Her face brightened. "No worries. That's why I'm here. My little brother turned two last week."

"Really?" My voice cracked.

"Half brother. My dad remarried a few years ago. I'd been the only child until then."

I couldn't tell if Marjorie welcomed the new sibling or not. "Ah." I nodded, adding, "Mine remarried last November."

"Maybe you'll have new siblings soon, then."

"My half brother just graduated from high school," I said, immediately wishing I hadn't. Maybe this was the reason my parents hadn't allowed me to attend birthday parties when I was a kid. Family secrets burbled out of me. Although, in all likelihood, Marjorie didn't know my family or my mom's incessant need for the ladies at the club to respect her.

"Fast work with the half sibling." She avoided my eye, making me wonder what she really thought.

"Something like that. Life can be… complicated." I shrugged again, obviously the one form of communication that worked in my favor.

"Tell me about it. I'm twenty-three, still in college, graduation not in sight, and working two part-time jobs while amassing a sizable student loan that will take a lifetime to pay off."

Never would have guessed she was twenty-three. Twenty tops. All I could think to say was, "Life." My ineptitude at casual conversation was a good indicator it was best to keep my interactions with students, current and former, confined to the classroom. But there was a nagging emotion I couldn't put my finger on that nibbled on the edges of my brain. Marjorie, either her personality or her youthful too-good-to-be-true looks made me realize I was rapidly approaching middle age. I hadn't considered myself the type of woman who would care about that, but maybe I did.

Marjorie didn't seem put off by my inability to pontificate further on her woes. She appeared to embrace my awkwardness. Smiling, she asked, "Anything else?"

"No, you've been great."

Marjorie led me to the register, quickly ringing up the purchases.

I paid with cash, feeling awkward, even though the total was less than two large pizzas, considering she'd mentioned her debt. Perhaps I was overanalyzing everything per usual.

"I hope the party is a smashing success." She offered a somewhat bashful grin. "I'm jealous. The only parties I get invited to involve kegs and frat boys, and I'm so done with both."

"If you're in my neighborhood, stop by," I joked, because what adult in their right mind would want to attend a birthday party for children?

"Really? It would be nice to get to know other..." Her face burned cherry-popsicle red. Clearing her throat, she asked, "Can I bring my little brother?"

"Yes, of course." Alarms blared in my head, but I managed to supply my address and time of the party. What option did I really have? Was it possible that Marjorie had a crush on me? That couldn't be the case, could it? What was she about to say? Other what...? Daughters whose fathers remarried and had second families? Maybe she was desperate for any type of attention since the birth of her half brother after being the only child for two decades. That made a lot more sense than a hot girl having the hots for me, the clueless one, as everyone liked to say. Although, did I really think she wanted to start a ditched daughters support group? Had I given any indication that I was interested? She was beautiful and, if my memory served correctly, quite intelligent. But a fling with a former student, or anyone, was simply out of the question. I'd heard stories from other professors about these types of situations, but never did I contemplate it'd happen to me. Whether Marjorie had a crush on me or simply needed any type of attention, I just invited her to the twin's one-year birthday party, and from the evidence of Sarah's party planning, she was having a crisis of... what? Feeling inadequate? Lacking confidence? Being bored out of her mind? How would Sarah react to me inviting a hot twenty-three-year-old? An uncomfortable social situation that could cause a ripple in my marriage was reason 456 of why I hated going to the mall.

This was the worst possible moment to upset Sarah, whose behavior of late had been troubling me.

I googled how to cheer up a stay-at-home mom. The ideas were chocolate, the occasional glass of wine, exercise, girls' night out (need to enlist Maddie), downward dog, which apparently is a yoga move, splurge—that could have explained the party, but, more likely, it meant Sarah should splurge on herself... I continued reading: hire a babysitter and date your mate. Now that was something I could help with. And, I could merge the splurge category by hopping into Victoria's Secret before heading home.

In the parking lot, after getting a few surprises for Sarah, I texted to explain the rudiments of the situation, leaving out my suspicions, and waited in the car to receive the demand to buy more supplies. Surprisingly, I got the all clear along with the news that they'd purchased two extra bags just in case two random toddlers crashed the twinks party. Did that mean my rush to buy replacement blowers was for the emergency stash and if I hadn't gone to the store, there wouldn't have been a need for said stash and I wouldn't have blundered into inviting Marjorie?

CHAPTER TWO

*E*than's six-year-old daughter, Casey, and two other girls around the same age raced by, nearly upsetting the tray of food I was transporting from the kitchen to the table set up on the edge of our backyard.

"I'd tell her to settle down, but you and your wife are to blame, really." Ethan, in khaki shorts, flip-flops, and a black Dune T-shirt with two blue moons—or possibly planets—and a red sky, seized the two-liter Coke bottle that was about to topple off the tray onto the grass.

"How do you figure that?" I placed the bowls of chips, salsa, fresh fruit, veggies, and ranch dip on the table already over-loaded with other summer picnic offerings.

"In my experience, soda and rock candy sticks make for dangerous kid experiences."

I eyed Casey and her buddies sitting at a table under an oak tree, decorating their own teacups. "They're completely out of control. Next, they'll be asking for whiskey shots to add to their tea." A thought struck me. "I would like to note that we put out healthy food, water infused with berries and mint leaves, and lemonade with agave nectar instead of sugar."

Ethan, ignoring the children and my comments, slugged my side. "Who is that?"

I followed his eyes, crestfallen that Marjorie actually came. "A former student with her half brother," I mumbled in an effort to blunt the reality of her presence as I tried to conjure up ways to shield Marjorie from Sarah's view.

Marjorie, in a halter top and shorts that barely classified as a garment, gripped her brother's hand. The boy, a redhead, stared wide-eyed. I could relate to him.

Making my way over, I had to suppress a groan, sensing Ethan was hot on my trail. My married best friend, who was teetering on relationship woes due to his wife wanting another child, couldn't control the urge to chat up my former bomb-shell student. It was as if the gods deposited Marjorie into my life at this moment to complicate the hell out of it. Wasn't having an air conditioner on the fritz during a heat wave a big enough challenge? Although, the air conditioner was a much easier fix and I'd already called a technician. As a Petrie, I excelled at calling experts, and I'd already programmed the company's name into my phone. Was there a relationship expert I could have on speed dial?

"Marjorie, so good of you to come." I hunched down to greet the boy. "Hello, there."

The boy buried his face in Marjorie's legs.

She laughed. "This is my baby brother, Max."

Sarah, the perfect hostess, noticed the new guests and left her mom's side. "Hi, I'm Sarah."

Marjorie shook Sarah's hand, but before Marjorie could speak, I jumped in. "This is Marjorie and her brother, Max." I threaded an arm around Sarah's waist. "And this is my beau-tiful wife, Sarah."

Maddie appeared out of nowhere. "I'm Maddie."

"Jorie."

"Jorie and Max," Sarah said as if engraving the names into

her memory bank. She proceeded to get to Max's level to officially greet him, pulling me down to do the same when Max stepped away from his big sister. He had kind green eyes and a timid heart-melting smile.

After ruffling his hair, I straightened. "I didn't know you went by Jorie," I said, wondering why she never corrected me in the past and why she chose to do so now. Another tick in the *be wary* column.

Marjorie laughed, her eyes boomeranging around all the party madness. "It's my way of rebelling. Everyone in my family has a name that starts with the letter M."

"I'd fit right in, then," Maddie said with a smile that could only be described as lecherous.

Jorie furtively gave Maddie, whom Gabe liked to call the blonde-bombshell, the once-over. If she was attempting to be discreet, she could use some pointers. Not from me, though. Clearly her attendance at the twins' party was proof positive I also needed flash cards on how to act in certain situations.

After a pregnant pause, although, I suspected she wasn't doing so for effect, she said, "I do believe Maddie qualifies."

Maddie's smile didn't appease the unease swirling inside over how Sarah would react to Jorie. Besides, Maddie was involved with Gabe, who was my half... no stepbrother and my half brother's older sibling. I hadn't met either of them until last year when Dad revealed his secret relationship with Helen. I squinted one eye, ascertaining if I got that right. What was Gabe's official title when it came to the twinks? Step-uncle? Did that make Allen a half uncle? A term I'd never heard or seen in print.

Jorie said something that caused Maddie to laugh, knocking me out of my head.

Ethan hadn't offered his hand, remaining mute, but his eyes roved over Jorie in a way that made me want to punch him in the nose. His wife was fewer than ten feet away.

"You're one of Lizzie's former students? Which class?" Sarah asked in a polite tone that I knew wasn't actually polite. Not that Jorie would pick up on it. I hoped at least.

Jorie smiled at me. "I was in Dr. Petrie's Weimar history class."

"Lizzie, please." My cheeks prickled, which usually happened whenever someone complimented me, although I feared Sarah would read it incorrectly. Maybe I could ask my former therapist for a note explaining how I'd mentioned never knowing how to handle positive attention after growing up with the Scotch-lady, who had dished out negativity like it was candy on Halloween.

"She's the best professor I've had. I almost switched majors." Jorie's adoring look spooked me.

"From what?" Maddie asked.

"International business." Jorie reassuringly patted the top of her brother's head as Casey and her crew zoomed past blowing bubbles and squealing.

"That would be quite the switch." Maddie gave me an appraising smile that made me stop breathing for a moment. If Maddie had picked up on the potential crush situation, no doubt Sarah had. I replayed the scene in my head when Sarah met Jasmine, a graduate student I briefly assisted before the twins birth at the behest of Dr. Marcel. My gorgeous and loving wife could become irrational when it came to me interacting with beautiful women. The time I made a pass at Maddie eons ago undoubtedly hadn't helped matters.

With her sparkling eyes on me, Jorie said, "Dr—Lizzie is that good."

Was she overtly flirting with me in front of my wife and friends at my twins' birthday party? I'd only known one woman in my life with bravado like this, and I never wanted to see *that* woman—or a copycat-version—again.

Or was I channeling Sarah and I should assume Jorie was

innocent until proven guilty? What evidence should I look out for? Standing too close? Casual touches lasting a moment too long? Excessive compliments?

A different handful of sugar-crazed kids raced by, chasing after an errant beach ball. Did none of the parents insist on them eating and drinking the healthy choices? I mentally flicked my hands in the air. Why did we even try?

Max wormed back into his big sister's legs.

Sarah knelt down once again. "Max, would you like some lemonade, berry water, or juice?" She glanced up at Jorie to gauge if that was okay. After receiving a nod of approval, Sarah put her hand out for the boy, who took it. The two of them wandered to the drink and snack table.

"Sarah, the shy-kid whisperer." I smiled, perhaps too widely, at my wife, who observed our new guest over her shoulder with curiosity.

Maddie rubbed her hands together. "Would you like something to drink, Jorie?" With that, Maddie steered the curvy brunette to the adult drink station.

My father and his wife of less than a year, Helen, approached, each with one of the twins on their hips.

"I think both need a change," Helen said, smiling in her grandmotherly way.

I reached for Freddie, but my father shook his head. "You have enough on your plate. Helen and I can manage."

They went inside.

"Your dad changes diapers?" Ethan asked, reminding me of his presence.

"Apparently." I doubted he had ever changed mine, leaving it to the nanny he'd hired to save me from having the Scotch-lady attend to me in any way.

Ethan, the fluid hater, pranced about as if he'd stepped into a cobweb, his lanky arms and legs adding to his ridiculousness.

His fluid aversion was another reason why his relationship with his wife was on the brink of collapse.

I rolled my eyes but turned my attention to the matter at hand. "On a scale of one to ten, how much trouble am I in?"

Without prompting, Ethan glanced at Jorie. "Twenty."

"What should I do?" I whispered, keeping Sarah in my line of sight.

"You should have asked that before inviting a former student who's majorly crushing on you to your children's birthday party." He brushed one index finger over the other, looking very much like the teacher he was.

"It just happened, and what proof do you have that she has a crush? I mean really, she could be super sweet to everyone and attend birthday parties every weekend."

"Sure. Happens to me all the time." Ethan blew on his nails and then buffed them on his shirt. "Students and their crushes," he said in a tone that implied he had no experience in the matter.

"No, seriously. Sarah sent me to the toy store. Jorie works there—"

"Now that's what I call customer service!"

I groaned. "Whatever I say, you're not going to listen."

"I'm channeling Sarah to help you prepare." He splayed his slender fingers on both hands and jostled them up and down in front of his face as if attempting to tap even further into Sarah's mindset. "Shall we ask for Lisa's help?"

Before I could respond, Ethan called his wife over.

"Who's the brunette everyone's eye-fucking? Me included?" Lisa asked, completely unprompted, tossing her red locks in an alluring way, purposefully trying to catch Jorie's eye. I wasn't sure if this was meant to rile Ethan. Like she was advertising she had options. Was Lisa bi?

Not wanting to delve further into the Ethan and Lisa rollercoaster relationship, I focused on my own problem. "Fuck," I muttered under my breath.

Ethan grinned and then whispered behind his hand, filling Lisa in. At least they got along well enough to gossip. Maybe there was hope yet.

She burst into laughter, quickly smothering it with her palm. "Your dad's wife owns a flower shop, right?"

Confused by the change of topic, I stuttered, "Y-yeah. She made all the flower arrangements. There's a lion, tiger, dog, and butterfly." I pointed to the carnation creations on the various tables spread out over the backyard. "She'd probably give you the family discount."

"The white dog is my favorite. The black button eyes and nose are adorable." Ethan's smile provided a glimpse of him twenty something years ago.

Lisa ignored us. "Good news about the discount, and I highly recommend buying everything she has in stock, because you're in the doghouse. And I'm not referring to the cute one the flower dog lives in."

"But—"

Both cut me off by elevating their hands in the air.

"I—"

They repeated the *don't bother* hand gesture and wandered off in the direction of their daughter, who was shrieking as she and her friends ran through a sprinkler on the far end of the yard.

"Lizzie!"

I wheeled about to greet Tiffany, who preferred being called Tie, Peter, and their baby girl, Dominique, affectionately called Demi. "Hey."

Peter rumpled his brow at my lackluster greeting. Tie took no notice and said, "Sorry we're late. Blame your brother."

"Oh, I do. For everything," I deadpanned.

Peter actually laughed. "This place is a madhouse." He

surveyed the groups of people, young and old, the different craft sections Maddie and Sarah had set up, the bouncy castle, blow-up pool with colorful balls for the little ones to play in, and random toys, streamers, and popped balloons strewn over the rain-parched lawn. "Glad we didn't have twins."

"Most of this is for the guests," I pointed out, knowing Peter was quite similar to me in one regard: not having had a normal childhood.

"Still, every day I say a silent prayer we didn't end up like you." His tone didn't imply he was joking, but I picked up on a twinkle in his eye. It was a new thing we did, teasing each other.

Gandhi, our neighbor's Yorkie, strolled by wearing a silver bow tie. I smiled at George, Gandhi's proud owner and a widower in the neighborhood Sarah had adopted.

Tie drilled her elbow into Peter's side. "What a terrible thing to say!"

"Are Kit and Courtney coming?" I directed to Tie since Kit was her sibling and Peter liked him as much as I imagined he'd enjoy having a prostate exam.

"Nope, my brother is off gallivanting in the south of France, and Courtney is… working, maybe. It's hard to keep up with them." She handed my niece to me and traipsed off in search of a glass of wine.

Kit and Courtney had been engaged for some time now with no signs of actually planning a wedding. The reason: Kit was gay, but relished pretending he wasn't as if playing a game. Courtney enjoyed stringing her well-to-do relatives along with the faux relationship out of revenge for forcing her into the family business.

It was hard for me to keep up with my ever-expanding family and social connections. Recently, I'd started a family tree and spreadsheet.

I turned my attention to Peter. "Just a stab in the dark but

I'm guessing you're late because you were golfing," I said, nuzzling the top of Demi's head with my chin.

"With clients." He put a finger out for Demi to hold. "Right, baby girl? Daddy was with clients?"

I held my niece, bobbing her up and down. "Does anyone ever believe Daddy?"

He started to speak but opted to shrug in defeat. He blinked. Not once but five times before uttering, "Who's that?"

I didn't need to turn around. "Trouble."

"Yours or mine?" he asked with a mischievous twist of his lips.

"If you could make it yours, I'd be eternally grateful."

Straightening, he said, "I'll see what I can do."

I about-faced and muttered after him, "I wasn't serious."

"About?" Sarah asked with a playful *gotcha* expression.

Not speaking, I waved my free hand at Peter, who had corralled Jorie and Maddie against two Aspen trees.

Sarah rolled her eyes and then kissed the top of Demi's head. "It's time for cake."

I handed Demi to Sarah. "On it, beautiful!"

Inside the kitchen, I found Janice, a friend from my grad school days, and Bailey, Janice's cousin and our new part-time nanny, which incidentally was one of the *cheer up a stay-at-home mom* solutions I'd stumbled upon yesterday. "Just who I was looking for," I said.

Peering out the window, Janice asked, "Who's that talking to Peter and Maddie?"

I rubbed my face. "No one."

Janice circled a finger in the air. "You did something wrong. You have the guilty hunch."

Bailey nodded in agreement.

"It's time for cake." I pressed my hands together.

"What'd you do?" Janice pushed.

"Cake!"

Janice looked at Bailey. "This is going to be entertaining."

"Cake!" I shouted as if I had a one-word vocabulary.

"Who was the evilest Nazi leader? Hitler? Goring? Goebbles? Himmler?" Janice beamed, odd given the context, but not so much if you really knew her obsession with teasing me. Not to mention both of us had studied early twentieth-century German history.

I stood my ground, shouting, "Cake!" once again.

Sarah came inside, her face flush from the heat. "What's going on?"

"Watch this." Janice looked to the ceiling for inspiration. "The worst dictator? Hitler, Stalin, or Mao?"

"Cake!"

Bailey shook her head, nearly dislodging her tortoiseshell glasses. Pushing them back in place with her finger, she said, "I think the heat has caused Lizzie to lose her marbles."

With a hand on her hip, Sarah said, "She's panicking because she somehow invited a former student, who obviously wants to get into her pants, to the party."

Janice and Bailey twirled around as if on the fastest merry-go-round. "Her?" they asked in unison.

"Her name's Marjorie. Goes by Jorie." Sarah removed the individual cupcakes from the bakery box, setting them on a platter, careful to mix them up so not all the hippo, tiger, giraffe, zebra, elephant, and monkey cupcakes were segregated. At least Jorie's presence distracted Sarah's mind from her usual, and frankly ludicrous, comments about her nonexistent extra pounds when around sweets.

Janice removed one of the twin's mini-cakes from a box, and Bailey removed the other. Both had purple icing with monkeys on top and one stick with a large marshmallow on the end in lieu of candles.

Through the window, I spied Rose, Sarah's mom, and Helen

situating Ollie and Freddie in their high chairs. Dad held Demi. The partygoers gathered around in anticipation.

Sarah, with the silver tray in her hand, asked, "Have you recovered enough to lead everyone in 'Happy Birthday'?"

Playfully, I chirped, "Cake."

She winked at me in that way of hers that put me at ease. Really, I couldn't be blamed for a hot chick digging me. Or did Sarah's wink imply Jorie didn't have a crush on me, the almost middle-aged mother of twins? Either way, I chalked it up to a win.

I led the group outside, bursting into a rousing rendition of the song.

* * *

MOST OF THE guests had left when Sarah rallied the remaining family members to clean up the mess.

Two employees, who had set up the blow-up castle, returned to take it away.

I opted to join Gabe and Allen's team.

"Great party," Gabe said. He was Helen's eldest son who technically wasn't a blood relation, but we'd grown close as of late.

"Thanks. It was all Sarah's and Maddie's doing."

"Now, that's sad to see." Allen, my half brother whom I'd only met last year, watched the castle slowly deflate.

Gabe slung an arm over his shoulders. "It's okay, Bro. You have plenty more bouncy castles in your future."

Allen shoved off Gabe's arm. "Whatever. Someone had to chaperone Ollie and Freddie inside the castle."

"And I had to rescue them when they started screaming their heads off and you were preoccupied chatting up Bailey." Gabe laughed.

"Money well spent," I grumbled, leaning over to pick

balloon remnants off the ground and toss them into a black garbage bag.

"Are you referring to the bouncy castle or the self-help books Sarah gave Allen to help him conquer his shyness and lack of organizational skills?" Gabe quickly stepped away from his red-faced brother. "Just kidding, Allen. I'm proud of you for hitting on Lizzie's new nanny."

Allen turned his back on both of us, taking the higher road or possibly retreating inside his bookish brain.

I admonished Gabe with a finger. "Not all of us can be sleazy business types."

Allen nodded but didn't flip around or join in his defense.

Gabe laughed, accepting the rake Sarah handed over before charging off in her party-military way. "Speaking of questionable business types, how are things with you and Peter?"

"Okay, I guess." I stood. "It's weird still, but at least we're speaking like normal people."

"As much as Petries are capable," Gabe joked. "Are we still on for golf next month?"

"Wouldn't miss it."

Gabe raked a pile of discarded cups and plates. "Remind me not to have kids."

"You say that now, and then…" I smiled at the twinkies sound asleep in their plush elephant chairs, gifts from Helen and Dad. "If you ever settle down, you may not have a choice. Sarah basically ambushed me with the idea, and for that, I'm truly grateful. Besides, for someone who says he doesn't want kids, you sure spend a lot of time with the twins."

Gabe's eyes found Maddie across the yard. From the looks of it, she was getting an earful from Sarah. When Sarah stormed off in her mother's direction, Maddie gave a sarcastic salute with her middle finger. The three of us laughed.

The employees walked back and forth over the now-flattened castle.

"It's hard to believe they're one already. Where did the year go?" I asked no one in particular.

Allen moseyed closer to me and whispered so Gabe wouldn't overhear, "Who was the girl?"

Not Allen, too. My half brother, who until this moment I'd thought was one of the good guys. Sweet. Innocent. Respected all women. Not the type to lust after a busty woman in skimpy clothes.

"Jorie," I said.

Gabe perked up. "You noticed her, Allen, with all the talking you and Bailey engaged in?"

That was a weird way to put it. I said to Allen, "You know, Bailey's grandmother put me in charge of making sure Bailey behaves and takes college seriously."

Allen, his cheeks pinking, nodded. "We talked about college. A lot."

A dubious claim, considering Bailey hadn't mentioned anything college-related since moving to town one week ago. The dorms weren't open yet, but Bailey was staying with a family friend in the interim. I'd tried on more than one occasion to get her to talk about her classes.

"Sure you did." Gabe prodded my arm with his.

CHAPTER THREE

*W*e tucked the twinks in, each of us kissing their fuzzy heads.

In the doorway, Sarah pressed her cheek against the doorjamb. "I can't believe it's been a year."

I encircled her waist with my arm. "I know. It feels like it just happened yesterday."

"Except I'm not sore." She stifled a laugh so as not to wake them. "I'd do it again, though."

I led her by the hand to the bedroom, both of us moving sluggishly after the long day in stifling heat.

Sarah collapsed onto the bed, rustling the gift I'd placed there an hour ago.

Reaching over her head, she seized the box, examining the purple wrapping paper. "Is it for the twinks?"

I shook my head. "It's for the best wife in the world."

She placed a hand to her mouth. Speaking through her fingers she said, "I didn't get you anything. Was I supposed to?"

"Not at all. I wanted to spoil you. For everything you do to keep the household running smoothly."

"Is it the Ninja blender I've been wanting to make juices?" Still on her back, she rattled the box.

I sat on the edge of the bed. "Nope, but considering the box isn't the right size, meaning you really want the blender"—I tapped the side of my head—"I'm making a mental note to buy one tomorrow." I waved for her to open the gift.

Sitting up, she sat cross-legged and tore off the paper. She held up one of the items, a red pepper satin kimono. "It's beautiful."

"There's a matching slip."

Sarah held it up. "Is this a gift for you?"

"Maybe it's for both of us. I know how much you love sexy things, and I admit I like it when you wear them." I twitched my brow in an exaggerated fashion.

She glanced down at her T-shirt with frosting and juice smears. "Not sure that's true anymore."

I laid my hand on her thigh. "Remember way back when, you said you didn't want people to put you solely in the mom box? I think you need to remember not to put yourself there either. You are, without a doubt, sexy."

She offered a crooked smile. "Really?"

I kissed her deeply. "Don't ever doubt it."

Sarah rested her forehead against mine. "It's been hard lately. To think about anything else besides the twinks."

"I know. What can I do to help out more? Not everything is on your shoulders."

"You have so much with co-parenting, teaching, and publishing."

I placed a finger against her lips. "Don't talk nonsense. If you need me to step up, I will. You've always been there for me."

Sarah pulled her head back, flicking away a tear. "Half the time, I don't know what's wrong with me. I'm crankier. Conflicted about my feelings of being a stay-at-home mom. I'm always tired…" She waved her hand to imply the list went on. Sarah shook the box. "This helps, though."

"There's more." I gestured for her to keep digging into the present under the tissue paper.

"Bath bombs!" She clapped her hands.

I laughed, looking over to the baby monitors to ensure the twinks were still asleep. "Never heard someone get so excited about bombs before. There's one last gift."

Sarah rifled through the tissue paper, finally pulling out a card. Upon opening it, she whooped. "A day at the spa for two." Her face became serious. "Wait a minute? Are you going with me?"

"Nope. Maddie volunteered to escort you to ensure you get all the necessary treatments or whatever you call them." I showed my palms to indicate I was clueless. "Shall I draw you a bath?"

"Please." She latched onto my hand. "All of this means so much to me."

I leaned over and kissed her forehead. "Anything for you."

After turning on the water, I ran downstairs for two more elements of the *cheer up Sarah* plan: wine and chocolate. I was fairly certain the article I'd read didn't mean to utilize everything in one go, but it didn't hurt to kick things into a higher gear. Christmas was just around the corner, and I didn't want another elaborate function so soon after today's.

By the time I was able to uncork the wine and locate Sarah's stash of chocolates, she was already immersed in the water with an eye mask on.

"Oh, sorry. I didn't mean to crash in here and wreck your Calgon moment."

Sarah hiked up one corner of the mask, taking in the offerings in my hands. "Okay, what's going on? Gifts, wine, and chocolates. Are you feeling guilty about anything or anyone?"

I inched into the bathroom. "Of course not. I just wanted to spoil you."

"And...?"

I perched on the side of the tub. "It would be helpful if you gave me some guidance as to why I should feel guilty. As far as I know, I've been a perfect angel." I rattled the chocolates. "Case in point."

"I can think of one reason, and it starts with an M or J depending on who you're talking to." Sarah eased the wineglass out of my clutched fingers. "No reason to let this go to waste."

"An M or J?" I glanced out the window overlooking the backyard, unable to see anything in the darkness. "Um, math or jammies?"

"That's what you're going with?" Sarah narrowed her eyes.

I jacked up one shoulder. "They were the first words that came to mind."

"Marjor—"

"Oh, geez. That should have been obvious. I didn't mean to invite Jorie. You know I can be awkward in certain situations."

"I'm aware." Sarah flipped the Kilwin's box open and selected one. After taking a bite and letting out a moan, she said, "Dark vanilla butter cream. So good."

"Really, Sarah. I never would have invited her if I hadn't popped in to buy party blowers."

"This is *my* fault?" It was difficult to determine if she was joking, given the hardness in her tone and sparkle in her eyes.

"Of course not. I'm only saying, when Marj—Jorie started talking to me, I didn't know what to say. I hardly ever run into my students in the real world. I..." I waved a hand pathetically in the air. "I didn't even know she went by Jorie. If I knew her better, don't you think I would have known that?"

"It would be a good cover, though." Her face was softening.

I massaged my already tired eyes. "I can't win."

She laughed. "Don't worry. I don't actually think you're

having an affair with Jorie. She's way too hot. You'd never stop babbling long enough to get to second base." Her coquettish smile was meant to ease the blow.

My jaw dropped. "I—what am I supposed to say to that?"

"I don't recommend arguing against it." Sarah set the wineglass down on the other side of the tub. "I think it's best to table the Jorie discussion. Get in here. I'm not the only mother who ran herself ragged today."

I stripped down and eased into the jetted tub, facing Sarah. "Shall I flip it on? Or will it cause the bath bomb to actually explode?"

"Explode, no. Mess up the jets, probably." She took a swig of wine. "How can I get my groove back?"

Proceed with caution! I asked in a toneless voice, "In what regard?"

"I was referring to Sexy Sarah."

I eased further into the water, wanting to work out the knots in my shoulders, although the way I had to hunker down to avoid the tap wasn't helpful. "What did you used to do to feel that way?"

Her forehead puckered. "I don't think I had to do anything. I just was."

I nodded. "You still are."

"I don't feel it." She popped another chocolate into her mouth.

"Okay, what do you think would perk up your sex... spirits? More lingerie? Porn? Erotica?"

She mulled over the options. "I've been meaning to read the sequel to *Fifty Shades of Grey*. Maddie mentioned some lesbian films she recently watched."

I wished I had a notepad or my phone to jot down everything. "What about a weekend away?"

"Who'd watch the twinks?"

"We could ask your mom," I said, again carefully dipping my toes into a potential Sarah land mine.

"Troy would probably be there."

Troy was Rose's new boyfriend, who Sarah wasn't all that keen about. As far as I knew, Sarah hadn't told her mom she disliked Troy, but his absence at the birthday party spoke volumes. Sarah's shoulders tensed, and darkness clouded her eyes. I needed to pull her thoughts away from Troy and back to Sexy Sarah. Fast!

"Not that you asked, but I vote for more sexy lingerie." I ran my hands up and down her smooth legs.

She rolled her head back, her hands gripping the edges of the tub. "That feels good."

"There's more of this if you want it. I've been working on my massage skills." I cracked my knuckles.

"Do I have Jorie to thank for that?"

I slapped her knee, splashing water. "Don't. Not when I want to take you to bed to show you how sexy you are."

CHAPTER FOUR

While Sarah made the twins oatmeal for breakfast, I set them up in their high chairs. Hank, our black cat, was curled up in the sunny spot on the charcoal mat next to the door leading to the deck.

Ollie fussed more than usual, which was a feat. There were times I thought she had four arms and four legs, calling her Octo-kid.

Fred, on the other hand, stared at me with his large blue eyes.

"You ready for your morning victuals, Freddie?" I asked.

He smiled his sweet little boy smile.

"He has no idea what you're talking about." Sarah set the communal bowl down on the breakfast nook table.

"Neither does the majority of the people on this planet." I turned to Freddie. "But when I'm through with you, you'll know more words than Merriam-Webster."

Sarah groaned her displeasure, seeming too tired to mount a verbal attack.

She put out her fist. "Rock, Paper, Scissors to see who feeds the twinks."

Ollie made a fist.

"You want to play Roshambo, Ollie?" I asked, bumping my hand against her fist and then exposing scissors. "Rock smashes scissors. You win."

She giggled.

I prepped for my round with Sarah by rolling my neck side to side.

Sarah sighed. "Ready, set, go." She threw paper and smothered my rock. "I'm going to shower."

I picked up the spoon, loaded it with an Ollie-sized bite of oatmeal, and made airplane sounds, accompanied by Fred's version, resulting with spittle oozing down his chin.

Ollie's mouth greedily clamped down on the spoon.

I repeated the process with Fred, who wasn't as exuberant as his sister.

Breakfast with the twins was not the easiest of times. None of us was fully functioning at seven in the morning. Ollie enjoyed her food, but she loved to fight the feeding process as if spooning her the food she craved was an insult to her independence. Fred, on the other hand, was easygoing, but his lack of appetite bordered on concerning. Our pediatrician, though, claimed he was a healthy weight and that we should heed his signs when he was done. But, what about his not starting in the first place?

By the time Sarah returned to the kitchen, freshly showered, she kissed each of their heads. "How's it going?"

"Just about done, aren't we, Twinkies?" I attempted to give Fred another bite, but he shoved the spoon away, smiling.

Sarah wiped his mouth, face, and fingers clean, lifted him out of the chair, and set him on the floor. He toddled away on wobbly legs toward the play area in the front room, which was within view.

Ollie accepted one more bite before making it known she

didn't appreciate being held captive while Freddie roamed freely.

"Why don't you go shower? I can manage now that I'm fully awake." Sarah flicked her fingers for me to make a break for it while I could.

"Okay, Twinks. Time for my morning ablutions. Ab-lu-tions."

"Knock it off. I don't want our kids turning into vocab freaks. One per family is the limit." Sarah offered a sweet smile that managed to convey a fraction of love with 99.87 percent sarcasm.

"Hate speak isn't tolerated by management."

"I'm the boss of all things under this roof." She raised her brow, knowing she had me there.

"Here's another word, Twinkies: *dictator*. It means a ruler with total power."

Freddie raised his purple stuffed monkey in the air.

"Your point, Lizzie?" Sarah crossed her arms.

"No point. Just defining your title so everyone's on the same page." I blew a kiss in Sarah's direction.

* * *

"Okay, Mom, I think we got everything." Sarah, in a turquoise floral sleeveless dress, seemed to run through a mental list of things the kids needed.

I laughed, standing in Rose's doorway, both of my arms overloaded with the twins' bags and stuffed animals.

Both of them ignored me, the twinkies' Sherpa.

"You two have fun tonight." Rose kissed Sarah's cheek. "We'll be fine."

Next to her stood Troy.

Sarah waved goodbye, taking a moment longer than usual,

her eyes not on the twins but on Troy, who reminded me of a heavier version of Clark Gable.

In the passenger seat of the car, Sarah flipped the visor down to inspect her makeup. "It's weird."

"What?"

"Mom and Troy. I thought after my dad she turned asexual or something."

I laughed. "Maybe she was waiting for you to be able to handle her dating."

"I'm married, with children, every day inching closer to middle age." She pointed to the crow's feet next to her left eye.

"Exactly!" I punctuated with an exuberant head nod. "Too busy and old to cause a stink." I backed out of Rose's two-car driveway.

Sarah flipped the visor back into place with a jolt. "It's just weird!"

Squeezing her thigh, I said, "I know, sweetheart. I didn't mean to sound insensitive. And for the record, I don't think you've officially hit middle age. Not for another handful of years."

She twisted in her seat, placing the side of her face against the headrest. "I know it's perfectly natural for Mom to date, but..." She shrugged.

"Weird," I supplied, putting the SUV into drive.

"Come on, Miss Vocab. Amaze me with your verbal skills."

"I'd rather use my tongue in other ways." I arched my brows but didn't take my eyes off the road as I turned onto a busy street.

"Can we cancel, you think?" Sarah perked up.

"Up to you. You're the one who planned this double-date with Maddie and Gabe."

"Yeah, yeah. You'd be perfectly fine staying home, reading the latest book on the Third Reich every single night."

"If I remember correctly, I *had* hinted about something else."

She ran a hand up my arm. "Go on."

I stopped at the red light on College Avenue and faced her full-on. "I want to eat your pussy until you beg me to stop. And you know what, I may not stop. Not until you pass out." Slapping my leg, I added, "I almost forgot. There's a gift for you in the back seat. I didn't have time to wrap it."

She reached behind her, grabbing the Barnes & Noble bag. "You got me the Fifty Shades series." She fished around in the bag and pulled out another book. "And *Twilight?*"

"It was in the Amazon's also boughts. It's usually spot-on when I'm buying history books." I shrugged. The light turned green, but the next one turned red, so we didn't get very far.

"Let me see if I understand. You went to the bookstore after looking up Fifty Shades on Amazon?"

"Absolutely. I adore you, but I wasn't going to ask someone in the store for recommendations of how to get my wife hot to trot. And after our conversation last night, I wasn't sure you could wait for a delivery."

She patted my leg. "Or you couldn't."

"Same thing."

"Maybe we should cancel. We can read passages aloud to each other."

Sarah's phone rang.

We locked eyes.

A car behind us honked, but the light was still red.

I glanced in the rearview mirror, laughing. "Hold that thought." I jerked my thumb between the two seats to Gabe's car behind us.

Sarah answered the phone. "Yes, Maddie?"

I heard Maddie's muffled voice but couldn't make out the words. Probably for the best.

"Why would I intentionally ignore you?" Sarah grinned at me.

They chatted until we pulled into the parking lot of the new Italian place twenty minutes from our home.

The four of us made our way to the entrance, with Gabe dashing ahead to hold the door.

The hostess led us through the darkened dining room, although it was still daylight outside. There was a large party in the back, no one under the age of sixty. The couples nearest our table were even older.

Each of us took a seat at the square table.

"This is a happening place," Gabe joked. "Maybe pasta is easy for denture wearers."

I glanced at Sarah, who'd picked the restaurant, wondering if this was adding another dent to Sexy Sarah and bringing her one step closer to Frumpy Sarah.

"Or there's a nursing home attached," Gabe continued, much to my horror.

"I'll have you know everyone has been raving about this place." Maddie pulverized my foot with hers under the table as if I should be the one to get my stepbrother under control. She was dating him.

"Who's everyone?" Gabe pushed.

"Everyone," Maddie spoke loudly and slowly.

Gabe nodded. "Got it."

Wanting to keep the conversation lighthearted, I said, "These two love to give others shit, but when it's dished back, they get a scooch testy." I held my arms out wide, smiling.

"I've noticed that trend." Gabe situated his hand on Maddie's forearm on the table, and she, in turn, stuck her tongue out at him. "The classic comeback."

I gave Sarah's thigh a pat, and she good-humoredly flicked my hand off. At least, I think she was being playful.

Gabe switched topics, maybe sensing the mood could

plummet to the level of *I'd rather eat a shit burger than pretend I'm having a good time*. "Who's watching the twinkies?"

"My mom and Troy." The way she pronounced *Troy* made it more than apparent that Sarah wasn't happy with the new man in Rose's life.

Gabe's eyes clouded with distress, and he looked to me to bail him out. Maybe it was time to teach him my Golden Rule when it came to irritable women, *Don't speak unless spoken to*.

Maddie jumped in. "He seems like a nice guy." Her voice was soft and lacked her typical southern sarcastic bite.

"Many thought Ted Bundy was a nice young man." Sarah flicked her menu open.

Whoa! Sarah had just compared her mom's boyfriend to a serial killer.

This was huge.

For once, I wasn't the one acting like a child.

Inside, I did a victory dance.

The waiter arrived, asking if we wanted wine. Maddie quickly ordered their best merlot, and I added grappa, which we usually reserved for after dinner, but the situation called for it. Maddie gave me an approving nod, and I mentally swiped my forehead with the back of my hand. Grappa wasn't on the *cheer up the stay-at-home mom* list, but I didn't think the creators of the list factored in the mom raising twins and her mother starting to date a man after years of not dating anyone following her husband's death.

"Do you want to talk about it?" Maddie asked, bracing herself for a tart response, making it clear Sarah wasn't only taking it out on me.

"About what? That my mother is sleeping with a man more than fifteen years younger? What's to talk about? She likes him. He's poor. My mother is rich. It seems like a match made in heaven." Throughout it all, Sarah kept her face purposefully neutral, and at the end, she offered her best Stepford wife smile. "I think I'm going to start with the Venetian crab cakes. Shrimp and crab Alfredo for the main course, and I have my eye on the salted caramel or triple chocolate cheesecake."

"Hell, why not get both?" Gabe said with an encouraging, albeit businessman, smile.

The waiter returned and did the whole uncorking routine that gave everyone a chance to focus on something other than my wife. After getting approval and filling everyone's glass, he placed a basket of breadsticks along with an olive oil and herb dip in the middle of the table, followed by getting his notepad ready. Had he sensed it would be best to move us along to avoid an ugly scene?

Each of us ordered, doing our best to pretend Sarah wasn't in the midst of a minor mental breakdown.

As soon as the waiter left, Sarah said, "I mean, what do the two of them have in common? He's never been married. That's odd, right? A man in his forties who's never been married? What do you think, Gabe?" She plucked a breadstick from the basket, more intent on shredding it than eating.

Gabe swallowed, his eyes watching as she tore another chunk off, swirling it in the olive oil concoction. "Well—"

Maddie cut him off. "Is it the age difference, money, or the simple fact that your mom is seeing someone after all these years? Or do you feel like she's trying to replace your father?" She held four fingers in the air.

Sarah shot the small glass of grappa, which I'd always assumed was the type of drink one should sip, and chased it with a massive dose of wine. "I'm being an asshole, aren't I?"

All three of us vehemently shook our heads. While Sarah's father died when she was so young, and Sarah didn't really remember him, I doubted she ever fully recovered from the loss. There were constant reminders in movies, books, casual conversation, Father's Day—the list went on. Over the years, Sarah had developed an idealized version of her father, and it was nearly impossible for anyone to compete with the sainted dead.

On top of that was the age and wealth differences between Rose and Troy, which I noticed were near the top of Sarah's gripes each and every time.

"Who cares that he's a first-grade teacher? I was… am a teacher. There's nothing wrong with a man who's never had children teaching six-year-olds, right? It doesn't make him a pedophile or something." She rooted around in her purse for her phone. "I'm going to check on the kids."

When she was out of earshot, Maddie said, "What does she plan on asking? Hey, is Troy alone with the kids?"

I sighed. "I wouldn't put it past her. She's been researching those nanny cams you hide in a teddy bear or something." I bolted upright. "She did insist I bring both of the twins' favorite stuffed animals even though Rose has duplicates of all their toys at her place."

"It's a sad day when you're the rational one in the relationship," Maddie said.

"Tell me about it. I'm totally out of my depth here." I ran a hand over the top of my head, staring at Maddie in hopes she'd have a magic potion to make everything go back to normal.

Gabe studied my face and then Maddie's to see if he was missing something. Shaking his head, he asked, "How'd they meet?"

"A seniors' cruise." I craned my neck to ensure Sarah was still outside the restaurant on the phone.

"I thought he wasn't old enough to go on a seniors' cruise."

Maddie scouted over her shoulder. "He isn't. One of Rose's cruising buddies mentioned her son lived in Fort Collins."

"Troy's mom set them up?" Gabe's voice squeaked.

Maddie waved the notion away. "No! Actually, the woman isn't speaking to either one anymore."

Gabe tapped his fingers against his wineglass. "Let me see if

I've got this straight. Sarah is upset Rose is dating Troy. His mother isn't speaking to him or to Rose."

"Families! They're not for sissies." Maddie selected a breadstick.

"How long have they been dating?"

"Not long. A couple of months, maybe. I haven't quite pinned down the exact date." I refilled my water glass from the pitcher.

Maddie pantomimed slitting her throat, using the breadstick. "Shush, she's coming back."

"Sad day all around," Gabe muttered to his lap.

"What'd I miss?" Sarah wore a fake smile.

"How are the twins?" I rose and pulled Sarah's chair out for her.

Sarah cupped my cheek. "Fine, I think."

"I'm sure they're happy. They love their grandmother." I retook my seat.

Sarah flicked her fingers to get the waiter's attention. Raising her empty grappa glass, Sarah queried the rest of us with an arched eyebrow. Maddie indicated she'd have another. I wanted to thank her for taking the hit for the team. Sarah clearly intended to get drunk, and drinking wasn't my strong suit, not to mention I had to drive us and the twins home.

Gabe pressed his lips together in understanding.

There was an uncomfortable silence.

"Now that the kiddos are a year old, do you have any plans for going back to work?" Gabe asked. "Or do you plan to have another baby?"

My heart stilled at the thought.

Sarah jostled her head to the left and right, as if contemplating the pros and cons. "We haven't decided yet about expanding the family." The way she breezed over this part troubled me some, as if the final solution—I cringed over the phrase that popped into my mind. How could I use a Nazis phrase when it came to any aspect of my family life?

Maybe sensing my mood, Sarah plowed on. "As for working, I don't want a full-time job. I've been brainstorming ideas of businesses I can start at home, but so far, I haven't landed on an idea that gets my blood going."

Unless she counted the pedophile app she'd proposed the other day. Perhaps I should do some research about socially acceptable part-time jobs for stay-at-home moms.

"What about hosting Tupperware parties? I recently read a book where one of the main characters made a ton of money doing them." Maddie buttered a piece of a breadstick.

Sarah crumpled her face. "Do those still exist?"

"In the book they did, although it was set in Australia. You may have to move Down Under." Maddie hitched one of her shoulders.

"If you want to get out of the house, you can work part-time in the flower shop," Gabe tossed out. "I'm sure Mom wouldn't mind if you brought the twins. Allen was practically raised in the Denver store."

Sarah did her head bob once again, weighing the possibility. "Maybe."

By the time we were halfway through our main courses, both Maddie and Sarah were sozzled. Now there was a great word to teach the twins. I snapped my fingers under the table, unfortunately snaring Sarah's attention.

"Yes, Lizzie?" she added five extra Zs.

"What? Oh, nothing." I set my fork and knife in the five o'clock position on my plate, indicating I was done.

"You were just snapping your fingers for..." Sarah narrowed her eyes. "Is this about Troy?"

"No! Not even close." I simulated waving a white flag.

"Then what?" If she weren't glaring at me with such hostility, I would have laughed.

"I just thought of a word I hadn't used in some time; that's all." I stared at the water glass in my hands as if the clear liquid could save me.

Maddie giggled. "Which word is it this time?"

"Uh... I don't remember." I shrugged in an aw-shucks way.

"Liar!" Maddie wielded her knife.

Sarah clumsily set her wineglass down. "That's not it, Maddie." She spun her head in my direction. "This *is* about Troy. Lizzie's gloating because, for once, it's my family causing a stink. Not her cruel mother—who's now dead—her cheating father, or the conniving Peter, who probably has wet dreams involving ways to steal Lizzie's trust fund." Sarah, with a victorious grin, turned her attention to Maddie for support.

Maddie, though, had buried her face in a napkin.

Shell-shocked by her verbal diarrhea, I curbed a nasty retort. Sarah enjoyed playful banter, but nothing about what she'd said was funny. However, she'd put up with plenty of uncomfortable family situations for my benefit, and deep down, I knew Sarah would regret everything once the grappa fugue dissipated.

Sarah's leap into the Troy zone was tenuous at best. But, that wasn't the troubling aspect with Gabe present. His mother had been my father's mistress for years.

Gabe let out a rush of air.

Realization slowly seeped into Sarah's expression. "Oh, Gabe—"

He showed his palms. "It's okay—"

"No, it's not," Sarah said. "I..."

"Sozzled," I blurted to save Sarah, even though I was hurt, knowing if the situation were reversed, she'd jump into a pit of vipers for me.

All three of them turned to me.

"I was thinking the word *sozzled*, because—" I pointed at Sarah.

Sarah blinked. "You were going to tell our children that I'm beyond drunk?"

"The thought did cross my mind." My shoulders shriveled inward, and I offered a weak smile.

She burst into laughter, Maddie quickly joining in. "Only you would s-see a t-teachable moment in this s-situation." Sarah slurred a few words.

"How often will the twins see you sozzled?" I joked, adding mentally, *hopefully never like this*.

"How long will my mom continue seeing Troy?" Her face had traces of merriment, but there was hardness in her tone.

"It's okay, you know," I said.

Sarah frowned. "What?"

"Not knowing how to handle a family situation. Families are hard, even perfect ones."

"My mom is not perfect!"

I darted my arms in the air. "Hallelujah! I've been trying to tell you that for years. All the times she's mimed mowing me down with her car, accompanied with sound effects."

"She does that?" Gabe asked, bewildered. "She seems so nice."

"She does that *all the time*." I punctuated each word by tapping my finger on the tabletop.

Maddie conceded with a half shrug.

Sarah rolled her eyes. "She has her reasons."

"Had a reason. I've done nothing wrong since—"

Maddie and Sarah chortled together.

"Don't get carried away. You still have your Lizzie moments." Sarah caressed my hand. "For the most part, I love your Lizzie moments."

"Last week, Lizzie was on a walk listening to an audiobook"—Maddie gestured I had on massive headphones—"using the Bose noise-cancelling pair Sarah gave her for her birthday, when a neighbor stopped her to talk. Lizzie didn't realize until two-thirds of the conversation that she'd left the headphones in place and was shouting at George."

"You weren't even there." I knifed a finger in the air.

"But I witnessed the whole thing from the window. Poor George winced every time you spoke, as if your words were assaulting his hearing aids. Even Gandhi tried to cover his ears with his paws. Why didn't you just turn off the book?"

"I did, but the headphones are great for blocking out most sound. Like when you're over."

"Maybe I can borrow them for when Mom wants to talk about how great her sex life is." Sarah's body tensed again, making it clear that the Troy issue was never far from her mind.

"She talks about that?" My mouth dangled open.

"No! I was being sarcastic—another word you can teach our kids." Her shoulders relaxed, and a smile transformed her face.

I slanted my head to peer into Sarah's eyes. "You're back."

"What does that mean?"

"Carefree Sarah."

"Not Sozzled Sarah?"

"Oh, no. You're still drunk. Speaking of, one more for the road?" I motioned for the waiter, wondering if Sarah would fall asleep in the car, forestalling what I believed was an inevitable blowup with her mother.

"Are you trying to take advantage of me?" Sarah didn't bother whispering.

"Please, that would be wrong," I said.

"It would take my mind off Troy." She acted as if that was a perfectly normal diversion.

I spoke to Maddie. "Does that count as a Sarah moment? Mentioning her mom's boy toy while trying to seduce me?"

Maddie crinkled her forehead. "I think it ticks all the boxes."

"You have boxes?" I asked, miming ticking one with my finger.

"Stupid? Embarrassing? Insensitive? Socially inept?" Maddie displayed four fingers in the air.

"Are you three like this all the time?" Gabe asked, tugging on the collar of his shirt.

We all nodded.

"Harsh, man. Harsh."

I squinted to see if there were beads of sweat on his forehead or upper lip. Not seeing any, I said, "I'm laying the blame on the grappa, but if you plan to continue dating Maddie, get used to this."

"The first time Lizzie had grappa was on a date with me. My mom had to pick us up, and Lizzie puked in the back seat." Sarah acted out the last bit in an exaggerated way.

Gabe burst into laughter.

"I didn't puke!"

"Got proof of that?" Sarah crossed her arms, pushing her breasts upward.

"My word isn't enough?"

"Not even close. It's the Petrie factor." The frivolity in her expression had returned, another pivot in her seesaw emotions.

"You're such a Cavanaugh!" I countered. "And if you keep it up, *you'll* be ticking more of Maddie's boxes. Not me."

Gabe prepped for another Sarah outburst, but she nearly spurted wine out her nose, laughing.

"Finally, the shoe is on the other foot." I waggled a finger at Sarah.

"And that's all the time we have tonight, folks." Maddie gestured for the check.

CHAPTER FIVE

After putting the twinkies to bed, I clambered under the covers, wrapping one arm over Sarah and tugging her back against me.

Sarah's body became rigid. "I shouldn't have said what I said earlier."

"What, exactly?" I kissed the back of her head, not wanting to fall into a Sarah pitfall.

"About your dad cheating."

"He did cheat. For years."

"Yes, with Gabe's mom. I feel awful." She snuggled closer.

"But not for tossing me under the bus every chance you got?" I tightened my arm around her.

"Never that," she joked.

I playfully groaned. "I'm sure Gabe understood, but it may behoove you to apologize again. Sober, this time."

"*Behoove,*" she parroted, and I sensed her rolling her eyes. "I'd send flowers if he didn't work for a flower business. Maybe a cookie bouquet."

"Can I sign up for one? I mean you've said much worse to

me and not just tonight." Before I could suggest a sexier apology, she cut me off.

"Honestly. What do you think about Troy?"

I sighed, carefully venturing back into the Troy zone. "Your mom seems to like him and vice versa."

"Is that your way of telling me to back off?" The hardness in her voice could almost be used as an axe.

Undeterred, I said, "Switch roles. What would you tell me if it was my mom?"

She assailed my gut with her elbow. "Sometimes I prefer the clueless Lizzie."

"She has her moments." I rolled Sarah onto her back. "Everything's going to be okay. Your mom isn't an idiot—"

Sarah started to speak, but I smothered her lips with my mouth. "You taste like grappa." I smacked my lips.

"That's better than tasting like a grandma."

I laughed. "Before we're ready, we'll have our own grandkids. Does that mean I shouldn't kiss you then?"

She goggled at me. "If you're trying to cheer me up, you're failing."

"How's this?" I planted a soft kiss on her cheek.

"Better, but do you know what would really do the trick?"

"Do tell," I said in a sexy voice.

She flopped onto her stomach, spreading out her arms. "Back rub."

"I think you're taking advantage of the situation."

"And your point is…? Focus on my lower back." As if I was unfamiliar with her anatomy, she tapped the area. "Next time, you can carry Ollie all day."

I spanked her butt. "Don't be cruel about our daughter."

"I'm not. She's absolutely gorgeous, but she does weigh more than Fred. Nothing wrong with it. She's going to be the enforcer on the playground, that's for sure. The world needs strong women, and we're raising a fierce one."

"Do you want to take your top off?"

"Nah. I'm too tired." To emphasize this, she released an exaggerated breath.

"I remember the days when you slept naked." I suppressed a *woe is me* sigh.

"That was BK, also known as Before Kids. I don't want to rush to the twins aid in the middle of the night with my boobs flopping around, sending them to therapy for the rest of their lives." She wiggled her butt for me to get busy.

I hoisted Sarah's tank top up and dug my fingers into her lower back. She let out a guttural moan.

"Now *that* feels good," she said. "Keep it up."

"Can we circle back to the naked sleeping conversation?"

"As long as your magic fingers don't stop."

"Never fear." To prove my point, I increased my efforts. "You can always put on a robe before dashing down the hall. Maybe I can ask Gabe to help me construct a device by the door so you'll have easy access. Like a mom superhero thingy." I made a mental note to watch superhero movies for tips.

She laughed. "Why Gabe?"

"Out of all the men in the family, he seems the handiest, which isn't saying much."

"Do you really want me to sleep in the nude again?" Her voice was teasing.

"I absolutely do. Your boobs don't traumatize me, although being deprived of seeing and feeling them every night might tip me over the edge."

Sarah motioned for me to get out of her way to allow her to roll over. "What does that mean, really? Tip you over to find your jollies elsewhere?"

I bonked the top of my head with my palm. "Not at all." I tapped her forehead with a finger. "When will you get this through that thick skull of yours? I think you're the sexiest woman, and I miss you."

Her eyes misted. "I need help feeling that way again."

*　*　*

THE NEXT MORNING, after losing Roshambo the third straight day in a row, I walked out onto our deck, freshly showered. Who knew feeding kids could be so messy?

Sarah and Bailey had set up a small plastic table under the oak tree for the twins to finger paint. A well-used canvas drop cloth protected the deck.

"Get the oatmeal out of your hair?" Sarah teased.

I ran a hand through my wet hair. "I think so. Not sure about my ears, though." I cleaned one out with a finger. "If I'd known it was art day, I would have delayed my shower."

Sarah, with red fingerprints on her cheeks, heaved a shoulder. "Maybe we should invest in Dove."

"Or invent a roving shower for parents." Bailey was creating her own masterpiece with Fred's help. Sarah hadn't reached the level of comfort yet to leave Bailey alone with the kids for long stretches, and Bailey's initial shifts had been more like a helper bee letting the twinks get used to her.

"That's what the hose is for." Sarah's tone didn't hold an inkling of humor.

Freddie held his rainbow-colored fists in the air, giggling.

"Let me see." I hunched down to inspect his creation. "Wow! This is great. I really like what you did in this corner." I pointed to the green handprint. "A bold statement. Bold," I repeated slowly. I swiveled to Ollie and her artwork. "How beautiful! Your use of red is striking. Red." Ollie smeared paint on top of her head, tingeing the spattering of blonde hairs.

Sarah and Bailey exchanged a look at my repetition of words.

I kissed both twins on the top of their heads, quickly

followed by rubbing my lips with the back of my hand to remove any trace of paint. Standing up, I said, "I'll be back in a few hours."

"When you get home, I thought we'd take the twins for a bike ride." Sarah cleaned Freddie's hand with a wet wipe.

"It's a date." I blew a kiss to both twins and Sarah. "Bailey, do you need anything from campus?" I asked, sounding overly hopeful.

"Nope, thanks." She avoided my eyes.

As far as I could determine, she hadn't purchased any textbooks or been to campus to find her classes, which started in less than five days.

"You look very professorial today." Sarah's tone conveyed the polar opinion.

I glanced down at my shorts, flip-flops, and green T-shirt that read: *If History Repeats Itself, I'm Getting a Dinosaur*, a birthday gift from Maddie. "Don't be jealous of my cool factor."

"I'll try to curb myself. Wave goodbye, Twinkies." Sarah exaggerated her wave to get the twins to copy her.

Both did, accompanied with adorable baby giggles I never tired of hearing.

"Now I don't want to leave them."

Ollie's face morphed into a strawberry, and she belted out a blood-curdling wail.

"Gotta run." I tossed a wave over my retreating shoulders.

Sarah hollered, "Coward!"

* * *

IN MY OFFICE, I quickly dashed off emails and finalized the remaining syllabus. This semester I was teaching three undergraduate courses: The History of the Weimar Republic, On the German Home Front, and The Nazi Propaganda Machine.

"Good morning, Jean." I smiled at the ancient admin dwarfed by her mahogany desk.

"Ah, Lizzie, I was hoping you'd stop in today." Her voice wavered, and I wondered how many more years she had left in this role or life.

"Problem?"

She shook her head. "Nothing like that. Dr. Murphy, one of the faculty advisors for the History Club has stepped down. Dr. Marcel thought you might be interested."

I could smell the frame-up job. "Oh… that's interesting." Did Dr. Marcel hate me?

"Quite," she said dryly. "Can I add your name to the website?" She held a fountain pen in the air, making me wonder how she intended to update the Internet page.

"It would be an honor." I wanted to add, "Can you please call the mother of my twins, who at this moment is covered head to toe with finger paints, to explain I had no choice in taking on more responsibility?" Actually, given the twins' attention span, finger painting was more than likely in the past.

"Thought you'd say that." She had the audacity to wink at me.

"Anything else?" A liver, kidney, full blood transfusion?

"If you need anything printed for the first day of class, I suggest you get it in before one o'clock."

I flaunted the papers in my hand. "Last one. Have a lovely day, Jean."

"You, too. Love the shirt, by the way. When I was a kid, I had a brontosaurus as a pet." Her laughter turned into a cough. Once it settled, she added, "Give those babies a kiss from me."

I flashed my *will do* wave on my way out the door before I got strong-armed into another dreaded role. History Club. Even when I was an undergrad, I never joined the nerd fest. This would seriously impede on my cool-points scale. Maybe Maddie could track down more snazzy T-shirts to help tip the scale. Wasn't branding the rage these days?

WE STOPPED at a picnic table outside a popular ice cream shop conveniently located next to the bike trail.

"What can I get my princesses and prince?" I rubbed my hands together.

"What if Freddie wants to be a princess?" Sarah, with a twin on each thigh, cocked her head in that way of hers.

"Who said I was calling *Fred* a prince?"

She smiled. "Vanilla for me and the twinks."

"Probably best for their first time now that they're a year and can have whole milk."

"I have a feeling your *first* was the definition of vanilla." She arched an eyebrow, daring me to contradict her.

"Really? In front of our children?" I shook a fist at her.

"They probably understand the shake of your fist more than my words." Sarah waved for me not to waste time given that Ollie was behaving.

Within moments, I had two vanilla cones. "I'll take Prince Olivia."

Exchanging Ollie while simultaneously giving Sarah her cone was awkward at best.

"You'd think we'd be better with that by now." Sarah licked ice cream that had dribbled down her hand.

I sat on the bench opposite Sarah, settling Ollie onto my left leg. "Do you want some ice cream, baby girl?"

"Wait!" Sarah boosted her hand to stop me. "I feel like we should say something."

"They aren't marrying the ice cream." I laughed.

"Be careful, Lizzie, or you won't get any. Not even vanilla style."

"Are you threatening to withhold S-E-X from me in front of our innocent babes?" I raised one shoulder to imply *what gives*?

"Take it how you want. Okay." She glanced down at Freddie, who was more interested in bunching the front of Sarah's shirt with both fists than the ice cream. "Hold on to your socks, Fred."

"That's your speech to commemorate this momentous moment?"

"Say that five times super fast."

Ollie reached for the cone, nearly toppling the scoop.

"Hold on to your socks, Ollie," I said, smiling at my wife and Freddie. I fished my phone out of my pocket and captured a photo of the two of them, with the foothills and blue sky in the background. Then I huddled down and snapped a photo of me and Ollie, who'd already owned the ice cream. "There was a day when I thought baby spit gross." I licked the ice cream oozing down the side.

"Yes, I think I remember those days." Sarah placed the cone in front of Freddie's lips, and he took a tentative swipe with his tongue, scrunching his face. "Seriously, your son is weird. Who doesn't like ice cream?"

"He has a discerning palate; that's all. Just you wait. Soon, he'll school us on what wine to pair with oysters."

"Oysters!" She laughed. "I know geography isn't your specialty, but we're landlocked. Or, are you talking about the Rocky Mountain variety?"

"Maybe with the right drink, fried cow balls would taste… okay." I bit down on my bottom lip.

"A ringing endorsement." She held her phone in the air. "Say cheese, you two."

"Oh my God!" There was a handclap. "All of you are adorable."

I cringed, hearing Jorie's voice behind me.

"Hey, Jorie." Sarah tried again to coax Freddie to sample the treat to no avail. She motioned for me to swap with her since mine was half gone and hers was barely started. "I don't need the calories," she said as explanation. Not that she had to. Many times, Sarah had mentioned her fears she'd never lose the baby weight, even though she already had. Yet, it seemed fruitless to argue with her.

"Do you work here?" I asked Jorie.

"What gave her away? The shop's T-shirt or hat?" Sarah asked.

Jorie laughed. "Yeah. It's really helped me define my arms—well, the right one." She mimicked scooping ice cream.

Sarah admired the bicep and then glanced down at her arm. "Maybe I should get a job here."

In my head, I screamed, "You're not fat!"

"What are you talking about?" Jorie gave Sarah the once-over. "I'd kill for a body like yours."

"Thank you," I said. "When I tell her that, she ignores me."

"Were you talking?" Sarah said to me with mock surprise, prompting a laugh from Jorie.

"You two are a riot." She donned the hat. "I have to run. Next time come when I'm working, and it'll be on the house. Oh, Lizzie, cute shirt."

Sarah, Freddie, and I waved goodbye. Ollie was otherwise occupied smooshing the cone with her fingers. I dabbed my thighs with a napkin. "I think this may be the first and last time I wear this shirt."

"I'm surprised you wore it at all."

"It's that bad?" I tugged on the front to get a better view.

"The opposite, it's adorable and funny."

"Two things I'm not?" I narrowed my eyes in what I hoped was menacing fashion.

Unperturbed, Sarah said, "Oh, you're coming around some. Having a family agrees with you." Her smile was genuine.

Ollie succeeded in dumping ice cream all over my lap again.

Doing my best to clean her fingers and my shorts with a previously used napkin, I asked, "Do you think there's something off with her?"

"Show me a one-year-old who doesn't play with her food." Sarah added, "Aside from Fred, who doesn't like food at all." She handed me a wet wipe from the mom bag strapped to the bike leaning against the picnic table.

"Not Ollie. Jorie." I made another go of cleaning Ollie and myself.

"You mean because there's a chance she has a crush on you?"

"Yes." I nodded a little too much.

Sarah tossed her cone into the trash can behind her. "We're quite the pair. I can't stop obsessing about my weight, and you assume anyone who thinks you're cute is an escapee from the lunatic asylum."

"Do you think she is?" I asked.

Sarah took a moment to ponder the question. "No. I don't think she *likes you*, likes you."

"Thanks," I said with a hint of snark, although I was relieved. "How is she suddenly everywhere, though?"

Sarah's laughter was pleasant. "If you're worried she's a stalker, don't be. I don't get the stalker or even obsessive vibe that can sometimes happen between a student and professor. If I had to hazard a guess, I think she's lost and is trying to find her sense of self. Unfortunately, she's probably learned to rely on drawing attention to her good looks to mask her insecurity. Maybe she's a lesbian or bi but hasn't come to terms with it. And you're her role model." Sarah's teasing tone implied *God help her*.

"Maybe she should join the History Club, then." I popped the tip of the cone into my mouth before Ollie had a chance to crush it.

"Because that's the hip place for college students to come out?" Sarah's eyes shone with confusion.

"She's not that young. Twenty-three."

She slanted her head. "What aren't you telling me?"

I sighed. "Guess who's the newest faculty member of the History Club?"

Her eyes tapered to nearly closed. "You're joking."

"I would never joke about History Club. That's the first rule." I raised a finger in the air.

"Why in the world did you volunteer for that? You've already committed yourself to churning out three peer-reviewed articles, one more than last year, and drafting the next book this school year."

I cupped my ear. "I'm sorry, did you say *volunteer*? I'm not the type to jump up and down shouting, 'I'll do it' when asked to take on extra responsibility with little to no recognition. That's more your style. Dr. Marcel and Jean tricked me. Or, at least, Jean did."

"How did an eighty-year-old woman trick you?"

"Hey, Dr. Marcel is almost as old, although he's not looking forward to retiring at the end of the school year. History is that cool." I shifted Ollie to my other leg.

"Uh-huh. Ever since I was a little girl, I dreamed of marrying a history professor." Sarah batted her eyelashes.

"And I made your dream come true. You see that kids? I opted to ignore Mommy's sarcasm. Always take the higher road." Ollie giggled. "Shall we get back on the bikes?" I said in hopes of ending the History Club conversation.

"Why? They're behaving, and it's a nice spot." She jerked her head to the creek on the other side of the bike trail. A family of five zoomed by on their bikes, clearly in a race. "Besides, I'm not ready to battle Ollie to get her helmet on."

"Fair point. Maybe we can call your mom to pick up the twins."

Sarah moved to straddle the bench. Bouncing Freddie on her leg, she said, "Can you see the gap in the mountain?"

Ollie wanted off my lap. She led me by the hand, still unsteady on her chubby legs, to the other side of the table. Upon reaching her sibling, she pinched Freddie's leg, not hard enough to warrant much of a response.

"Such a pot stirrer." Sarah shook her head. "Let's show them the creek. We can leave the bikes here for a moment. No one is going to steal bikes overloaded with baby stuff."

At the creek, the two of us sat on a large rock, a twin in each of our laps. "Why can't every day be like this? Not too hot or cold. Endless blue skies. You, me, and the twinks." I raised Ollie's arms in the air, and she howled in delight.

"I don't think I can ever trust Troy," Sarah blurted.

"Okay, that's the perfect example of a non sequitur." I spoke to the twins.

"Don't repeat the word for the hourly vocab lesson."

I looked skyward.

"Are you trying to come up with a Hitler quote or story?"

Slowly, my eyes met Sarah's. "You're funny." I stood Ollie up on my thighs so she could see Sarah's face. "Hitler isn't funny, but your mom is."

Freddie wiggled happily in Sarah's lap. "He's so cuddly." After kissing the top of his head, she asked, "So, were you?"

"Actually, I was praying Maddie would parachute in to save me. She's so much better at these types of conversations." I let out a puff of air.

"Translation, you want me to stop harping about Troy."

"Not at all. I'll do my best to fumble through it, Lizzie style." I tried to look confident.

Sarah laughed. "I feel bad—"

"For hating Troy?" I jumped in.

"No, for being hard on you when dealing with your family situations. Like your father and Helen. Maddie sleeping with

Peter—not when they were engaged but after Peter married Tie. I rode you hard sometimes. Now the shoe is on the other foot. For so long, it's always been just Mom and me. Smooth sailing, while your family... And now, with Troy..." She smoothed a few errant hairs on top of Freddie's head. He was falling asleep. "We may have to call Mom to pick us up after all."

I stared into our son's face, smiling. "You're right, you know. Having all of you in my life has helped me become a better person. More relaxed. Confident. Loving."

Sarah beamed, holding Freddie tighter in her arms. "Look at you, growing more comfortable in your role as wife, mother, and History Club leader."

"I'm going to take the high road yet again and ignore that last part."

"But you wanted to point that out. Again."

"Absolutely, but—" I orbited a finger to stop her. "Let me say the most important part. None of it would have happened until I learned to trust you. You, Sarah Cavanaugh, are the most amazing woman I've ever known. And your mom, who is even harder on me than you, raised you right. She's loved our children as if they were her flesh and blood, even though we used my eggs—"

She snorted, but I think it was unintentional or meant to be subtler. Either way, she said, "I think I know where you're going with this."

"I'm glad one of us does." I laughed. "You don't have to like Troy, but maybe you owe it to your mom to give him a chance. This world needs more love and happiness."

"I can't believe you're taking Mom's side," she said in a defeated, albeit much calmer, tone than she usually used when discussing Troy.

"Why does there have to be sides when it comes to love? Besides, before we had these two"—I smiled at the twins—"I remember you encouraging me to repair the relationship with my family for their sakes."

Before Sarah could jump down my throat, Ollie started to fuss, giving us limited time until it turned into her typical screaming meltdown.

Sarah was on the phone with her mom within two heartbeats, and I got to my feet, walking and bouncing Ollie in my arms. "Look at the birdie, Ollie. Isn't she cute? So small and hopeful someone will feed her."

Judging by Ollie's wailing, she wasn't going to be a bird watcher.

Sarah crossed the bridge to prep for Rose's arrival. "We're in luck. She's only a couple of blocks away."

"She's always there for all of us," I said pointedly to Sarah to reinforce my earlier comments, and then I spoke to our fussy daughter. "Do you hear that, Ollie? Grandma's super powers have kicked in once again to save the day!"

Ollie ceased crying, reaching for my face with her tiny hands.

"Do it again?" Sarah urged. "In the cartoon voice."

I repeated the line many times until Rose's SUV pulled up with Troy in the driver's seat. That was going to go over with my wife as well as a turd sandwich. Her blazing eyes confirmed my gut instinct.

After loading the twins, Sarah said, "There's not enough room for both of us. Lizzie, you go with Mom, and I'll ride my bike home."

"Are you sure?" I asked.

Her nostrils flared. "I could use some alone time."

"Totally get it." I kissed her cheek and then managed to squeeze into the back seat between the two car seats.

"Since when do you prefer riding your bike?" Rose, with one hand on the vehicle door, asked in a disbelieving tone.

"Please, Mom. I've been with the twins all day. I'll see you at home. Troy," she said in a forced polite voice after turning her back to hop on her bike.

Troy hefted my bike into the back of the SUV, whistling "Twinkle Twinkle Little Star." Did he do that all the time as a result of teaching first graders or only when nervous?

I encouraged Ollie to wave goodbye to Sarah as we pulled out of the parking lot.

Rose peered between the front seats. "What'd you do this time?"

"N-nothing," I stammered.

"Lizzie…?" She seemed determined to have me be at fault, but surely, she'd picked up on Sarah's coldness toward Troy. Even I, the clueless one, had. Or was she like Neville Chamberlain during the lead-up to World War II, determined to stick his head in the sand and trusting Hitler to keep his word?

Troy placed a hand on her thigh, and Rose retreated, facing forward, although, I caught a few glimpses of her observing me in the visor mirror. Each time, I offered a weak, innocent smile.

For the entire twenty-minute ride home, thanks to traffic, both twins fell fast asleep. The only sound in the car was Troy's whistling. I wanted to scream, "How I wonder what you are!"

* * *

UPON ARRIVAL, the twins awoke ready for their next adventure. We set them up at the craft table with large colorful buttons they couldn't swallow and flat plastic sticks.

Sarah, who didn't have to contend with traffic, beat us home and prepped the supplies in anticipation.

"I never knew parenting involved so much playtime," I joked in an effort to diffuse the unease.

"I use art and games all the time to keep my students involved." Troy sat down on one of the tiny chairs like a seasoned pro, immediately joining in on the fun.

"Sarah, can I have a word?" Rose asked.

My wife stared as if Rose had asked her to eat a dirty diaper. Finally, she said, "Sure. Let's go in the library."

They left in silence.

Troy glanced at me with a sympathetic expression. I wanted to say I wasn't the issue; he was. Would Sarah confess to her mom? Or would she throw me under the bus? I kinda hoped she laid the blame at my feet to avoid even more awkwardness. At least until I figured out a way to ease Sarah's concerns, if I could. This was a whole new side of Sarah, and quite frankly, I was mystified. Sarah the rock was crumbling.

I took a seat next to Ollie and said to Troy, "How long have you been teaching?"

"Since I graduated from college." He plucked a bright red button, half the size of his hand, to be the head to the rainbow stick person he was making.

Was that last week? *Come on, Lizzie. Give the man a break, and don't act like Sarah.* "Did you always want to teach young children?" I fished for Sarah's benefit, although I didn't subscribe to her pedo theory.

He laughed. "Not at all. When I entered the teaching program at CSU, I wanted to teach high school students. But, then I volunteered at an elementary school and fell in love with the job. Seeing the excitement of a child reading for the first time. Writing their names. It's almost addictive to be around them." Troy ruffled the top of Freddie's head, which had much more hair than his sister's.

"And they probably don't have cell phones they're surreptitiously trying to read to stay on top of social media. Heaven forbid someone miss the latest tweet about national donut day or whatever."

"I do love donuts." He glanced down at his slight paunch.

"Who doesn't?" I agreed.

"Why'd you decide to become a history professor?" he

asked, craning his head to see Ollie's masterpiece. His graying temples added a sense of gravitas. "It reminds me of a creature in a Stephen King novel. I wonder if she'll be an author."

I studied Ollie's stick person, with more arms than an octopus, and then compared it to Fred's fort-type stack of buttons that leaned more than the Tower of Pisa. "And, we may have an architect." Ollie swiped her creation with a tiny hand, sending the buttons and sticks skittering to Fred, who started to stack them on top of each other. Ollie, not getting the reaction she wanted, began a new project.

Raised voices drifted into the room. To distract Troy and the twinks, I said, "As for your question, I didn't set out to teach. I loved studying history and stayed in school until I had to do something. Lecturing helps me learn even more, now that I have to understand the material in order to explain it."

There was a shout.

A slammed door.

The creak of the door reopening.

Heavy footsteps.

Rose rushed into the room, her purse slung over her shoulder. "Troy! It's time for you to take this old, easily manipulated, and desperate fool home."

Troy quickly got to his feet.

Sarah stood defiantly behind her mother.

"I'll walk you to the door," I said.

"I know the way!" Rose flipped around, not meeting Sarah's eye on her way to the front door.

Troy gave a supportive smile to me and then Sarah before tailing Rose, his head tucked down.

"I take it your conversation went well." I gazed at Sarah to judge her willingness to talk.

Which apparently turned out to be zero percent.

After she rushed upstairs in a huff, I asked the twins,

"Looks like it's just the three of us for dinner. What shall we have? Caviar and champagne, Fred?"

Freddie responded with a giggle, one arm over his head, and Ollie chucked one of the buttons at me.

"You, Ollie Dollie, take after your mother."

This prompted even more giggles from Fred. Ollie clapped her hands.

CHAPTER SIX

"*D*on't shoot!" I shimmied into the bedroom with my arms reaching for the sky.

Sarah, sitting up in bed reading a paperback, glared at me, but her face softened after a few seconds. "Are the kids in bed?"

"All quiet on the Western Front." I put a finger to my lips.

She rolled her eyes. "A World War Two comparison to our kids?"

"World War One actually, but I think you know that, English Teacher Extraordinaire."

"Why are you being nice to me?" Guilt flooded her expression.

I lay down next to her. "It's a new thing I'm trying."

"When did you get funny?" She smiled, although her eyes brimmed with sadness.

"When my wife started acting like me. Isn't this opposite day?" I squeezed her arm.

She sucked in a breath and released it with force. "I screwed up."

"Want to talk about it yet? Or shall I draw you a bath, ply you with wine, and then force you to talk?"

"To talk?" Her voice oozed sex appeal.

"You're taking impersonating Lizzie seriously." I propped my head on a bent elbow. "Yes, to talk. I know you. You need to talk about things."

Sarah chewed on her bottom lip, mulling over her words. "Maybe I've been wrong this entire time. It's best not to talk. Look what it got me earlier."

"I can make a strong case that not talking causes problems as well. Or do I need to remind you about couple's therapy?" I cracked a smile.

"Where's the middle ground?" She placed *Fifty Shades Darker* on her lap, spine up to keep her place.

I shrugged.

She laughed. "Look who I'm asking."

I playfully scouted over my shoulder.

She flicked the cover of the book. "I've been staring at the same page for the past hour."

"Maybe you should try the audio version." Inexplicitly, I tried to imagine listening to a BDSM book while walking across campus. What would my students think?

"I don't know why it bothers me." She yanked the covers higher over herself, knocking the book onto the carpet.

"What?" I asked just to be on the safe side, knowing she wasn't referring to reading or listening to smut.

"Troy."

"It's different—"

"If my mom was a man, it wouldn't matter to most."

I couldn't suppress a smile. "I was going to say, before I was so rudely interrupted,"—I rapped a finger against the tip of her nose—"that it's different for you. Your mother hasn't dated much since your father died." I paused to evaluate her reaction before plunging on. "I think it's telling that you cut me off. If this wasn't your mom, I think you'd be high-fiving Rose. Girl power and all that hoopla." I waved etcetera.

"But it *is* my mom. And Troy isn't my father. For so long it was just the two of us, and now there's someone else always hanging about, not always in person, but his existence is never far from either of our minds. I don't see her as often as I'm used to. Then there are the age and money factors." She leaned her head back, squishing her eyes shut.

"Which is why it's hard. You're invested emotionally, and you don't want to see your mom get hurt. What aspect of their relationship concerns you the most?"

"That he's using my mom. Her money and connections." Sarah stroked her left eyebrow. "Do you think it's weird that Troy finds my mother attractive? She's not a fitness nut or anything." Sarah removed her right hand to allow her eyes to bore into mine.

I forced the image out of my mind and suppressed a shudder. "Uh… I don't know how to answer that."

She gouged her eyes with the heels of her hands. "Probably for the best. Can we take that bath now?"

I launched off the bed. "With wine?"

"Maybe I should call Maddie."

"To take a bath with you?" I tutted. "I know I'm being über supportive and understanding, but really, don't press your luck. You're my wife, meaning no one else gets naked with you."

She inclined her head. "Is it odd I'm turned on now?"

"I have that effect—"

"Don't say it." She waggled her finger in the air, smiling with ease. "Go, get the wine." She dismissed me with a flourish of the hand.

I bowed. "At your service." Before heading downstairs, I slipped into the bathroom to turn on the water. The deep-jetted tub took ages to fill. Passing the bed, I asked, "Anything else?"

"Chocolate."

I bonked my forehead with a palm. "I should have known. Maybe Maddie can compile a checklist for these types of situations." I grinned at Sarah and skedaddled before she had a chance to add her two cents.

* * *

SARAH EASED INTO THE WATER, resting against me. She sipped her wine and then nibbled on a dark cashew cluster. "Thanks, Lizzie."

After kicking on the jets, I wrapped my arms around her. "Everything's going to be okay. You and your mom have a strong relationship."

"Even after I called her an old fool? And desperate?"

I had hoped Sarah hadn't actually used those words, but it was difficult to subscribe to this completely since Rose uttered them in my presence. At best, I hoped Rose had deduced from Sarah's comment. This didn't seem like the time to point out she should be more judicious when bashing her mom's boyfriend. So, I said, "Yes. Look at me. I never thought my dad and I could mend fences, and now he comes to birthday parties for our kids."

"I shouldn't have said it, though."

I attempted to wipe away all expression from my face, which had busted me on more than one occasion. "I won't argue with that."

Sarah quenched whatever feelings roiled inside with a deep tug of wine, clearly numbing the pain, which wasn't the best of signs. Given the argument she'd had with Rose earlier, I opted not to raise my alarm at the moment.

"I happen to know someone who owns a chain of flower shops." I snapped my fingers to the best of my ability, considering they were wet. "Just in case you want to apologize the Lizzie way."

"Without words?"

"Exactly. Even a word lover like me avoids them when situations are overly complicated." I wrapped my arms around her.

"I find that especially so when it comes to idiots uttering the words."

I squeezed her tighter in my arms. "Don't be so hard on yourself," I joked.

She laughed. Really laughed. "I never thought you'd be the one talking me off the ledge."

"That makes two of us. Being sensible is exhausting." I rested my head against the lip of the tub. "Any chance I can talk you into a massage?"

She drilled her elbow into my stomach. "You're comforting me."

"I thought I already did. How much do you need in one night?"

Sarah craned her head over her shoulder. "All of you."

"You may be in luck, because I want all of you. All of the time." I cradled her right breast in my hand.

She reciprocated by taking my hand and running it down her slick torso and back up.

Soon, our hungry hands explored her body while we kissed to the best of our abilities given our position in the tub. The jetted water helped keep her body afloat, but her neck could only twist so much.

"Take me," she urged, tossing her head into the crook of my neck. "Now."

My right hand teased her clit before I inserted two fingers inside.

Sarah reached around the back of my neck, tugging. Her free hand continued to trail up and down her body.

"I love it when you touch yourself," I said into her ear.

"I love—" Her breath hitched when I drove in hard, ignoring the pain in my wrist from the difficult angle.

It didn't take long for Sarah's body to start trembling. She came soon after.

Breathing heavily, she went limp. "I needed that. And this." She swept her wineglass to her lips.

"Ah, you have to get drunker to reciprocate. I get it."

I sensed her gaze zooming to the heavens. "You know that isn't the case. I need some Dutch courage to call my mom," she said in all seriousness.

I nodded, wondering if now was the best time for them to chat.

Sarah stood, water dripping from her. Bypassing toweling off, she eased into a plush robe. "I'll be in the library."

"Good luck."

She left, but I stayed in the tub.

CHAPTER SEVEN

*I*n the garage, I had one foot inside the SUV, preparing to swing my body behind the steering wheel.

Sarah stuck her head out the kitchen door. "Hey, can you pick up diapers on your way home?"

I pried a manila folder out of my mouth. "Sure. Anything else?"

"Surprises are always welcome." She rested her cheek against the doorjamb, chocolate eyes imploring. "Your shirt is inside out."

I glanced down, swearing under my breath. "Why didn't you tell me earlier?"

"I thought it'd be funny if you showed up the first day like that, but I just couldn't go through with it." She shrugged.

I tossed the folder and bag into the passenger seat and removed my blazer.

"Are you going to give the neighbor's a striptease?" Sarah's hand darted to the garage door control panel. The door started its downward descent.

"I'm running late," I growled, lifting my shirt over my head.

Sarah whistled. "Do you always wear one of my sexy bras on the first day of school?"

I sighed. "It was the only clean one I could find."

"Uh-huh."

With my shirt back on, I said, "See you this afternoon."

She blew me a kiss.

I thrummed my hands on the wheel, waiting for the garage door to reopen. "The woman loves to test me," I said to my reflection in the rearview mirror.

The parking lot outside the history building was full. As was the next one. Half a mile away, I finally nabbed a spot and had to make a run for my office to grab all the syllabi. At the far end of the hallway, a familiar and terrifying figure emerged out of Dr. Marcel's office.

I ducked back into my office, using my satchel as a cover, breaking into a cold sweat. This was the last thing I needed today of all days. Correction. This was the last thing I needed ever.

What the fuck was she doing here?

Why was she speaking to Dr. Marcel?

There were a zillion other questions and fears raging inside, but it was difficult to focus.

Think, Lizzie!

I peered furtively into the hallway to see if the coast was clear. Luckily, Meg, my blackmailing ex, had her back to me as she retreated through the exit on the far end of the hallway.

I sucked in a deep breath, releasing it in hopes of cleansing my aura, or whatever therapists called it. Fortunately, before therapy, I had trained myself to force down any type of emotion to focus on the matter at hand: my first class of the semester was starting in under three minutes.

Lecture first. Then, if needed, have a mental breakdown in my office before my next class.

I dashed down the two flights of stairs and arrived with

seconds to spare, out of breath and still slightly shaken from the Meg sighting. My voice warbled some when I greeted the students, but it became stronger with each word as I forced myself to step away from weak Lizzie to professor Lizzie.

* * *

LATER IN THE DAY, Dr. Marcel poked his head out of his office as I happened to be walking by. "Lizzie, do you have a moment?"

"Of course." I entered, easing into the wingback chair, praying to the history gods this conversation wouldn't have a thing to do with Meg. My fingers dug into the leather armrests.

He took his seat behind his desk and folded his hands. "How was your first day?"

"Not bad, aside from the usual craziness of students petitioning, some practically begging, to enroll in a course that's already full."

"Ah, yes. As if they didn't know all along they needed to fill their history credits in order to graduate." He looked around his office. "It'll be weird not being here next fall. I may even miss the frantic pleading of seniors." His watery eyes glistened with fondness.

"I imagine so. The department won't be the same without you."

He waved a wrinkled and spotted hand. "It's time for new blood to sit in this chair." Dr. Marcel cleared his throat and shifted in his leather chair. "Meg was here earlier."

"Oh," I forced out, hoping my tone didn't match my Code Red panic level whirling through every fiber.

Dr. Marcel bobbed his head absently. "She came to talk... to me."

"I see," I said, not understanding why I needed to be informed.

He sucked in some air and tossed his hands up in a desperate way. "She's, uh..." He shifted in his seat again. "Meg asked if I thought you'd be okay hearing from her."

"Umm..." Proper words wouldn't form on my lips.

"I understand your hesitation." He leaned on his forearms. "But, perhaps it'd be helpful for the two of you to talk. Closure. Isn't that what experts say?"

I nodded, dumbstruck. Not speaking to Meg was enough closure for me.

"She doesn't want to blindside you, which is why..." Even Dr. Marcel seemed incapable of seeing why I should agree.

Blindside? The word was entirely inadequate. It was as if Meg dropped Little Boy, the atomic bomb that devastated Hiroshima, into my lap.

"Do you know why she wants to talk?" It was my turn to clear my throat. "After all this time?" Not to mention the last time I saw my ex was when I shoved Meg into a cab after finding her in a hotel *working*, using this term loosely, as a prostitute to support her addiction.

"Yes, but she should really be the one to tell you her purpose. That is if you meet up with her, which is entirely up to you." Dr. Marcel stared at the bookshelf behind me, clearly uncomfortable having this conversation. He was the one who had arranged rehab after the hotel incident, and while he didn't know all the details, he was aware Meg's behavior had been deplorable. Not just her prostituting herself but how she'd treated me.

To head off having to say no to my mentor in case he once again pressed the issue of Meg contacting me, I asked, "Does she have the same phone number?"

"I think so." He looked it up on his phone. "Here, just in case." He grabbed a pen and jotted it down on a notepad, the university's seal at the top. It seemed so inappropriate to have

Meg's name on anything related to the university after she'd flushed down one opportunity after another.

I took the paper from him.

"It's up to you to call or not," Dr. Marcel said in his fatherly way.

I nodded, rising from my chair. Considering my work number and email was on the university website, if Meg really wanted to get a hold of me, she could. Not to mention I'd never bothered changing my personal phone number.

He stood, walking me to the door with his hand on my back. "We still on for dinner at the end of this month?"

"Yep," I said in the least peeved tone I could manage since it wasn't his fault Meg the home-wrecker was back in Fort Collins.

"Good." His lack of a more verbose response made it clear I wasn't the only one who wanted to end this awkward conversation.

I forced a smile and left his office, heading straight for mine with my head down, avoiding eye contact with fellow professors as students chased them down in the history wing hallway. After shutting the door, I started to tear the phone number up but stopped myself.

Why did my blackmailing ex want to meet, and why had she gone to Dr. Marcel to arrange it?

* * *

I GOT HOME AROUND four after teaching my second class.

Sarah, with Fred on her hip, met me at the kitchen door. "How'd it go?"

"Fine," I muttered, patting Sarah's head and kissing Freddie's cheek. "Where's Ollie?"

"You okay?" she asked, taking a step back to get a better look at me.

"Yeah. Why?"

"You just petted my head like I was Hank." Her face crinkled with concern.

I kissed her cheek. "Sorry. Long day."

"That doesn't bode well for the semester."

We wandered to the front room, where Bailey and Ollie sat watching television. Or rather, Bailey was engrossed in *Judge Judy*, and Ollie was reaching for me.

I took her in my arms. "How's my favorite girl?"

Ollie clapped.

"I thought I was your favorite girl," Sarah teased.

"I'd put you in the woman category." I held Ollie close.

Sarah jiggled her brows. "I'd put you in the baby momma one." She motioned for us to switch twins. "He needs to be changed."

I rolled my eyes. "Nicely played."

Bailey stood. "I better get to class." She stretched her arms overhead as if waking from a deep sleep.

"What class?" I asked with too much eagerness, a rookie mistake when dealing with the likes of Bailey.

"Um… geology or maybe Scientology." She wore an evil grin. "See ya tomorrow."

Sarah said goodbye.

Bailey bolted.

When the coast was clear, I said, "Are we sure Bailey is actually enrolled at CSU?"

"Just because she isn't jumping up and down with excitement doesn't mean she's conning everyone."

Perhaps, but even the so-called cool freshman showed some excitement about being out of the family home and starting college. "Let's hope you're right. I don't need any m—" I stopped myself from saying *more* and opted for, "drama this semester. Ready, Freddie?"

Sarah followed me to the nursery with Ollie in her arms.

"Our little girl doesn't want to be left out." She waved a hand in front of her nose to alert me to Olivia's stink bomb.

"She takes after you with her timing." I bumped the nursery door open with my hip. "How'd it go today?" It was the first time since summer started that I was away for the majority of the day.

Sarah set Ollie down on her changing table. "Good. Bailey was a great help, and Maddie stopped by for lunch. You?"

"Fine." I cleaned Fred's bum, holding his legs in the air, while he twisted and turned, having a great time.

"That's the second *fine* since you got home. Let's get the kiddos in their bouncy chairs so you and I can talk."

I bottled-up a groan, not wanting to dump my Meg drama in Sarah's lap. She had enough going on with the twins and her mom.

"Don't bother," Sarah said in tune with my feelings. "I can feel it."

"What?" I looked over my shoulder.

"The eye roll or whatever." She held up Ollie, completely changed. "I win again."

"Not sure you're setting a good example for our children with the way you race me with everything." I finished securing Fred's diaper.

"Says the woman who loses in all baby-tending categories." Sarah nuzzled her head against Ollie's. "What happened today?"

I sighed. "Can we talk about it later?"

"Helen and your father are coming over for dinner."

I squeezed my eyes shut momentarily. "That's right. After that, then." I paused. "I thought your mom was joining us."

"She cancelled." Her voice was flat.

Their talk on the phone had cracked the door open to getting past the Troy situation, but as far as I could tell, neither was willing to settle the matter completely. Not yet.

By the time Dad and Helen left, both of us were the walking wounded, and the only thing either of us wanted to do was get some sleep, leaving the Meg conversation for a different time. Or maybe I could avoid her and not have to open the wound all over.

CHAPTER EIGHT

"*L*izzie!"

    I whipped around on the quad, trying to locate the voice, dread bubbling in the pit of my stomach.

"Lizzie!"

I groaned.

Meg reached me simply because my legs had failed to move. We eyed the other, unsure where to go from here.

"Hi," she said with a shyness I didn't know she possessed.

I nodded, my fingers gripping the strap of my bag across my heart.

"You aren't going to make this easy, are you?"

"W-what?" I stuttered.

"Talking."

"Not my strong suit."

She bobbed her head, shoving her hands into the pockets of her jeans. "Right. You prefer sticking your head in the sand."

I nipped the retort, "Better than tucking into booze." Instead, I remained silent.

"You never responded to the voice mail or email..." She

trailed off while students streamed past us as if we were unwanted obstacles.

It was the third week of the semester, and everyone was starting to hit their stride when it came to schedules and overall business associated with university life.

Meg puffed her cheeks full of air, held it for several seconds, and then let it seep out. "Can we go someplace more private?"

Nope, I screamed in my head. "Uh…"

Several nicknames for Meg rolled through my mind. Hooking Meg. Blackmailer Meg. Home-wrecker Meg.

"Lizzie, please. I need to say something to you." She looked vulnerable.

That extinguished my nerve to say no, turn around, and walk away for good.

"My office?" I posed.

She put out her hand for me to lead the way.

My mind continued to scramble for words to get me out of this situation. I hadn't seen Meg in years. Not since she'd reached her rock bottom, after skimming the surface of it for many months and making me wonder if she'd ever reach it. Back then, she blamed me for much of her woes, including selling her body since I had stopped handing over wads of cash. Even though the cerebral part of me knew I wasn't to blame, the emotional side bobbed in guilt, like a child tossed into a pool on the first day of swim class. Leveraging my guilty conscience was one of Meg's greatest weapons in her destroy-Lizzie arsenal. Maybe it was time for me to re-read *Macbeth*, Shakespeare's masterful play where guilt was the motivating factor for all the crimes and drove everyone insane. Would it be rude to thumb through my copy while she spoke?

We reached the nearly deserted history wing, relief flooding my system. Not everyone knew Sarah's animus for Meg, but it wouldn't take Einstein to put two and two together. Ushering her inside, I closed the door before anyone got an eyeful of my ex, who was also a former student often seen in these halls.

I skirted around the visitor's chair and desk as if Meg was a praying mantis. Plopping down in the safety of my chair, I picked up a cheap green pen with CSU written on it. "So?" I focused my attention on the pen in my hands, clicking it repeatedly.

"How have you been?" She tried not looking at the pen, but it was hard not to.

Click.

"Good."

Click.

Meg readjusted in her seat, the vinyl cushion creaking. "I hear you have twins."

I nodded.

"A boy and a girl."

I nodded again followed by a click.

"And you're married..." Meg motioned with her hand for me to fill in the blanks.

Was she stalking me? Several clicks. And did she expect me to open up about marriage and my two beautiful children? They represented everything good in my life. Meg was the snake in the garden. Mixing the two would bring down my entire world. She had to know that. Was that why she mentioned them? Years ago, she leveraged threats to my career to get me in line. Was she hedging my family was my weak spot? She was right, of course. I'd do anything to protect Sarah and my children.

As if in tune with my worry she was stalking me, Meg said, "I visited Janice in California. She seems to be settling into domestic life well."

"Oh." I didn't know what to say.

"We had a good talk." She perked up. "I hear her cousin Bailey is your nanny. Small world."

Much too small at the moment. *Click, click, click.*

"I finished my PhD, and I'm shopping for a teaching gig. A permanent one to get back on my feet," she tossed out.

"Oh." Slowly, I looked up. As far as I knew, Dr. Marcel wasn't looking to fill any entry-level positions, and I had a hard time believing he'd hire her after... everything. The office grapevine reported she had her sights on Boulder, a city known for being granola and quite possibly more accepting of a woman with a sordid past. Their love for pot was slightly worrisome. My biggest concern was its proximity to me. Although it was a forty-five-minute drive, it was way too close, but it wasn't like I could stake claim on the entire state or region. Or could I? How good were Dr. Marcel's connections there? Should I remind him the majority of Boulderites had their alarms set for 4:20 as a way to discourage Meg from being hired?

Meg's deep green eyes roamed over the items on my desk as if searching the open books and journals for a blueprint for whatever she wanted to say to me. "I'm going through the steps."

I tapped the pen on the edge of the desk. "I'm not following."

"The steps for recovery. I'm on step nine."

"Which means?" I wiped my left palm on my trousers.

"Making restitution."

"How's that going?"

"At the moment, not well." She offered a bashful smile.

I blinked.

"There's your *deer in headlights* look." There was a trace of humor in her tone. "I know I can't take back all the pain I caused you, but..." She straightened in her chair. "I'm sorry, Lizzie, for—" Her voice faltered, showing a crack in her bravado.

My instinct was to comfort her. *Damn that guilty conscience!*

Then the memories of Drunk Meg killed that desire.

I didn't know if she had chutzpah for coming here as if she'd never blackmailed me, or sold herself, or if she'd blocked out all the memories to survive. Kinda like how I had weeks earlier to survive teaching.

I fidgeted in my seat, knowing I resembled a first grader who didn't prep for show and tell. Finally, I said, "It's okay—"

She shook her head adamantly. "No, don't. It wasn't okay. What I did. The things I said. How I treated you. My behavior. None of it was okay."

Maybe she remembered some of it, then. I focused on my breathing. In. Out. In. Out.

"Not a day goes by without thinking of you." She spoke to her folded hands in her lap.

I couldn't see her face, but I took the opportunity to note the normal skin pallor of her forehead. Not booze-soaked and splotchy. Her blonde hair had a shine. Her V-neck sweater hugged her curves, instead of hanging limply. "You look good— better, I mean."

"I'm trying." She met my eyes.

"I'm glad." I rested on my forearms. "Really, Meg. I want the best for you." *As long as you stay away from me and my family.*

The left side of her mouth tugged up. "Thanks. I'm happy everything is going so well for you. I never thought you'd have kids, though."

I cracked a smile. It was hard not to with the mention of Ollie and Freddie. "Neither did I back... then." When I'd barely started my graduate program and was naïve, making me easy pickings for the likes of Con Artist Meg.

"I'd like to meet them. And Sarah." She added, "Officially."

Like that was ever going to happen. I'd rather have Mussolini over for tea. "Sure, sure," I said in the placating tone I'd used with her many times in the past.

Meg, naturally, picked up on it. She rose. "Thanks for listening. I know it wasn't easy for you."

I rushed around the desk and reached for the door handle, relieved to end the meeting. "Nor you, I imagine." I hoped she understood her old power was useless without me coming out and saying that. I'd moved on with Sarah and the twins and nothing she said or did could help her weasel her way back in.

Meg stood inches from me, staring into my eyes like she had a thousand other things she wanted to say. Then a curtain came down over her face. "Bye, Lizzie."

"Bye, Meg." My tone was resolute, and I mentally high-fived myself, following it up with a celebratory spike of the football in the end zone.

She left. Closing the door, I rested my forehead against the wood, completely zapped of positive energy.

* * *

"WAS YOUR DAY THAT BAD?" Sarah asked immediately upon my entrance into the kitchen.

"What? No." I set my bag on the barstool. "How goes the battle with the twinks?"

"Battle is an appropriate word choice today." Sarah jerked her head upward. "Bailey is giving them their bath."

"Should I even ask why so early?" I glanced at my watch. Didn't Bailey have Scientology class? Although, I was 99.98 percent sure that wasn't the name of the course.

"It involved an art and food project gone awry. Let's leave it at that. Do you want to shower before going out?"

I sniffed my armpit. "Trying to tell me something?"

"Looks like you could use alone time, and that's really the only place in our house for privacy these days."

"You know, I'll take you up on your offer." I kissed her cheek.

In the bathroom, I pulled my phone out of my left pocket and realized I'd forgotten to turn it back on after my last lecture. After flipping it on, I put it on the counter and then rummaged the walk-in closet for a clean pair of jeans, a shirt, and a sweater.

Outfit selected, I hopped into the shower. Sarah was right. This was exactly what I needed. The hot water streamed over me, doing its best to obliterate the weirdness pinging throughout my body.

The shower door opened.

"I was hoping you'd join me." I turned around, and my smile fell when I spied Sarah's face. "What's wrong?"

Sarah held up my phone. "You got a message."

"And?" I swiped water droplets from my forehead. Sarah wasn't the type to read my texts or emails, nor was I one to keep them from her.

"I caught a glimpse of the name when it lit up."

I rinsed conditioner out of my hair, massaging my scalp, my mini-version of Cloud Nine. "Who was it?"

She waited for me to shut off the water so I could hear the name. "Meg."

My entire body went cold despite the steam swirling around. Drying off my face, I wrapped a towel around my body and stepped out. "She stopped by my office today." I added, "She's on step nine," to explain what I still didn't fully understand. While part of me could see the purpose of instructing an addict to say sorry to those they'd hurt, as a way of realizing the magnitude of their actions, the other part didn't like the addict tracking down loved ones after they had, hopefully, healed their wounds inflicted by said addict. Did they, whoever *they* were, realize it was putting the innocent in a terrible predicament by accepting an apology and likely opening the door to becoming a crutch to keep the addict clean and sober?

It was beyond selfish, and frankly typical of Meg, which

worried me more than I wanted to admit. Meg's addiction wasn't solely booze. Adoration also fueled her. When she couldn't achieve that, she turned to terrorizing to keep subjects under her spell. Time to reread Machiavelli's sixteenth century political treatise *The Prince* as guidance. Meg was more Machiavellian than the author.

"And you didn't think to tell me?" Sarah staggered back a step.

"I was going to after dinner. I promise." I pressed my palms together like I was praying for absolution.

Sarah's expression wavered from angry to believing me and then back to angry. "What's step nine?"

"Telling people sorry or something. It's part of her recovery." Perhaps step nine didn't really exist or it was meant to be handled differently. I needed to look into that.

"Is she back in Colorado for good?" She leaned against the counter with her arms folded over her chest.

"Boulder, according to the office grapevine."

Sarah inhaled deeply and released it. "I don't like it."

That makes two of us. "Did you want to hop in?" I gestured to the shower.

"I—" She looked to the shower and then back at me, her shoulders slumping. "Why didn't you call me after it happened?"

I sighed. "It literally occurred less than an hour ago. I didn't call because I wanted to tell you in person." I put a hand on each of her shoulders.

"Because you knew I'd be upset?"

"No—"

"You don't think I should be upset that the woman who tormented you is back?"

I lumbered back a step and showed my palms. "That's not what I meant. Not at all. It was the last thing I expected today, and... I needed time to process." I shrugged. "I'm sorry you found out this way."

Seeming somewhat mollified, she said, "I don't trust her."

I snorted. "Join the club."

"How do you feel?" Kindness seeped into her eyes.

"Cold." I raised my arms to show her the goose bumps.

Sarah started to speak but released a soul-cleansing sigh. "Fine. Get dressed for dinner, but we aren't done with this conversation." She gnashed her teeth.

Dealing with an angry Sarah, given her irrationality as of late, was one of the last things I needed to juggle on top of the Meg bombshell.

Although, Sarah had helped me through the situation before. Would it be prudent to let her in and admit this was beyond my personal survival skills?

I squirted lotion, which was jasmine with a hint of cedarwood, into my hands and placed my right foot on Sarah's makeup chair. "It was strange, you know? Seeing Meg... after everything. And she acted... I don't know, like everything was normal. I mean, she was nervous, but at the same time, she wasn't." I repeated the lotion routine with my other leg. "I'm not doing the meeting justice. I wish you'd been there. You're better at picking these things apart." It'd played over and over in my head for the past sixty minutes, yet I couldn't find the words to let Sarah in completely. Not because I didn't want to. Nor because of the Troy situation.

Maybe I was embarrassed that Meg still had some kind of power over me, Independent Lizzie. In the past, she had blackmailed me for money. Now that she was looking for a teaching gig, she still held something over my head. I never wanted my colleagues to learn the truth about our relationship. The blackmail or Meg's methods of making money to support her habit, which would be embarrassing for her if that got out, but there was a nagging thought Meg might not see it that way. She excelled at playing the victim and laying all blame at my feet.

Sarah bobbed her head, unusually quiet.

"Talk to me." I slipped on a pair of plain cotton panties.

"I don't know what to think, really. I thought you—we were done with Meg."

It wasn't like I could control or stop Meg from seeking me out, but from the fire in Sarah's eyes, it didn't seem pertinent to bring that up. I laughed nervously, which wasn't the right emotion to express, while putting on a matching bra. "I am. It's not like I requested the meeting. And the way she put it, as part of her recovery… and Dr. Marcel and Janice had already spoken to her. What could I say?"

"Do you still love her?"

Love, no. Was I conflicted? A thousand times yes. Was it evil of me to wish I'd never see Meg again? Not that I wanted her to get mowed down by a bus, but couldn't she set up her new life far away from me? Like Mars? Or, were there any experiments, like the Biosphere, I could nominate her for? Sealing her off with a handful of people to test the practicality of settling on different planets or the moon even? Maybe it was time to foster alliances with science professors.

Right now, though, Sarah needed reassurance. She'd been my rock for so long. It was my turn to shoulder everything. "I'm in love with you." I took her hands in mine. "Our life together. The twinkies. Sarah, you have absolutely nothing to worry about." I so wanted that to be true.

"I… I'm sorry." She rested her head against my shoulder. "I'm not myself these days."

I kissed the top of her head. "Take your own advice. Hop in the shower. Let the news wash off. Hot water does wonders for the soul."

* * *

We almost literally bumped into Dr. Marcel and his wife outside the glass doors of the Vietnamese restaurant.

"Imagine meeting you here," Dr. Marcel joked, dropping his wife's hand to greet us.

"I secretly hoped the babysitter wouldn't show up, forcing you to bring the twins." Mrs. Marcel pulled Sarah into a comforting hug. "You look like you need a break, though."

Dr. Marcel air-kissed both sides of Sarah's cheeks. "If your two are anything like our boys..." He left the rest unsaid, a trend I'd started to notice loving parents used when not wanting to bad mouth their own flesh and blood.

Inside, the lights were dim, making the large and colorful fish tank pop into view. Green vine-like plants resided in the corner with a trickling waterfall and small pond. Several people were squeezed onto the bench off to the side of the entrance, probably waiting for a table.

The hostess offered a warm smile, and Sarah supplied her name for the reservation. The woman promptly escorted us to the table. "Anything to drink?"

"Wine. Loads," Sarah said, coupled with a joking smile.

The wine list was offered to Sarah, who immediately handed it off to Dr. Marcel with the usual *you know better* reason.

"He likes to think he's an expert, but his method involves selecting the third most expensive," Mrs. Marcel said behind her hand, although she'd spoken loud enough for all to hear.

"It hasn't let us down yet," he defended with a gleam in his eyes.

"Lizzie goes for the most expensive," Sarah offered.

Dr. Marcel perked up in his seat. "Wait until the twins get older. The bills really start to stack up."

I groaned. "Maybe my boss will take pity on me and give me a raise."

Dr. Marcel pointed out his selection to the waiter who had stepped in for the hostess, before saying, "Wish I could, but our budget was slashed for the fifth straight year. Soon, computers will be teaching history courses, robots will take over administrative tasks, scheduling, serving coffee..." He motioned that the list went on and on. "Have you considered teaching an online course?"

"Not an appropriate dinner conversation when trying to entertain parents of young twins on a rare night of freedom." Mrs. Marcel admonished her husband with a finger wag.

"We dissect the effects of war on societies for a living. You really expect Lizzie and I to have an upbeat conversation?" Dr. Marcel offered a teasing smile.

Sarah and Mrs. Marcel locked eyes. "Maybe we should guide the conversation," Sarah said.

"Fine with me." I brushed my hands, showing my relief. "I have to talk for a living."

Both spouses rolled their eyes.

"Careful, Lizzie. I think they're on to us." Dr. Marcel sipped his water.

"The pretending you're exhausted from working and shouldn't be expected to do anything else?" Mrs. Marcel arched a thin eyebrow.

Sarah and I exchanged a smile. Many times, we'd commented on how we wanted to be like the Marcels. Playful, loving, and honest.

"Woman!" was all Dr. Marcel had.

Mrs. Marcel turned to me. "What's new with you, Lizzie?"

I wondered if Sarah had alerted Mrs. Marcel via text about the Meg bombshell as a test. Normally, she'd reach out to Maddie and her mom, but Rose was out of the question at the moment, leaving me to wonder if she'd reached out to a different mom-like figure for guidance.

I went for it. "I did have an interesting meeting today. With Meg."

Sarah's face hardened.

"She finally got a hold of you," Dr. Marcel said, showing zero indication of his true feelings.

I nodded, chancing a stealthy peek at my wife, who seemed to be frozen in time, and from the static expression on her face, I was in for a very long night of explaining and reassuring.

"And?" Mrs. Marcel asked, eyes wide.

"It was okay, I guess." I recrossed my legs. "Weird, actually."

"I hear she's speaking at the conference in Boulder next month," Dr. Marcel said. "It's good she's focusing on work."

"Aren't you slotted to speak at CU next month?" Sarah asked me in a confrontational tone.

I swallowed. "I'll need to check my calendar, but I think you're right." *Why oh why didn't I just confirm right then and there?* I hadn't known Meg would be speaking, but fluffing the simple question made it appear like I did. If I could palm-slap myself without drawing more ire from Sarah, I would have. Possibly hard enough to knock myself out. I channeled my therapist: Sneaky Lizzie would only complicate the hell out of this situation, and it was already mired with land mines.

Mrs. Marcel honed in on Sarah's anger, her face registering support. "Frank will be there." She said it as if I needed a guardian. The Marcels didn't know the whole story, but I'm sure they gleaned enough to realize Meg was bad news. Like when Hitler marched into Poland, unleashing World War II.

"You've always wanted to see me in action. Maybe this is a good time to come," I offered to my wife as a peace offering.

Sarah didn't commit, but I could practically see her brain kicking into action, determining who could watch the kids all day on a Saturday. Bailey typically didn't work on the weekends, and if Sarah asked her mom, that would involve Troy.

"What's your topic?" Dr. Marcel asked, and Mrs. Marcel didn't attempt to derail the comfort of a safe conversation.

The waiter returned to take our orders. After glancing at the menu, I selected pork dumplings as a starter and lemon chicken with steamed rice. Sarah opted for crab cheese wontons and lemongrass salmon.

While the Marcels ordered, I reached for Sarah's hand under the table. Knowing why I was reassuring her, she gazed at me with the look that had made me fall in love with her so many years ago. If Meg messed this up for me, I would...

After the waiter left, Mrs. Marcel turned to Sarah. "Are the twins talking your ears off yet?"

Take note, Lizzie. When in doubt, bring up the safest of conversations.

"Ollie is saying *mama* like a pro now, along with a few other words. Fred seems to be taking his time saying more than *no.*" Sarah's shoulders relaxed and her eyes twinkled. "Lizzie is praying he's holding out to say something that will instantly qualify him for Mensa."

"I am not." I feigned being indignant, but she wasn't too far off the mark. I figured Freddy was holding back for a reason.

Ignoring me, she continued. "She loves to repeat words. Slow-ly."

"I'm sensing sar-casm," I mocked, much relieved Sarah was willing to put the conference kerfuffle aside for the sake of the dinner.

The Marcels laughed, and conversation broke off into Sarah and Mrs. Marcel discussing twin stuff while Dr. Marcel and I veered into work talk.

"Well, this is a surprise," a voice said behind Sarah and me.

From the way Sarah flinched, it wasn't a welcome one. Dutifully, Sarah stood and said, "Mom, how lovely to bump into you." She neglected to address Troy, who was standing right next to Rose.

Inwardly, I winced over Sarah's formal manner, so unlike the way she usually acted around Rose.

Dr. Marcel, ever the gentleman, got to his feet and greeted

Rose with his sophisticated but easygoing kisses. Had he picked up the trait while living in Europe?

All eyes were on Troy, and I expected Rose to introduce him, but she focused her attention on Sarah. Was this the Cavanaugh version of High Noon? It was hard to imagine an Old West shootout in a stylish Vietnamese restaurant with a large mural of three ladies in colorful full-length dresses and white cone hats carrying baskets, but stranger things have happened, especially lately.

I headed off any fireworks by saying in the friendliest voice I could summon, "Troy, this is my mentor and boss, Dr. Marcel, and his wife." Turning to the Marcels, I said, "This is Troy, Rose's... dinner companion." I was certain Rose would have preferred I'd said *boyfriend*, or maybe *partner* was more fitting for a woman of her age, but my wife wouldn't have been happy and I was already on her shit list.

The fire emanating from Rose's eyes was proof positive Sarah had failed the test. How ironic, considering the test Sarah had lain before my feet earlier.

"Would you two like to join us?" Dr. Marcel asked.

"We wouldn't want to intrude," Troy rushed to say.

"Not at all. We're like family," Mrs. Marcel said.

Sarah, usually the observer of my awkward family situations, quailed in her four-inch heels.

"We'd love to," Rose accepted with too much glee.

Several scenarios ran through my head. One, faint. Two, jab a chopstick into my chest. Three, scream *rat*, and step aside for all the diners to run outside. Could I be sued for that?

Nixing all three, I sat down and replaced my napkin in my lap, because that clearly was the only civilized response to the situation.

The hostess procured two chairs, placing Rose and Troy in Sarah's direct line of sight. Sarah, much to her credit or not—I wasn't sure if this was a continuation of the High

Noon scenario—didn't wither under Rose's penetrating brown eyes. Again, I rethought the third option, the least painful, but lawsuits could take years and drain our trust funds.

Mrs. Marcel came to my aid. "Thank goodness you arrived when you did. Frank had that look in his eye. Like he was going to break out into a depressing lecture about life on the home front."

Dr. Marcel slanted his head in a professorial way. "Don't tempt me. I perform better with a larger crowd, and everyone loves to hear a rousing lecture about the French resistance during the war. Just ask my adoring students."

I was willing to bet the couple sensed the tension between mother and daughter. Of course, their staring competition wasn't discrete. Not to mention Troy's hangdog expression.

"Troy's also a teacher," Rose said.

Mrs. Marcel gripped the tabletop. "I'm surrounded!"

Dr. Marcel, Troy, and I laughed, all of us putting on a show, not feeling at ease.

"Oh, you're safe with Troy." Rose smiled at Mrs. Marcel.

Sarah nearly choked on her wine, and I prayed Rose didn't catch it.

Rose said, "He teaches first grade. Kids love him, and he loves kids."

Luckily, Sarah had set down her wine. When was the last time I took first aid classes? Probably time for recertification for adults. Or, did I need to freshen up on the one for babies since the twins were now a year old? I reached for my phone but thought better of it.

"So, you're the only one at the table making a difference. Teaching young minds." Dr. Marcel refilled his wife's glass and held the bottle up for Sarah.

She nodded for more.

Dr. Marcel leaned over to fill the glass.

I motioned to the waiter, indicating we needed another bottle.

There was a lull at the table.

Mrs. Marcel smiled at me expectantly. I wanted to say, "You're barking up the wrong tree if you expect me to guide the conversation away from the edge of despair."

Sarah gleefully led the way. "Troy is the son of one of my mother's cruising buddies. Or was."

"You aren't her son anymore?" Dr. Marcel attempted to lighten the mood with a joke.

"Perhaps not," Troy said without levity, fidgeting with his chopsticks.

Rose narrowed her eyes. "I think my English-teacher daughter meant I'm no longer friends with Troy's mom since I started dating her son."

"That's too bad." Mrs. Marcel flagged down the waiter. "Are you ready to order?" She posed to Rose and Troy and then added to the waiter, "Can you arrange for all the meals to come out at once?"

"Of course."

Why not extend the misery? Or impending gunfight? Rose may be the type to carry a small pistol in her purse. I'd recently watched a newscast about the NRA channel and the accessories they sold women, including purses with hidden compartments for guns. That would be right up Rose's alley.

Sarah furtively pulled her phone out of her clutch, and I wondered if she was going to fake a twin emergency. I hoped she would. Sarah replaced the phone without uttering a word. Disappointed, I forced a smile.

"Did you two meet on a cruise, then?" Mrs. Marcel asked.

"No, Troy gets seasick. I met him on solid land." She gave him a smile that implied it was an inside joke.

Troy, slightly green around the gills, nodded. Teaching first graders probably didn't prepare the bachelor for tonight's impromptu family dilemma. Silently, I cheered for him to break out into a stirring rendition of "Twinkle Twinkle Little Star."

"You can't handle being on a ship?" Sarah asked.

"He gets seasick," Rose repeated.

"But you love to cruise," Sarah said pointedly to her mom.

"There's more to life than cruising."

"No, there isn't." Sarah held firm.

"Yes, there is," Rose said through gritted teeth.

"You'll never go on another cruise again?" Sarah's expression was fierce.

"Maybe not."

"This is what you want? A cruiseless life?"

"Would that be so bad?" Rose cocked her head in a threatening way.

"You tell me. You've dedicated your life to making friends. A support network after Dad died. And now, you've alienated yourself and for what…?" Sarah seemed to realize what direction she was going and changed tact. "No more vacations with your friends who have been there for you for three decades."

If the Marcels hadn't picked up on the tension, they surely did now. The timing couldn't have been better if we were in a RomCom. "There are always seasickness pills," I said, inwardly kicking myself for getting in the middle, but watching these two bicker about conducting a so-called cruising lifestyle in front of the Marcels was excruciating.

Sarah shook her head. "Sometimes they're useless."

"Sometimes they work." I squeezed Sarah's leg under the table.

She shoved my hand off. "I'm only thinking of Troy's well-being. Getting out in the middle of the ocean, realizing he's made a mistake, and…"

"And, what?" Rose barked.

"I can't fly, either," Troy said. "I've taken pills, but on the last flight, I had a panic attack and paced in the galley for the majority of the flight. I swore I'd never fly again."

This nipped Rose and Sarah's battle of wills. Had Troy missed the subtext? He did teach first grade. Was there subtext in Dick and Jane stories? Wait, weren't they siblings? Maybe Ollie and Freddie could replace them. If my memory served correctly, the stories were coma-inducing. *Snap out of it, Lizzie.* Troy whistled when nervous, and apparently, I entertained inane internal thoughts.

"Lizzie, what are you thinking about? By the intensity of your expression, it has to be a doozy," Mrs. Marcel said.

"Oh, nothing." I waved.

"Your latest research topic, perhaps?" Mrs. Marcel urged.

Picking up on her intent, I said, "Well, yes, actually."

Dr. Marcel jumped in. "Her topic is fascinating. Go on." He motioned that I had the floor.

* * *

"DID THE TWINKIES BEHAVE?" I whispered to Bailey, noticing she didn't have any textbooks or notes out. She'd mentioned earlier in the evening she had a test or quiz the following day.

She stood from the couch, stretching her arms overhead. "Perfect angels."

"Did you drug them?" Sarah teased.

"Got extra?" I added.

Sarah led Bailey to the front door, while I headed to the kitchen to prep tea.

Moments later, Sarah staggered in, looking like a child preparing for a lecture. "You staying up?" She parked her butt on the barstool.

"Thought I'd get some work done." I avoided her eye. Earlier, I had thought this talk would have been all about Meg and how I had lied about the conference, but after Rose showed up, Sarah quickly shot up the naughty list. Part of me wished we could deal with the Meg issue. I was used to being the source of trouble in the relationship and knew how to navigate that, mostly.

"Talking about your research all night wasn't enough?" She yawned.

Ignoring the dig, I said, "It inspired me."

"Or you're using it as an excuse."

"Two cups, then?" I pulled another mug out of the cupboard.

Sarah rested her face in her hands, sighing. "What's wrong with me?"

"Hey, this has been an exhausting day and night. No trick questions." I reached for the purple Earl Grey box. "What kind of tea do you want?"

Not responding to my question, she launched into, "Mom is going to kill me."

I nodded, selecting chamomile and honey for Sarah. "With good cause," I wanted to say but thought better. Or should I get it out in the open? All signs pointed to Troy being a good man, and I'd known many snakes since childhood.

"Why doesn't Mom see he's using her?" Sarah said.

"That's never an easy thing to admit." I added, "If true."

Her head popped out of her hands. "What does that mean?"

"Do you have concrete proof? You know what they say about assuming." I left it at that, trying to determine how much she was willing to hear at the moment.

"Do you honestly think he likes my mom?"

I met her eyes. "I do. Yes, he's a bit odd, but really, aren't we all? Maybe instead of battling your mom, you should try getting to know him. If I remember correctly, I was a hot mess when we met. Luckily, you gave me a chance. And so did your mother."

"You still lied earlier at dinner," she said, although I noted her tone suggested she understood why.

With a hand over my heart, I said, "I did. I don't know why." I let my hand fall. "Yes, I do. Dealing with Meg again scares me." Saying that made me feel stronger. "Earlier, when I said goodbye to her, I foolishly thought that was the end of the Meg saga." I ran a hand over my forehead. "I had absolutely no idea she'd be speaking that weekend. I know attending a history conference isn't your idea of fun, but if we can find a babysitter, I would really like you to be there. I'm asking for help."

Her eyes misted. "Thank you for saying all that. It scares me, too." Sarah licked her lips and then took a deep breath.

"I want to keep our line of communication open, especially since you're falling apart with the whole Troy thing." I smiled to blunt the statement. "Tell me how I can help you." Because I was clueless.

She buried her face in her hands. "I don't like acting like this. It makes me feel so dirty." She pulled her hands away, her eyes imploring. "When did I turn into this person?"

"Maybe your true self is finally coming through." I jabbed my hands in the air. "Just kidding."

Before the teakettle could whistle and wake the kids, I killed the flame. I poured water into both mugs and scooted Sarah's chamomile over to her.

Holding the paper tab, she dabbed the bag in and out of the water. "I don't want to be this woman. So judgmental. Cruel—"

"It's hard to watch. Rose dotes on the twins, and she's always there for them and you, I might add. How many times have we called her when in a jam?" I mimed too many to count. "And now with Troy in the picture and your instant dislike— You're teetering on the edge of the Scotch-lady zone."

"I am not—" A look of disgust slammed into her eyes. "Oh, God. Am I?"

I held my thumb and forefinger in the air. "A smidge. But admitting you have a problem is the first step."

"Does step nine involve apologizing?" Her shoulders stiffened.

"In your case, I think that should be step one."

"Should we talk about how we should handle Meg tonight?"

"Seriously? You're giving me the option?" I leaned against the cupboards, cradling my mug in my hands.

"I'm hoping you say no, because I don't think I can muster enough rancor needed for *that* conversation."

"At me or Meg?" I blew into my tea, grateful the steam blurred my vision.

"What do you think?"

"Fingers crossed, my confession absolved me completely." I took a hesitant sip.

She chuckled quietly. "I probably should apologize to you for how I acted earlier when I saw the text."

Not wanting to prematurely jump for joy, I prompted her. "Please explain as if I were a total idiot."

"Covering your bases?" Her smile was becoming more natural, and her upper body wasn't as rigid.

"Absolutely."

"It couldn't have been easy for you."

"Go on." I motioned for her to fill in all the gaps.

She laughed. "I know how much Meg hurt you. And, I know she was probably the last person you expected to bump into today. You did bump into her?" Her eyes were teasing.

I wanted to nip it in the bud anyway. "Don't go there. You were doing so well. Besides, we also bumped into your mom and Troy, so things like that really do happen."

"I hate this. Acting like you and vice versa."

"It's less stressful on my end. Not having to try to think of ways to spin the truth or avoid admitting anything. Or if I do take a wrong step, admit it and move forward." I tapped the side of my head. "I'm finally seeing the allure of the Sarah way. Another plus to channeling Sarah is the discovery that I like crab cheese wontons." I smacked my lips.

Sarah beamed. "You demolished most of my appetizer."

"The more I ate, the fewer chances for you and your mom to rope me into the middle of your... I don't even know what to call it."

She sighed.

"Have you learned any lessons switching roles with me?" I asked.

"How exhausting it is to be pigheaded."

"Don't hold back." I grinned over my mug.

"Do I ever?" She expertly arched one eyebrow.

"As Sarah, no. But if you continue to channel Lizzie, you need to follow the rules. No back and forth." I bobbed my head as if trying to follow a tennis ball. "My brain can't handle it."

"Can you handle holding me? In bed?"

"Naked?"

"Now look who's pressing her luck?"

"Come on," I cajoled. "Naked cuddling is the best type of cuddling. We don't have to do anything. Feeling you against me is more than enough."

"I just got a glimpse of you in high school, bumbling your way to losing your virginity."

"I didn't bumble."

"Delusional Lizzie is back." Sarah hopped off the barstool. "Take me to bed and prove me wrong." She sashayed out of the kitchen, putting effort into the swing of her hips.

CHAPTER NINE

*T*he sun overhead obscured my sight but didn't warm my body all that much. The vibrant green grass was testimony to the amount of care that went into tending it after months of dry, hot weather. Peter, in a yellow polo and green sweater vest, swung his golf club as if his life depended on it.

Gabe, shielding his eyes with his gloved hand, followed the ball's path. "Ooooh, nice shot."

"I gave him a few tips," I said. "Not about the outfit, though." I pointed my club at him. "I may never wear a sweater vest again."

Gabe looked at ease in a crisp red polo and black slacks. "I'll believe it when I see it."

"Like I could learn anything from you." Peter shoved his club back into his bag.

"Stand back, boys. Let a woman show you how to play the game." I inserted the tee into the turf. After making a show of practicing my swing, I hit the ball, knowing right away it was on target.

Allen, the only brave soul to wear shorts on the somewhat

cool September day, patted me on the back. "She's getting the hang of it."

"Nothing to it, really. Maybe I should get an agent."

"You got the BSing part down." Gabe prepped his shot.

"Talking a big game is the most important part. Like fishing." Allen waited for Gabe to begin his swing before goosing his brother with his club.

The ball headed right for the lake.

"Sabotaged by my own brother." Gabe wasn't all that put out.

"Go ahead. Try again," Allen said.

"I've never taken a mulligan in my life, and I'm not going to now. But watch out, little brother. Paybacks are hell." He shook his club menacingly at Allen.

I wondered how many injuries resulted from golf clubs, intentional or not.

Everyone headed for the golf carts.

"Lizzie, ride with me," Gabe said.

"Don't let her drive," Peter warned.

"Oooh, good one. Not." I hopped in.

Gabe laughed, easing into the driver's spot. Peter's cart took off with Allen hanging on for dear life. "This is going to be a long afternoon."

"Whose idea was this?"

"I believe it was yours."

"Correction. Sarah's. She thinks family time is good for me." I held on as Peter's cart inched closer.

"How's the situation with her mom?" He peeked at me out of the corner of his eyes.

"I won't compare it to the Middle East peace process, since that seems too easy."

"The comparison or do you mean solving the Middle East problem seems more achievable?" Gabe turned the steering wheel to avoid Peter's cart. Were all golfers terrible drivers or only competitive siblings?

I held on to avoid tumbling out. "Haven't decided yet. Let's just say I'm glad Rose won't be attending dinner at your mom's —I mean our parents' house."

"Sometimes I wonder if all families are effed up." Gabe pulled up next to Peter's cart. "Let's kick some ass."

* * *

"There you are!" Tie charged toward us with Demi on her hip. "Your daughter misses you."

Peter took Demi, nuzzling her head with his chin.

I never thought my uptight and selfish brother would take to parenting, but all evidence pointed to my being wrong. Maybe Demi could help select her father's golf outfits in a year or two so he wouldn't be a dead ringer for the Easter Bunny. She couldn't do much worse.

"Who won?" Tie asked.

"We're family. Keeping score would be rude." Gabe tossed an arm over Peter's shoulders.

Tie clapped her hands and said to Peter, "You lost."

"They cheated," he said, baring his white teeth.

"Whatever, Mr. Mulligan." I met Sarah's eye off to the side of the deck. "It's time for a congratulatory kiss." I made a beeline toward Sarah and Helen, each with a twin in their arms.

"Golfing definitely agrees with you." Helen smiled.

"Not sure about that but beating Peter does."

"You won?" Sarah crinkled her brow.

"Third. Peter came in last." I raised my hand for a high five, and Freddie slapped his fist into it. "Thanks, little man."

Sarah laughed, shaking her head. "I hope you and your sister get along better." She tickled Freddie's side, much to his delight, and he made a noise that sounded like the letter O.

"What can I get you two to drink?" I offered, placing my hands together in my best servant manner.

"Actually, take this one. I think your father needs assistance at the grill." Helen handed off Ollie. Taking Ollie's hand in hers, she said, "Can you say, *hello, Mama?*"

Ollie stared indignantly.

"She takes after me." Sarah laughed.

Helen rushed to Dad's rescue.

"Say *Mama is beautiful*, Ollie. Beau-ti-ful."

"Trying to get into my good graces?" Sarah narrowed her eyes.

"Wasn't aware I was on the outs with you." Ollie grabbed my ponytail, giving it a good yank. "Did you teach her that?"

Sarah redirected Ollie's hand by scooping a stuffed giraffe from the goodies bag. She handed Fred the elephant. "Did you have fun golfing?" She shook her head. "Really, I never thought I'd ask you that."

I laughed. "Think I missed my true calling."

"Not sure three out of four is LPGA worthy."

"Nope, but beating Peter—golden." I blew on my fingertips.

"Ah, now I see." She tsked. "At least you two are spending some time together. That's a step in the right direction."

I glanced over at Peter, who was chatting with Gabe and my father at the grill. Dad now held Demi, but she had her tiny fist wrapped around one of Peter's fingers. "Maybe fatherhood has tamed him some."

"Possibly. Or maybe he's realized life is so much harder swimming upstream all alone." Sarah held Freddie tighter.

"I feel like you're trying to impart some type of wisdom." I planted a peck on her cheek. "Are you trying to teach me or yourself?"

Sarah swatted my side. "Play nice!"

"But I like winning."

She held Fred in front of her at eye level. "I hope you don't inherit the Petrie competitive streak. No, not my Freddie-Weddie."

He giggled, swinging his arms and legs as if on a carnival ride, saying, "Weee..."

Ollie let loose a wail.

"I think she has. It's time for their dinner. Help me get them inside." Sarah led the way in her momma-general fashion.

There were two high chairs at the kitchen table. After securing Ollie, I grabbed the already prepared chickpea patties, steamed broccoli, and carrots and placed them in the microwave. I arranged cheese cubes in one of the ears of the elephant-shaped travel plates. When the microwave dinged, I put the veggies in the other ear and the patties in the center of the face.

Setting the plates down in front of the twinks, I said, "I'm not sure about these plates. They make me feel guilty. Like we're serving them elephant."

Ollie reached for a patty, clumsily feeding herself.

"She doesn't seem to mind." Sarah pushed one forward on Fred's plate. "Freddie, however, takes after you, snowflake." She joggled my arm.

"Just for that, I'm heading outside to gloat about my golf skills." I kissed both twins on top of their heads and gave Sarah a *good luck* smile.

Peter, Gabe, Allen, and my father congregated around the grill; however, the only one paying any attention to the steaks was Gabe.

After several minutes, the conversation rounded back to golf and rubbing Peter's face in coming in last.

"She's an amateur. I have to let her win so she won't get discouraged." Peter flashed a condescending smile at me.

"Is that your excuse? Do you lose to clients as a way of buttering them up?" I eyed Gabe and Allen.

Gabe laughed. "Can't blame him. Oscar and Reggie love to play with Peter."

"Fishing for stock tips?" Tie, in a sundress that didn't suit the clouds overhead, sidled up next to me, a wineglass at her lips.

"That, my dear, is illegal." Peter didn't look entirely comfortable around his wife.

"When is Oscar Mendez going public?" she pressed.

"Are there rumors about an IPO?" my father asked, his expression more than curious.

"Not you too, Charles. Learning about an Initial Public Offering ahead of time can land you in jail." Tie swigged her wine.

Gabe laughed. "Sounds like someone has been boning up on finance lingo."

Peter wore a priggish grin. "She loves the movie *The Wolf of Wall Street*." He whispered behind his hand, "She has a crush on Leo."

Tie's smile reminded me of a high school girl trying to school a group of boys who didn't take her seriously. But she said, "Who doesn't have a crush on Leo? Even Lizzie probably does."

"Leo who?" I asked.

Everyone laughed.

"I wish your brother developed a sense of humor like you." Tie linked arms with me. "Maybe you can teach Demi."

"She's not funny," Peter scoffed. "Go on, Lizzie, tell us who Leo is?"

"DiCaprio?" Helen approached the group. "He was fantastic in that finance movie. Has he been in a movie since?"

"Saved once again," Peter sneered.

"Please. Everyone knows him. Sarah has made me watch *Inception* God knows how many times trying to figure out the end."

Sarah, holding a twin on each hip, approached the group. "I've made you? You're the one who jots down clues. You probably belong to a nerdy club who discusses theories. Oh, wait, you're too busy cochairing the History Club."

I took Freddie from her.

"History Club," Peter chortled.

"Yuck it up now, Peter. You won't be laughing when I become dean." I jiggled one of Freddie's socked feet.

"Is that your goal?" Dad puffed out his chest.

"One of them."

"What else?" he asked.

"*New York Times* best-selling author."

Dad nodded encouragingly.

Peter rolled his eyes. "Might want to turn to romance if you want that to happen."

"There's a list for fiction and nonfiction," Tie came to my defense. However, I suspected she did so simply to needle Peter.

"What's at the top of the nonfiction list?"

"*Hillbilly Elegy.*" She stuck her tongue out at Peter.

"Gabe, are the steaks done? I'm famished." Helen inserted herself between Peter and Tie, a trick she utilized on a regular basis.

"I'll set the sides out." Dad corralled Allen with his arm. "Help out your old man."

We moved inside to the dining room. The early autumn night was mild, but with the darkness descending, the temperature would drastically drop. Sarah and I placed the twins in their respective seats on our side of the table. For the moment, Ollie was content, and Fred stared at the crackling fire with his usual stoicism.

Everyone took their places at the table. Allen sat next to me, while Gabe diplomatically inserted himself between Peter and Tie. Sarah wasn't quick enough and had to sit directly across from Tie. My wife turned to me, thinning her eyes without anyone else witnessing the act. I feigned it was an accident. One of Tie's tactics was to loop the person within eye contact into her assaults on Peter.

Sarah mouthed, "Later."

"Sarah, how's your mom?" Dad peeled back a crispy husk from his corn.

"Fine," Sarah said. "Can you please pass me the cornbread?" She bumped my elbow.

"I'm having lunch with her and Troy tomorrow," Helen said, her voice a bit too cheery.

"Really?" Sarah's leg bumped into mine. Was she attempting to garner my attention, or was it accidental? "Where?"

"Three Amigos. Care to join?" The way Helen said it made it clear she knew about Sarah's issue with Troy. Had Gabe or Rose filled her in? Both?

"Can't. The twinkies have a playdate with the daughter of one of Fort Collins' famous residents."

"Who?" I asked, stupefied.

"The daughter is Mia. Her moms are Claire Nicholls and JJ Cavendish."

"Ah," I nodded. "Claire is the publisher of the local paper."

Sarah's smile conveyed *You can't be serious*. "True, but her wife, JJ, is the famous one."

"I love her show *Confessions with JJ*. One of my goals is to appear on it." Tie chomped into her corn.

"You have to be famous, dear." Peter brandished his fork in the air as if punctuating a sentence that didn't require anything all that forceful.

"If Lizzie can be a best-selling author, I can be famous." Tie flourished the corncob at Peter.

Peter leaned forward to glare at his wife. "How do you plan on doing that? Riding my coattails?"

"Even Ruth Madoff, Bernie's wife, became famous."

Peter bristled. "Are you calling me a crook?"

"Please. You aren't even in the same league as Bernie. His Ponzi scheme was worth billions. With a B." Tie licked her lips.

"JJ Cavendish. Is she the one who wrote that memoir about her drug use?" Helen tipped more wine into her glass just as easily as she redirected the conversation.

Sarah nodded. "Yep. Their daughter is in the twinks' music class."

"Since when do the kids have music class?" I asked.

"Some mother you are," Peter said before placing a piece of bloody steak into his mouth.

"It's new, and they've only been there once. I'm almost certain I mentioned it to you." Sarah looked upward as if consulting a mental diary.

I was 94.35 percent sure she hadn't, but not wanting to call my wife a liar in front of my family, I fibbed, "It's ringing a bell."

"Anyway, Bailey thought it'd be a good idea, and one of her bandmates teaches the class. It's cute, seeing all the little ones wiggling their butts. Fred loves banging on a drum."

I smiled at the thought before pinpointing the troublesome aspect. "Bailey's in a band?"

"Yep. The Rockies Chicks. I think it's a play on The Dixie Chicks." Sarah peered over her shoulder to ensure the twins were okay. "They haven't booked any gigs yet."

"Bailey and her band or the twins?" Allen laughed at his own joke.

Gabe socked Allen's side. "Please, you know everything there is to know about Bailey." He sang, "Allen and Bailey sitting in a tree—"

Helen cleared her throat.

"Dottie's going to kill me." I groaned, remembering Bailey's grandmother's parting words when she moved Bailey to Fort Collins. *Anything happens to her and I'll skin you alive.*

"Extracurricular activities are healthy, like the History Club, which supposedly will land you in the dean's office." Sarah's not-so-innocent smile should have angered me. Instead, it turned me on.

"Mock all you want, dear." I whispered the last word in a tone that implied I couldn't wait to get her home.

"I plan on it."

To keep everyone from knowing the true meaning of her words, my eyes darted toward the ceiling. "Heaven help me."

"You're an atheist," Sarah chimed in, giving me the smile I outwardly pretended to hate, but it revved my engines even more.

"This family is driving me to religion. I need all the help I can get."

Helen heartily laughed. "Tell me about it."

"I hear Meg Shaw is giving a lecture at CU about the Russian Revolution. Didn't you two study together?" Allen forked a bite of potato salad.

Not expecting the change of conversation or the reference to Meg, I mumbled, "Um, yeah."

"*Meg*, Meg?" Peter asked.

Sarah, probably in tune with my unease, answered, "She and Lizzie have lost contact over the years."

"Now, there was someone who had a great sense of humor, unlike you, little sister." He leveled his eyes on me.

I glared at Peter. Booze played a huge part in Meg's *playfulness.*

"Can you introduce me?" Allen asked, completely oblivious to the unease swirling overhead like a Category 5 storm.

"I'm giving a talk at the symposium," I said in the most noncommittal way.

"I reserved my spot. Mom and Dad are going as well." Allen sliced off a chunk of steak.

"Are you?" I asked, looking my father in the eye.

"Wouldn't miss it." Dad seemed genuinely interested.

Peter, on the other hand, didn't show any interest. Just in case I didn't pick up on his body language, he said, "Too bad I have to work."

"It's on a Saturday," Allen helpfully offered, brushing some hair out of his eyes.

"Which one?"

"A week from today."

Peter rubbed his chin. "I'll have to check with my assistant, but I think I'm golfing with clients."

"Translation, he's going to make sure his assistant wrangles up some clients so he can't go." Gabe laughed. "I'm manning the store in Fort Collins, so I can't. To be honest, though, it's not my cup of tea."

"I appreciate the honesty. No worries. Sarah doesn't like going either. It's possible I may burst out into lecture-mode too much at home."

"Oh, I'm going to this one." Sarah perked up in her seat as if suddenly interested in history, but I knew her true reason for wanting to be there.

"Does that mean you found a sitter?" I asked.

"I'll convince Bailey to help if my mom can't commit to the whole day."

Dubious, I asked. "How?"

She rubbed her fingertips together, implying bribery. "She let it slip last week that she's desperate for cash. Apparently, it's not cheap to get off the ground." She drummed the table with her fingers. "That reminds me, we need to get some instruments for the twinks."

"When Lizzie was two, she had a drum set she loved," Dad said.

"I did?" I peeked over my shoulder at Freddie, who was watching the adults at the table as if following every word.

Dad nodded.

Tie leaned forward to ask Peter, "What was your instrument? The triangle?"

Peter frowned. "I didn't have time—"

Dad cut him off. "Maracas. Of course, he used to hit the other kids with them."

"He hasn't changed. Except today, he threatened to whack everyone with his nine iron." Gabe laughed.

"Don't buy Ollie maracas. She takes after Uncle Peter," Allen offered.

"Smart kid," Peter plucked a piece of cornbread off Gabe's plate.

"How are your classes going, Allen?" I asked to pave the way for my real question.

"Fantastic." He filled me in for several moments.

When I saw my chance, I asked, "And Bailey? How are her classes?"

He sipped his water. "She doesn't talk about school much."

"Has she at least mentioned her favorite course or any of her professors?"

Allen shook his head and turned to ask Gabe a question about CU's opponent for this evening's football game, which I had promised to watch with him.

"Oh, Peter, before I forget, Samuel stopped by the house to speak to you about some deal you two have cooking at work." Tie chewed on her bottom lip.

"He knew I wouldn't be home today." Peter lobbed a piece of bread into his mouth.

"Must have slipped his mind." She shrugged. "Not everyone follows your every move like you're some kind of finance rock star."

* * *

THAT NIGHT, after tucking the already asleep twinkies in, Sarah found me in the library.

"Preparing for Saturday?" She eased onto the couch facing my desk, one leg tucked underneath her.

I leaned back into my leather desk chair. "Did you know my family was going to be there?"

She shook her head. "Does that make you nervous?"

"A little," I confessed, tossing my pen on the yellow notepad.

Sarah's smile lit up her face. "This isn't your first rodeo. You'll be fine."

"I'm used to students ignoring me, but…"

"Is it your family being there or Meg that's keeping you up?"

In hindsight, I should have seen that one coming. "She's heard me speak. Many times."

Sarah's eyes hardened. "You know what I mean."

I scratched the top of my head. "Guess I better get used to it. We hobnob in the same circles. Academia is more incestuous than… I don't know."

"Let's hope your inability to make a comparison isn't a sign of how your presentation will go next week."

"Hey." I tossed a wadded paper at her, missing completely. "Don't start planting thoughts like that in my brain."

"Come over here and shut me up." She spread out her arms.

Briskly, I made my way to her, laying Sarah on her back on the couch to allow me to climb on top. Brushing some strands of hair off her cheek, I said, "Please don't worry about Meg."

"Are you going to introduce Allen to her?" There was a splash of anger or fear in her eyes.

"Hopefully, he'll forget about that. She really isn't the type I want him associating with."

"He doesn't seem like the forgetful type." She pressed a finger to my forehead. "And he's laser-focused on the Russian Revolution. Meg's specialty."

"I'll cross that bridge when I come to it. Besides, Allen's an adult and can associate with whomever he wants. Right now, my *focus* is on you." I nuzzled into her neck, planting soft kisses on her skin. "Shall I put you to bed?"

"I'm not tired."

"I was counting on that. Come on, beautiful." I hopped up and put my hand out.

"Don't you mean, beau-ti-ful?"

"It's your turn to play nice or I won't tuck you in."

"I think you will." She wore her *come hither* expression.

"Are you really willing to test my stubborn streak?" I tapped my right foot on the Oriental rug.

"Yes." She tugged her shirt up high enough to give me a sneak peek of her breasts.

"Not going to work."

Sarah sat up and removed her shirt. "Remember when I was pregnant and you couldn't touch them. We need to make up for lost time." She squeezed her tits together, forcing them to spill over the bra cups, before slowly letting her hands fall to give my eyes full access.

I sucked in a breath, zeroing in on her black-lace pushup bra doing wonders for her impressive rack. "Take back what you said. When you mocked me."

"You don't think I'm beautiful?" she said, her voice playful and sexy, running a slender finger from her throat to the top of her pajama bottoms.

"You know I do."

"What am I taking back, then?" She cupped her breasts again, using my weakness to draw me in further.

Not willing to admit I didn't mind her tactics, I said, "Your attitude."

Sarah leaned back on her arms, arching perfectly to put her goods on show. "It's hot in here." She eased her pajama bottoms off.

"Was this your plan all along?"

"What are you talking about?" She was able to come across as completely innocent, making her even more alluring.

"Since when do you keep your lingerie on when getting into your pajamas?" I waved an accusing finger in the air. "Usually, you go commando."

"Are you accusing me of riling you up as part of my seduction plan?" Her breasts heaved up and down. She knew my every weakness when it came to her body.

I inched closer to the couch. "Y-yes, I am."

"You think that little of me?" She swung her legs over the edge of the couch, each on one side of me. Her fingers reached for the top button on my jeans.

"I think the world of you, especially when it comes to this?" My breath hitched as Sarah slowly lowered the zipper.

"To what?"

"Getting me hot and bothered."

She tugged my jeans down. "Are you hot? Let's find out." Sarah buried her face in my panties, pulling back way too quickly. "You're warm."

"Oh, I think I've reached hot level. Try again."

Sarah supported herself on her arms. "Hmmm… I think I have the upper hand right now. How does that make you feel, Ms. Control Freak?"

"Again, you're testing my stubbornness?" I stepped out of my jeans, kicking them to the side.

Her eyes fell to my discarded baggy Gap jeans. "Clearly it's failing."

I stifled a groan, not of anger, but desire. "Keep pressing my buttons and I'll take you right here, not in the comfort of our bed."

She tossed her head back, laughing. "We need to work on your threats."

I shoved the coffee table up against the other couch, not bothering to right the empty vase that tumbled from the force. "Floor. Now!"

Sarah didn't mess about.

"Nope. On all fours," I commanded.

"Yes, ma'am."

I got on my knees behind her ass, yanking her panties down hard, nearly tearing them. "You want punishment?"

Sarah nodded.

My hand reached under her to fondle her wet pussy lips. Without warning, I shoved two fingers inside.

Sarah's upper body crouched down on her forearms, allowing me complete access.

I moved in and out of her, provoking moans.

This made me hammer her harder.

I relished the slapping sounds my hand made, moving in and out.

Faster and faster.

My other hand reached underneath, slipping under the bra to tweak her left nipple and to massage her breast.

One of Sarah's hands moved to stimulate herself.

"Is this how you wanted it? For me to fuck you?" I breathed heavily.

"Yes," she groaned. "Harder."

I complied while her fingers stimulated her clit with deliberate intensity.

She was so wet.

So willing.

And so beautiful.

Her tremor alerted me to how close she was to exploding. I jammed my fingers deep inside and pulled to hit her G-spot.

Sarah's upper body bucked up off the ground, and I

supported her against me with one arm. Her quivering ebbed, and she fell back to the carpet.

I lay on top of her backside.

Kissing her shoulder, I asked, "Was that okay?"

Sarah mumbled a yes.

"Are you ready to go upstairs?"

She shook her head.

"You want more?" I laughed.

"Maybe."

Surprised, I moved to her side and said, "My way, this time."

Knowing what I meant, she rolled onto her back.

Her pussy glistened.

"I can't go to sleep without having a taste."

My mouth went to work.

$\mathcal{T}$he following morning, I woke early. Before the twins, my usual routine every morning had been to jump out of bed, hop on my bike, ride for at least an hour, and return before Sarah woke. Since the twins, I tried to go for rides when I could, mostly every Sunday. Now that Bailey was with us, I hoped to return to my usual morning rides, although that hadn't worked out yet.

Sarah didn't stir when my feet hit the carpet. Sitting on the edge of the king-size bed, I stretched my arms overhead, yawning. The sun wasn't up, and it took my eyes several seconds to adjust to the darkness. Squinting, I made out the time on the antique art nouveau—Maddie's term—naked ladies clock on my nightstand. Not even six.

"Excellent," I whispered.

Not wanting to waste a moment, I rushed through my morning routine, put on shorts and the dinosaur T-shirt since I'd slept naked, and skedaddled downstairs. My bag was ready to go by the garage door.

The air was crisp, a sure sign the pleasant autumn temperatures were about to give way. On my bike, I headed north with the foothills on my left, although I could only make out their darkness against the even darker sky in the west. My LED headlight illuminated the way as I sliced through the predawn hours. The best part of the light, aside from being able to see, was drivers could spy me over 1000 feet away. Being a Sunday, this wasn't a huge issue. I dispatched with the side roads, turning right onto Taft Hill Road. It wouldn't be long until I turned left on County Road.

My destination was merely five miles, give or take, from my home. Faint fingers of light edged over the eastern horizon. County Road used to be one of my gateways to a much longer ride through the canyon. Lately, a diner was my stopping point every Sunday I managed to escape.

There were several pickups and one work truck in the parking lot. At the gas pumps on the side, a man in tight Wranglers and a long-sleeve plaid shirt filled his F-250.

I locked up my bike and made my way inside.

The hostess smiled. "Morning, Lizzie. I saved your favorite table in case you made it today."

I smiled. The majority of the tables were vacant, but it was the thought that counted. "Thanks. How you been, Ada?"

"Too early to tell. Right now, it's just the regulars. Who knows what the day will bring. Yesterday a group from California came through. It took them ages to order. Asking if the eggs were free range. Could they only get egg whites? Organic this. Organic that. I swear they'll die younger stressing about what they can or can't eat."

I took my seat under the massive bison head mounted on the wall. One of the reasons I preferred this seat was so I didn't have to look at the poor creature. The other was the accessible socket for my laptop.

"Your usual?" she asked with an expression that claimed she knew the answer but felt compelled out of politeness to ask.

"Yep."

She rested her hand on my shoulder. "Another reason why I like regulars. You guys never mess up our inventory. Biscuits and gravy coming up. And your tea will be here in two shakes." She playfully wiggled one leg, acting out the two shakes before heading off.

True to her word, the tea arrived before my newly acquired ASUS Chromebook, purchased because of its size or lack thereof, had time to boot up. The battery was full, per usual, but I still claimed this table and had the power cord just in case inspiration struck and I needed longer than a few hours. While the size of the laptop was ideal for dragging it on my supposed bike rides, the battery life was only so-so.

That wasn't a huge issue. Being a mother of one-year-old twins made it difficult to carve out large chunks of time. Another reason why I cherished Sunday mornings.

Getting a chill, I slipped on my black fleece jacket and stifled a smile, knowing Maddie would razz me for pairing black with navy shorts, a pet peeve of the designer. It was all I had packed in my Sunday bag, though, and I doubted Ada or the bison minded. I opened the Word doc and got to work.

Ada, not wanting to disrupt me, placed my meal to the side without much fanfare, and my Bose headphones blocked out any sound.

I hadn't been able to work on this project since Thursday, but that didn't stop my muse from bombarding my brain with ideas. My fingers flew over the keys to get as much down before the guilt crept in, wrecking my concentration.

After my first bite of cold biscuits and gravy, it dawned on me that I'd been typing for longer than thirty minutes without stopping or thinking. I'd read that was a good thing. Writing sprints. But, this project was my first go at fiction, so the academic in me worried about the quality, and I had to stop the impulse to insert endnotes. Blocking this out, I focused on eating a few more bites before beginning another sprint. More than likely, this project wouldn't go anywhere. It was mostly my way to blow off steam. Something for me that no one knew about. Not even Sarah.

Before I tortured myself with thoughts about whether or not it was wrong not to tell Sarah, I started the next sprint.

* * *

A QUARTER AFTER EIGHT, I packed up my laptop.

Ada placed the box containing four cinnamon rolls on the table. "Get some work done?"

"Yep."

A group of ten crashed through the entrance. Judging from their *just off the rack* hiking outfits from REI, I determined they were out-of-towners.

Ada groaned and whispered behind her hand. "If one of them asks if our products are organic..." She left the threat unsaid.

I laid cash on the table, adding an extra five for Ada. Giving the excited tourists a wide berth, I headed for safety. Outside, I texted Sarah, letting her know I was only five miles away. Not waiting for her reply, I shed the jacket, secured the box behind my seat, and strapped my bag on tightly.

* * *

"GIMMIE!" Sarah demanded as soon as I entered the kitchen via the garage.

I handed over the cinnamon roll loot. "Where are the twinks?"

"In the front room with Maddie and Mom. How was the ride? Maybe I should start going with you if you keep bringing these bad boys home."

Not wanting to address her non-existent weight problem and the possibility of her joining me for bike rides, I diverted, feeling slightly conflicted. "Your mom is here?" I whispered.

Maddie flounced in with an extra pep in her step. "I hope you have one of those for me." She pointed to the massive roll on a plate Sarah was about to pop into the microwave. "It's the only reason why I get out of bed this early on a Sunday. Can't you go for a bike ride later and make this a Sunday brunch tradition? And, if possible, can you share your Graves' Disease so the calories won't add up?" She walloped my arm.

"You do know the disease can kill you if you don't treat it?" I asked.

"Yes, you keep telling me that every time—"

I butted in, "Every time you discount how miserable I was when I had to fight doctors to take me seriously when I felt like hell, then having blood tests every month, and taking medicine that didn't agree with my system all the while working my ass off in grad school."

Sarah added two more rolls to the plate, and using her knuckle to avoid getting fingerprints on the keypad, she plugged in twenty-five seconds and hit start. In an effort to diffuse the Graves' disease brouhaha, she steered to a safer topic. "Brunch. I think I remember what that is."

Knowing the battle with Maddie was fruitless, I added, "It's something parents of one-year-old twins never attend." I disappeared around the corner to bring my bag into the library and take a few moments to gather my thoughts before joining everyone.

Freddie's giggles greeted me in the front room.

"Good morning, Rose," I said, taking a seat on the carpet between the twinks.

"How was your ride, Lizzie?" Her voice was overly kind.

The thought of FDR cooperating with Stalin to fight Hitler entered my mind. Was Rose Stalin? Surely, I hadn't meant to compare Sarah to Hitler. My brain fumbled for a second too long to curb saying any of this aloud, and finally, I was able to get out, "Refreshing." I paused, searching for something to say. "I hear you're having lunch with Helen today."

"Yes, I popped over in hopes of convincing Sarah to go."

I peered at my wife, who had entered holding a tray with the rolls, a chrome carafe, and small blue and white porcelain plates, which according to Maddie were chic and only for casual dining. She set the tray on the table and then took a seat across the room from her mother.

"Why don't you?" I asked, getting up to sit closer to Sarah but still on the twins' level.

Her chocolate eyes turned molten. "Because the twins have a music lesson today."

"I think I can manage that." I gave it more consideration. "I don't have to play anything, do I?" My voice sounded nervous even to myself.

"You *might*," Sarah said with emphasis.

"I don't have plans. Gabe's working. I'll go with Lizzie." Maddie chomped into her roll, icing oozing over her fingers, prompting her to lick them clean. "These really are the best, and I consider myself an expert in all things tasty."

"It's settled, then." Rose sneezed, more than likely an allergic reaction to Hank, who wasn't present, but getting all of his hair and dander out of the carpet, off the drapes, and out of the furniture was quite the challenge for Miranda, our cleaner. This was the biggest reason why every time Rose babysat the twinks, she did so at her house. The humidifiers helped some. Rose sneezed again and stood. "I'll pick you up in a couple of hours."

Wisely, she left before Sarah had a chance to think of another excuse.

"Really, you two. Really!" Sarah's face turned redder than Spiderman's face on Ollie's shirt.

I put my hands up. "I'm sorry. I only thought you'd want a break from the twins. I go riding every Sunday, and well, you and your mom used to go shopping every Satur—"

"That was before Troy," she said through clenched teeth.

"Yes. BT, not to be confused with BCE."

Maddie's brow creased as she took a massive bite of cinnamon roll.

"Before common era. It's the PC version instead of saying before Christ and after Christ."

Maddie scoffed but had her mouth full and couldn't really let her opinion fly.

I switched my focus back to Sarah. "You really should set time aside for a break."

"Some of us don't mind spending so much time with *our* children." She crossed her arms. "And some of us don't work outside of the home. Tell me, Lizzie, why do you need Sunday mornings all to yourself?"

I knew Sarah's anger had nothing to do with my bike rides, since she'd never given two hoots about them before. But I also suspected bringing that up would be the worst possible decision at the moment. Pointing out a spouse was in the wrong was pitfall number 58 for married couples.

"Lizzie's right. You need time to yourself. Join a club. Find a hobby. Take Gabe up on his offer of working in the shop part-time. You need to get away from the twins and have time to yourself. That way you won't be wound so tightly." Maddie added piping hot coffee in her half-full cup.

"I'm not tightly wound!"

Freddie, momentarily startled, got to his feet and stumbled over to Sarah, handing her his stuffed elephant. "M-mama."

Sensing a golden opportunity, I said, "Maddie's right. You really do need some time to yourself."

Sarah swept Freddie onto her lap, cradling him tightly. "And who'll watch the twinks?"

"Me, of course." I patted my chest with an open palm.

"This isn't your way of finding another way to get alone time, is it? Hire a babysitter or have Bailey, who's only part-time, clock in more hours without telling me?" Her voice lacked the venom she was going for.

I shook my head. "Don't take the Troy situation out on me, please."

Maddie gave me an *atta girl* head bob. "I rarely say this twice in one day, but Lizzie is right. And maybe you two need to institute a date night. I can watch the kids, or Jorie can. She's desperate for cash."

Stunned by this development, I asked, "You hang out with Jorie?"

"We exchanged digits at the birthday party." She mimicked dialing a phone.

"And what should I do with all this free time?" Sarah steered us back on track.

"Anything you want. When's the last time you read a book? From beginning to end, not just snippets every so often?" Maddie asked.

"I read to the kids every night."

Maddie rolled her eyes. "Not a children's book."

Freddie flailed in Sarah's arms, and she put him back on the carpet. "I don't even know what's popular right now, and I don't have the mind-power for literature."

"Read what you want. Who else will introduce the Red Room of Pain in our lives?" I whispered only for Sarah to hear, since I didn't want to clue Maddie in that I'd read *Fifty Shades of Grey*, some portions aloud to Sarah.

Sarah's eyes flickered, but she kept my secret.

Maddie hopped off the leather ottoman, heading for her purse. "Take this." She handed over a battered paperback of *The Girl on the Train*. "Start today. Head upstairs, draw a bath, and read. It'll help you relax before having lunch with your mom and Helen."

Sarah didn't budge from her seat.

Maddie extended her arm toward the staircase. "Go!"

Sarah snatched the book and her half-eaten roll. "Fine!" she said with defiance, but I sensed she was relieved to be banished from the room. At least this way she didn't have to face the Maddie inquisition about Troy.

When the coast was clear, Maddie turned to me. "Make her a cup of tea. Something soothing."

"You're bossy today." I pushed myself off the floor, my back making a cringeworthy popping sound.

"You two need a life coach or something."

Not wanting to concede she was right, I sought refuge in the kitchen.

"Make me a cup while you're at it," Maddie barked. "This coffee is making me jittery."

After taking Sarah a cup, I carried two mugs of tea into the front room.

Maddie, cross-legged on the floor with the twinkies, had a spiral notebook out. Without looking up, she said, "Does Sarah own a gun?"

"Worried?" I sat on the leather chair Sarah had recently vacated.

She met my eyes. "She needs to get this aggression out some way. Maybe join a gun club."

"You want Sarah, who, in your own words, has some aggression issues, to purchase a gun? Are you forgetting she's a democrat?"

"Democrats own guns." Maddie accepted the tea, resettling on the couch in order to avoid tiny fingers getting scorched.

"In the past, Sarah, the high school teacher, made her views on guns pretty clear, but just in case you need a refresher, watch a documentary on Columbine." I eased back into the leather chair, propping my feet up on the ottoman.

Ollie pounded on her Turn and Learn toy, which had a bright yellow base and red steering wheel, while Fred silently looked on. The annoying voice sang about the puppy wanting to go for a ride. The green light flashed. There was an *oink oink* followed by the voice announcing, "Pig."

"So, guns are out?" Maddie asked.

"Afraid so. What else is on your list?"

"Fencing."

"No sharp weapons. Actually, no weapons." I made a slashing motion with my hand.

Maddie scratched off a couple more items from her list. "That leaves shopping, which will remind her of Rose—"

"Leading back to the Troy issue." I walked my fingers along the arm of the chair.

"Yeah. We're back to reading. Not sure that's going to work."

"She is an English teacher."

"That's the problem. It may seem like work for her or make her miss teaching or… It's hard to tell with her these days." Maddie stared out the window, the street outside still Sunday quiet.

"What about your Tupperware idea?"

"You want your wife to get a job. Are you two strapped for cash?" There was worry in her eyes as she scanned the carpet littered with toys and stuffed animals.

I set my mug on the side table. "No, but I've been thinking."

"Dangerous for you." She smiled not so innocently.

I had to laugh. "Before the twins, Sarah loved working, and unlike me, she actually took on extra roles at the high school without being railroaded by Jean."

"Who's Jean?"

"The head secretary in the history office."

"They're called *admins* now," she scolded, running an index finger over her other one, teacher-like.

I waved it off. "We're trying to come up with a way to help my distraught wife. Stay focused. Maybe part of Sarah's restlessness is not working. She doesn't want to work outside of the home. And I looked into the Tupperware thing. Did you know Earl Tupper developed the first container in 1942 but didn't introduce it to the public until after World War Two?"

Maddie groaned, tossing her head back. "You want Sarah to sell Tupperware because of its connection to World War Two?"

"Don't be ridiculous. And I don't plan on buying Silly Putty for the twinks because of the connection, either."

"Silly Putty and World War Two?" She tapped the side of her head. "Doesn't compute."

"An engineer invented it in the forties when looking for ways to make synthetic rubber, due to rationing." I tossed my hands up, conveying *duh*.

Maddie stared at me as if I were insane. I didn't invent the stuff. Finally, she said, "I don't think hosting Tupperware parties will solve Sarah's issue."

I sighed. "Meaning you think *all* of her angst is because of Troy?"

"Did you do something?" Maddie's tone was way too eager.

"Not to my knowledge. Did I?"

"Why are you asking me?" She placed a hand on her chest.

"Please, you two love to dissect all the ways I've gone wrong." I picked up my mug again, adding as an afterthought, "There is the Meg issue." I took a sip.

"I heard." Maddie flinched when she realized she'd confirmed my statement, but she pushed past it. "I don't think that's really the problem. At least not yet." She cast an accusatory glance. "If you make it an issue, I may loan my gun to Sarah."

"You keep it locked up, right? Especially when the twins are over?"

"Of course and I've taken gun safety classes."

I still didn't like the idea.

Ollie's toy made croaking sounds, and Freddie put his arms in the air, doing his take on a frog croaking.

"You like froggies?" I asked my son. "Say *frog*."

"Ffff-fruck…"

I smiled. "Close, little man."

"There's a word I didn't think he'd say for at least another six months, and I hoped to be the one to teach him." Maddie encouraged him to repeat his pronunciation of frog, with Ollie chiming in, getting much closer to articulating it correctly. Not that Fred noticed. "I like frog legs." Maddie tickled Freddie's belly.

He giggled.

"When did you eat frog legs?" I asked.

"When I was in Paris last May." She kissed her fingertips and made a smacking sound.

"Maybe you shouldn't be the one to brainstorm hobbies for Sarah. You scare me."

"All right. You toss out some ideas and not jobs relating to World War Two."

"Knitting?" I said in an unsure voice.

"I thought you said no weapons. A knitting needle can do some damage." She mimicked hacking someone.

I sighed. "Reading it is."

There was a mooing followed by Ollie mimicking the sound.

"Maybe you're on the right track, though. Sarah wants to be in charge of something again." Maddie tapped her chin with an index finger.

I let out a bark of laughter. "Trust me; she is in charge. Of me. The twins."

Maddie glared at me. "Obviously, she doesn't see it that way."

"Not to mention she can't tell Rose to dump Troy."

"Exactly."

Taking advantage of Sarah being upstairs, I asked, "What's your opinion of Troy?"

Maddie checked the door and then the entrance to the kitchen to ensure Sarah wasn't in earshot. "I like him, and Rose seems gaga over him."

CHAPTER ELEVEN

*A*fter the applause died down, I retrieved my belongings from the podium and cleared out for the next speaker, who wouldn't start for twenty minutes or so. Everyone in the room milled about, stretching their legs or networking. Allen approached me. "You were fantastic!"

"Thanks." I glanced around for Dad and Helen, but they were nowhere in sight. Had I bored the crap out of them and neither could face me? "You alone?"

"Yeah. Mom needed to take an emergency call. Did you know florists have emergencies?" He said it in all seriousness.

"Hadn't ever considered it. And Dad?"

"His other office."

I crimped my brow.

Allen laughed. "The bathroom."

Both seemed like acceptable reasons, but...

Sarah, all smiles, joined us. "Who knew history could be fun?"

I was about to inform her I did, but she plowed on, hooking her thumb over her shoulder. "Two historians are shouting at each other in the hallway." She leaned in so only Allen and I could hear her. "Apparently, one of them slammed the other's book."

"I'm glad something kept you entertained," I said a little defensively.

"There's Dr. Shaw." Allen jostled my side with his elbow.

It took me a moment to realize he was referring to Meg. I'd never thought of her as Dr. Shaw. Probably because after the hotel lobby incident, when she was with a paying client, I never believed she'd get her act together to finish her PhD.

Sarah glanced away, her lips pursed.

"You promised to introduce me." Allen's eyes were wide with anticipation.

No one else in the family showed a lick of interest in my profession except for Allen. Was it a cruel twist of fate that he focused on the time period my abusive ex did? But how could I brush him off without getting into the details of why I avoided Meg like she was Heinrich Himmler rounding up victims? "Come on."

Sarah's eyes bored into mine as if trying to use her mind powers to force me to reconsider or to eliminate the problem once and for all.

I led him by the arm, Sarah charging right behind like Dwight Eisenhower. We could have used Omar Bradley, who led the First Army on D-Day.

Meg was conversing with Dr. Marcel. When she turned to me, I cleared my throat and said, "Dr. Shaw, Allen my... b-brother... wanted me to introduce you since... uh, you know a lot about the Russian Revolution."

Allen blushed, but was it because he was in front of an academic idol or because of my idiocy?

Frustrated I'd babbled, I turned to safety. "Dr. Marcel, how are you?"

"Not bad." He put his hand out to Allen. "Wonderful seeing

you again, my boy. Would you excuse me?" He retreated to another gaggle of historians anxious to talk.

"Hi, Allen." Meg shook his hand, her expression showing curiosity. "Are you really interested in the Russian Revolution?"

Sarah quirked her brow at me, and I wondered if the same thought penetrated her mind: did Meg think I was using Allen to get close to her?

Clearly, during her reconnaissance with Janice, Meg hadn't learned anything about the Dad/Helen/secret half brother intrigue.

"Yes!" He slammed a fist into his open palm. "I read your paper on the Lena River massacre. It was brilliant."

Sarah rammed her fingers into my back, causing me to stumble forward.

Meg and Allen gawked at me.

"These new shoes are giving me nothing but trouble." I pointed to my black loafers, which had lost their shine from years of wear and tear. "Have you met my wife, Sarah?" I asked Meg.

"It's a pleasure." Meg stuck out her hand.

Sarah smothered it with force. "Likewise."

Wanting to keep the introduction as short as possible, I said, "We don't want to keep you. I know you're next to speak."

Allen's face fell, but it was for the best. The last person he needed in his life was Meg. Adult or not, I could still teach my brother some things. Not to mention the last thing I needed was for Meg to think I wanted to be friends.

Meg picked up on Allen's disappointment. "Do you have time later to chat? It's not every day I run into someone with such passion for Russian history."

I was about to mention the roomful of people waiting to hear her speak, but Allen jumped in. "We're having dinner at the Mediterranean place in between the hat shop and bookstore on Pearl Street after Lizzie finishes the cocktail hour with all the academics. Maybe… if it's okay"—he shuffled on his feet —"with Lizzie, you can join us?"

I could have strangled my usually reserved half brother. Recovering, I said, "Allen, I'm sure Meg has dinner plans." *Please, please with a cherry on top say you have plans.* Evidently, drawing a line in the sand wasn't in my arsenal yet.

"Actually, I don't. My social calendar has been gaping open for months." Meg gave her attention to Sarah. "It would be lovely to get to know each other."

Sarah offered a noncommittal thin-lipped smile.

Zero words came to me to get out of the situation.

"I better get up there." Meg motioned to the podium.

"Good luck. Can I say that? Should I say break a leg?" Allen's words came out like rapid fire.

Meg situated a hand on his arm, but her eyes were on me when she spoke, "Thanks, Allen. I'm looking forward to dinner."

* * *

"How could you invite her to a family dinner?" Sarah paced the hallway outside the lecture hall. Aside from the older woman sitting with her hands folded at the welcome table on the opposite side waiting for stragglers, we were the only two present.

"I seem to remember Allen extending the invitation. And I recall you buying him books like *Eat That Frog, How to Win Friends and Influence People,* and others to encourage my younger sibling to be more efficient, confident, and determined. Who knew books could lead to this disaster?" I palmed the top of my head, struggling for air.

"He asked for my help so he could be more like you: successful!" She waggled a finger in my face.

"Well, he successfully invited Meg to our family dinner!" I shouted back.

Sarah sighed and spoke through gritted teeth. "Let's get back on track to the issue at hand."

"Do you want me to disinvite her?"

"And let her know she's a threat?" She made several hand gestures and seemed to be having an internal debate about the pros and cons. "She'll feed off of that."

"She's not a threat," I scoffed, taking a step back, troubled Sarah felt the same about showing weakness to the likes of Meg.

"Have you forgotten everything she's done?" Sarah's eyes blazed.

"Of course not! But—" I looked to the ceiling. "I meant she's not a threat to us."

"What? You think I'm worried about that? I'm worried for you. She was horrible to you. It's my job"—she clawed her chest with the tips of her fingers—"to protect you from the likes of Meg Shaw."

I mulled over the options. Let Meg join and become further acquainted with Allen. Call off the dinner and quite possibly bring Blackmailing Meg back to life. Would cancelling threaten her sobriety? Obviously, she didn't have anyone to go to. Why else was she hounding me? Her mother had blamed me for turning Meg into a lesbian, so calling her more than likely wouldn't be fruitful. I cradled my stomach with both hands. "I don't know what to do."

"You okay?" Sarah's voice was soft and supportive. "You're turning green."

Squelching the bile back down, I ran the possibilities by Sarah, while she did her best to stay mum by pacing.

Finally, I settled on a choice. "Allen is excited to speak with her." I stepped into her path, taking her hands in mine. "Let's not let Meg ruin the night. I presented my latest article, which went over well. Dad and Helen listened to me speak for the first time. We should celebrate. Besides, Meg can be very charming when she puts her mind to it. Maybe we can get through the night without incurring the wrath of Meg and then be done with her."

"Charming!" Her lips snarled. "I know the true Meg. Alcoholic Meg. The woman who struck you!"

I put a finger to my lips. "Please keep your voice down. You're the only person who knows the whole truth. There are details I would prefer stay between you and me." I glanced at two gray-haired historians slipping into the lecture hall, praying their hearing aids weren't on. "You thought the fight about the bad review was entertaining... if one of my peers learned the truth..." I swiped my forehead with the back of my hand. "I'd never be able to live it down. No matter how brilliant my books or articles, that's all they'll associate me with."

"Of course, I won't say anything," she said in a hushed angry voice she was struggling to control. Maybe she realized the impact of her tone since her facial expression softened. "I'm sorry. It's been years since she left your life. I don't know why it's affecting me this way. Once again, I'm making this about me."

"It's been your latest thing. Honestly, how'd you put up with my self-centeredness for so long?" I bumped my shoulder into hers.

"Good question." Her shoulders slumped.

"I'm sorry." I let out a rush of air. Taking her hands in mine, I said, "Meg reappearing in my life now after everything—I don't know how to process it. Being with her was hell, and she almost ruined my chance at real happiness with you. I know she's trying to turn a corner in her life, or at least she's claiming that. If it's true, I don't want to do anything to jeopardize her sobriety." I squeezed her hands. "But does her moving on have to involve me and now Allen, who reminds me so much of myself when I was his age? Eager to be accepted. Meg craves adoration." I pressed the heels of my hands into my eyes. "I hate this. Not knowing what to do."

She sucked in a deep breath. "Let's get some fresh air. Maybe that will help us focus on the first issue we need to tackle."

"Which is?"

"Getting through dinner without ripping Meg a new asshole."

"Maybe you can arrange to *stumble upon* her in a dark alley." I tried to laugh, but it didn't fully materialize.

"Tempting."

In the stairwell, I pulled her into my arms. "Your neurotic Lizzie side is adorable, by the way." I added, "In small doses."

She pressed her forehead to mine. "It's exhausting, acting like you."

"And vice versa." I captured her lips in a kiss before she could say something I didn't want to hear.

* * *

"Do you think she'll actually come?" Allen stood shoulder to shoulder with me, while Dad conferred with the hostess. Helen and Sarah stood next to a massive flower arrangement. Helen was pointing to a tiger lily, confiding something in Sarah's ear.

"I'm sorry, what?" I focused on Allen.

"Dr. Shaw—Meg. Will she come?"

"She's been unreliable in the past." I brushed a stray hair off my forehead.

"Quite true," said a familiar voice from behind us. Meg had stealthily infiltrated our group like a KGB agent.

Allen's face reddened.

I whirled around, taking a defensive stand. "Hey, there. Your biggest fan was concerned," I said in hopes of alleviating the awkwardness. For Allen's sake. Not that Meg looked out of her element, which I found extremely irksome.

Meg flashed a million-dollar smile at Allen. "I'm not used to the adoration."

Yeah right. Before Meg's drinking got out of hand, she was a rock star in academic circles. I used to look up to her.

Helen and Sarah gravitated to us as if sucked over by a strong vacuum vortex usually seen in sci-fi shows. Maybe it should be called the Meg Effect. Or was it due to the motherly instinct to circle the wagons? Had Sarah intimated to Helen that Meg wasn't to be trusted?

"How do you two know each other?" Helen was all smiles, alleviating my fear that Sarah had blabbed.

Although, Sarah's predatory stance made it clear Meg wasn't wanted. I tugged on the back of her silk blouse to ease up a bit.

Meg said, "Oh, we dated." Maybe Sarah's *I wish you'd die on the spot* expression made Meg add, "Years ago."

"I didn't know that. Another history connection that's practically in the family!" Allen crowed.

I needed to educate Allen about the protocol of leaving exes in the past, although the Maddie/Peter situation muddied the waters. Being a member in our family complicated knowing how normal people functioned.

From the displeasure and disapproval on Sarah's face, I had a feeling she was on the same page. Maybe we should find Allen a book outlining how to navigate awkward social situations, like having dinner with an abusive ex who worked in the same profession, making it difficult to tell her to fuck off out of fear of retribution. Was that too heavy for chapter one?

"Our table is ready." Dad put his arm out for Helen.

I did the same for Sarah, and Allen, taking our cue, crooked his elbow for Meg. I squeezed Sarah's hand on my arm to reassure her. She offered a brave smile. Or was it a threat? To whom, though? Me? Meg? Was poor Allen in her crosshairs? He was still very much a boy—the one who'd invited my ex.

One dinner.

With Meg and my family.

What could possibly go wrong?

The hostess sat us at a round table in the back. Behind us was a blue and yellow tiled mosaic water fountain. The ceramic table sported the same colors and pattern. It was as if the designer was trying too hard to transport customers to the Mediterranean.

"Shall we order wine?" Helen shook out her napkin, placing it in her lap.

"No! I mean, I have to drive, and—" I managed to stop myself before inflicting more awkwardness on the situation. If there wasn't a book on how to deal with certain situations, Sarah should write one. Maybe that could be her hobby. Helping me, the clueless wife, and my half brother who had been hidden away for years. The Brady Bunch had nothing on us.

"It's okay, Lizzie." Meg turned her attention to Helen. "I'm in AA, but please don't feel inhibited."

The first skeleton I'd hoped to keep in the closet sprung out into the open.

"That's so cool!" Allen immediately pinched his eyes shut. It was a classic case of not knowing how stupid something sounded until spoken aloud with so much excitement. Another way Allen reminded me how alike we were.

Helen cleared her throat.

Allen added, "That you're so open about it."

"I find it's easier to get it out there. Much easier than thinking of a million and one reasons for turning down a drink. People hate when you refuse a drink." Meg seemed so relaxed. Confident. This was the Meg I'd met so many years ago. The one I'd fallen for. This was how she roped people into her life, to feed her need to be loved, and how she seized unrelenting control.

My hackles rose.

Sarah placed a hand on my thigh.

The waitress, with notepad in hand, asked, "Drinks?"

"Iced tea," I said.

Allen dittoed.

"Mineral water," Sarah said. Was she making a point that no one should tempt Meg, or was she afraid if she imbibed, terrible things would escape her lips?

Dad and Helen followed suit.

The waitress looked to Meg.

"Iced tea for me, Lizzie, and Allen"—she pointed both of us out—"and a bottle of pinot grigio for the people being too polite to order booze around the alky. Or would you prefer a red?" Meg directed her question to Sarah.

"White's fine." Sarah's voice sounded as if she hadn't had any liquids for more than seventy-two hours. Could a person last that long? The guy who had to cut off his own arm, how long had he lasted before he drank his own pee? I took a deep, but silent, breath to knock myself out of my head.

The waitress absconded.

Everyone buried their noses in their menus, which was typical in a restaurant, although everyone's purposeful concentration, avoiding making eye contact with anyone, brought the awkwardness front and center.

"Whatcha getting, Allen?" I asked.

"Margarita pizza." He set his menu on the table. "You?"

"Same."

Sarah laughed, but it sounded forced. "You two are so alike sometimes it's creepy." Her eyes flittered to Meg and then to Allen.

Meg slyly studied Allen, then me, before her eyes casually

slid to my father and his new wife of less than a year. Was she trying to determine if we all looked alike?

Helen, perceptive as ever, watched Sarah closely as if she were a weathervane, waiting to see how the wind blew.

"Did you two date during undergrad?" Allen asked.

I tried to keep my eyes from bugging out in frustration.

"We met in grad school. I was ahead of Lizzie in the program, but she finished before me." Meg's eyes traveled to Allen, appraising his gray and white striped polo with Ralphie's logo on the left chest. "Are you attending CU?"

"Started this fall. History is my passion, like you and Lizzie." It was evident that Allen's desire to launch into Russian history bubbled under the surface, but his shyness and the weirdness at the table curtailed him somewhat. Not enough for my comfort level. But he was my youngest sibling, and didn't I have a duty to help him out?

"He wants to specialize in the Russian revolution," I said and added, "You might know a thing or two about it."

She laughed. "Not more than three, though."

Allen chortled. His willingness to gobble up everything Meg said worried me. Then again, Meg would never date my younger sibling. Would she? Yes, she'd slept with men for money to support her addiction, but Allen was just a kid, even if he was legally an adult. And, my brother. Did Meg have some boundaries? It wasn't like we ever chatted about this possibility, but surely even Home-wrecker Meg wouldn't stoop to that level.

"How is it I haven't met you before, Allen? Only Peter." She lowered her voice. "He only cares about making a buck."

"He has... some good qualities," Allen came to Peter's defense, but he didn't put too much effort into the message.

"Peter and his wife recently had a baby girl," I offered, hoping to sidetrack Meg from the second secret—Dad's affair with Helen—I'd hope to keep out of the conversation.

"Demi." Sarah reached for my hand under the table, turning her attention to Meg. "She's such a sweetheart."

I wanted to kiss her for coming to my aid.

"Nothing like Peter, then." Meg laughed, Allen joining in.

Dad met my eye as if asking if Meg was for real. His protective gaze switched to Allen, although that was the only indication he wasn't happy. Did I inherit this trait from him? Hide most everything under the surface so others couldn't take advantage?

The waitress parceled out the iced teas, poured wine for everyone else, and set the bottle in the wine bucket at my dad's elbow. "Are you ready to order?"

"Shall we get some tapas to start?" Helen picked up the menu. No one declined, so she proceeded to point to a handful.

I focused on taking deep breaths without looking like I was in the midst of a panic attack. Tapas. Main course. And then freedom.

Everyone placed their dinner order.

"Would you excuse me?" I rose.

It took effort not to dash for the exit instead of the bathroom.

At the sink, I doused my face with extra cold water.

The door opened, and I squinted with one eye to see who was coming.

A woman in black old lady shoes shuffled into the first stall.

I released a puff of air.

Sarah stood outside the door, keeping an eye on the table by craning her head around the corner.

"What are you doing?" I asked.

"Making sure everything's okay."

"Why are you here and not there, then?"

"I wanted to check on you. How are you doing?" She peeked at the table again.

I shrugged.

"Here's the plan. Tapas. Dinner. Then we can politely vamoose for the drive home. Not that anyone would suggest the club I mentioned to Helen the other day. Not after Meg's AA confession and Allen's faux pas."

"What club?"

"Oh, I read about a swanky jazz place that's in a basement. It's a bar reminiscent of the 1920s called Prohibition. I thought the historian in you would get a kick out of it."

"That's sweet. Rain check, though?"

"Of course." She kissed my cheek.

I moved to rejoin the group, but Sarah didn't budge. "Now what?"

"I'm going to call Mom. Make sure she picked up the twinks."

"You mean check on Troy." I squeezed her arm. "Don't be too long. I need you."

She already held her phone to her ear.

Dad raised an inquisitive eyebrow when I returned alone. He plucked a cheese-filled pepper from one of the plates of hors d'oeuvres that had arrived in my absence.

"Sarah's checking on the twins."

Helen's eyes softened. "I remember those days. Wanting to get out of the house but then missing the kids. Not to mention worrying myself sick."

"She'd excuse herself at least three times during every dinner." Dad looked to his wife, the corner of his lips slightly askew.

Meg met my eyes again but didn't press. Sober Meg had much more control. Or maybe AA Meg could only focus on one thing: not drinking.

Sarah retook her seat, hearing the last bit of Dad's comment, clearly able to deduce the topic of conversation. "I keep having this dream something is wrong or I'm about to die, and I'm trying to call the twins but can't dial." Her face paled.

"That won't happen. Not ever," I said with absolute conviction.

"Which part? Dying or not being able to call?" Sarah eyed me in her curious way when she thought I was being cute.

"Both, because nothing is ever going to happen to you."

"And the twinks don't have phones," Sarah joked, perhaps in an effort to ease the look of panic that surely was present in my entire being.

Meg said something that only I could understand, after I took a second to process it. Everyone turned their attention to the blonde, but only Sarah's posture contained a threat.

It'd been years since I had to speak Russian, but I responded, "Without a doubt" to her "You really do love her" comment.

Allen's eyes grew three sizes. "You speak Russian?"

Meg nodded.

His eyes questioned me, and I indicated a little with my hand.

Sarah pressed her foot on top of mine.

"What'd you say?" He looked eager for the answer.

Meg mimed zipping her lips. "One of the advantages of being able to speak a language most don't is keeping certain things private. Like spies."

"Surely you aren't on the Russian payroll and my family is your target," Sarah said with forced lightheartedness, followed by a tittering sound I'd never heard her emit before. Her nails digging into my thigh was testimony she was doing everything she could to keep from jumping over the table to punch Meg in the face.

Allen peered in my direction, but Meg laughed it off. "You have nothing to fear," she said with a tinge of terseness. She pivoted to Allen. "Are you taking any language courses?"

He nodded but with a grave air. "French. Russian was full this semester."

Helen said, "I imagine a lot of hopeful academics think learning Russian will be useful considering how much Russia has been in the news lately."

"I'm so sick of hearing about it." Dad plucked an olive from a tiny brown bowl.

I'd always assumed my father, given his stature in the business world, was Republican. But, politics, along with many other topics, had always been taboo between us.

Helen planted a hand on his arm. "Yes, but sticking one's head in the sand isn't going to help."

He stared at her, giving the impression they'd gone rounds about the issue before. I wondered if Allen's interest in Russian history played a significant role.

"If you'd like some lessons, I'd be more than happy to help," Meg said to Allen, turning her face away from the couple at the end of the table.

"You'd do that?" He squeaked, adorably so, which made me worry even more about Meg getting her claws into my impressionable sibling.

Allen's jubilation swayed me from interjecting an objection. He was an adult now, and he'd have to learn how to handle people like Meg. Maybe if I repeated this nonstop for an hour, I'd actually believe the words. Did we know each other well enough for me to play the Big Sister Card and tell him to stay away without having to proffer an explanation?

"I'm sure Meg has her hands full with finishing her PhD," Sarah said.

"Actually, teaching Allen would help me brush up. It's been some time since I've had a need to speak the language." She turned to Allen, one of the stuffed peppers in her hand. "You can impress the ladies," Meg teased, jouncing his shoulder with hers and popping one of the cheese filled peppers into her mouth.

Allen sat up straighter in his chair, in all probability imagining saying something clever to a girl as if he were James Bond in a tuxedo.

If she hadn't been speaking the language much, why had the comment she'd made to me rolled off her lips?

"Are you staying in Boulder, then?" Sarah asked Meg with a warning in her tone.

"For the moment. I have some friends in the area, and I'm applying for a position at the university." Meg sipped her iced tea and then casually said, "I'd love to meet your little ones. Honestly"—her eyes skimmed to me and then back to Sarah —"I never thought of Lizzie becoming a parent."

Her casual way of chatting as if nothing had ever happened between us vexed me more than I expected.

"She's a different person now," Sarah countered.

"I have no doubt. Teaching. Twins. And you. I have a feeling you're the most important part of the equation." Meg seemed to speak with earnestness, but I didn't want to allow myself to trust her. When I shut the door on Meg, I promised I'd never let her back in. I had to build walls when it came to Meg, which was slightly confusing since I'd spent years in therapy tearing them down for the sake of my marriage.

"I would be lost without her." I took Sarah's hand in mine and lifted it to my lips, placing a gentle kiss on her fingertips. "So, stop having those dreams. It ain't happening."

"I can tell when you're passionate about something. You start using words like *ain't*." Sarah pressed a finger against my nose.

"Do the twins take after Lizzie?" Meg asked. "Janice told me you used Lizzie's eggs."

The next time I saw Janice, I planned to give her a piece of my mind.

Helen rushed in with, "Freddie, does for sure. He's the thinker of the two. And more sensitive."

"And Ollie?"

Sarah recoiled, and it was as if I could see her replaying the conversation to pinpoint whether or not anyone mentioned our daughter's name.

Again, Helen responded. "She's going to make her moms go completely gray before she graduates from kindergarten."

"Do you plan on having any more children? One of your own, Sarah? Although, it's quite romantic—you having Lizzie's babies."

Thank God two waiters arrived with our main courses. While Sarah had mentioned having another child using her egg, I didn't want to open that can of worms with Meg. Sarah had never insinuated that she wanted one of her *own*, as Meg had put it, and I never thought she felt that way. I still didn't, no matter how much Meg hoped to get into my head.

Helen steered the conversation with Meg and everyone else in a masterful way, allowing me to relax to the point where I didn't have to worry about having a heart attack.

Yet, I knew to stay vigilant. Meg was many things, tenacious most of all.

* * *

IN THE CAR, after dinner, Sarah sank into the passenger seat. "She's nothing like what I expected."

Knowing she was referring to Meg, I asked, "And what did you expect?"

Sarah hitched a shoulder. "A hot mess. Like the last time I saw her."

"You saw her at her worst." I conceded with a half shrug.

"And, by that, you mean drunk in a hotel lobby, screaming about a John stiffing her," she added, "twice, if you get my meaning."

I peeked at her, not wanting to take my eyes off the road for too long, considering the dark back road from Boulder to Fort

Collins. I was mentally and physically drained from the conference and surprise dinner party invite.

Sarah continued. "If I didn't know anything about her past,
I'd consider her pleasant. Charming, even." Her voice was
much harder given the sentiment spoken. "She got a few not-
so-subtle zingers in that even your father seemed to notice. I'm
pretty sure Allen is the only one who thinks the dinner was a
smashing success."

I nodded, not wanting to acknowledge that was my biggest
worry when it came to Allen. His naïveté and Meg's ability to
win him over with the same ease she did with me. How had I
not seen her for what she was? Admitting this to Sarah would
be akin to disclosing I was desperate for love, making me weak.
Even after years of therapy and being in a loving relationship,
this was still a major obstacle. Not just knowing my Achilles'
heel but dealing with it and letting Sarah in completely. I gave
her glimpses but hadn't reached the full disclosure stage at all
times. What was wrong with me?

"What did she say to you? In Russian?" She slipped off her
heels and rubbed the bottom of her right foot. "I'd forgotten
you could speak the language some, and I wasn't thrilled when
she ventured into this secret communication."

"Neither was I, especially in front of you and Allen." I
pulled on the seat belt to loosen it some. "I'm surprised it took
you this long to ask. I half expected you to use the twins as an
excuse to get me away from the table."

"The thought did enter my mind, but I didn't want to leave
her alone with Allen. So, what did she say?"

"She said it was clear you were the one and only. Or something like that. Admittedly, even when I practiced, my Russian
was rudimentary, and I fear it's much worse now. You know
what they say, use it or lose it."

"And you said…?" She gave me her full attention.

"'Without a doubt.' Or possibly I asked if she had any goats to sell." I passed a car traveling slower than a grannie in a wheelchair.

"My guess is you got it right. How else do you explain her asking if I wanted a child of my own?" Sarah huffed. "What kind of bitch asks that about our children?"

I merged back into the right-hand lane. "One who never thinks she's in the wrong, even after all the shit she's pulled." My fingers wrapped tightly around the steering wheel.

"You don't feel that way when I mention having another kid, do you?" Her voice displayed vulnerability.

"Never. There are a lot of things I don't know or understand in this world, but I know with absolute certainty that you love our children and would do anything for them."

Sarah placed her hand on my thigh. After several moments of quiet, she sighed. "What are we going to do about Allen? Do you think he's developing a crush on Meg or is only interested because of the Russian history connection?"

"Surely he wouldn't drop Bailey for the likes of Meg."

Sarah tapped her fingers on the side window. "Allen is a sweet kid, and people like Meg know how to lure them into their trap. You know that better than most."

Not liking the turn in the conversation, I bristled. "What do you suggest I do, then?"

She let out a rush of air, but before she could respond, her phone lit up, illuminating the darkness in the car. "Mom says the kids are sound asleep and we should leave them be 'til morning."

Just thinking of our sleeping babes blunted my bad mood. "What do you think?"

Sarah stared at the phone, holding it up so I could glance at it. "The photo of them sleeping is pretty convincing."

"Settled, then. I won't lie; I'm beat." I let out a whoosh of air.

Sarah yawned. "Who knew history conferences could be so draining?"

"You're drained? I spent weeks prepping." I tapped her leg with my right hand briefly, assuming the nine-and-three position on the wheel.

"Please, I'm surprised you don't lecture in your sleep." Sarah leaned over the console. "You, my dear, were born to teach and surprisingly, you're able to make stuffy history bits somewhat entertaining." She kissed my cheek.

"Did I impress today?"

"Some," she purred in my ear. Abruptly, she retreated to her side of the car. "Now, Meg and Allen."

"Oh, I'm pretty sure we're on the same page."

"You're going to talk to Allen. Tell him about the Meg you know."

Stunned that was the course she thought I should take, I tried to stall. "Uh, not exactly what I had in mind. I was thinking more along the lines of banning Meg from interacting with Allen."

"How in the world do you plan to accomplish that? Allen's your brother and would do anything for you. Meg is… not to be trusted. Are you afraid of how she'll react?"

Yes!

But I didn't answer. "I'm sorry we didn't make it to Prohibition. Maybe we can talk your mom into watching the twinkies for a long weekend. Would you like a night in Boulder? Just the two of us?"

Sarah sighed but dropped the Meg conversation. She leaned into the SUV's back seat to retrieve my Patagonia insulated jacket, which I'd brought but didn't end up needing. She proceeded to bunch it into a pillow of sorts and placed it between the window and seat. "That sounds nice."

CHAPTER TWELVE

"*H*ow was the history nerd fest?" Maddie sat on the barstool with Ollie in her lap.

"Careful, I may pick up on your derision." Standing on the other side of the island, I flipped the *New York Times* over to skim the stories below the fold.

"I should hope so. I wasn't attempting to hide it. Right, Ollie Dollie?" She wiggled Ollie's feet.

"Don't egg her on. I have a feeling she'll give me enough grief once she starts talking in complete sentences." I grinned at my daughter over my *Sit down and shut up; I'm about to teach history* mug, a gift from Sarah.

Sarah returned to the kitchen with a freshly changed Freddie. "What'd I miss?"

"Maddie was mocking me, so nothing." I poured a cup of coffee for Sarah. It was a little before ten, but we both needed extra caffeine.

"You say it like I only ever mock you." Maddie had the gall to appear innocent.

Before I could respond, Sarah butted in. "Lizzie's ex Meg—"

Maddie interjected, "No need to name her. Lizzie doesn't have many—"

I jumped in with, "And you were saying you don't mock me twenty-four—"

"You two are horrible examples. Bickering like children." Sarah took a seat next to Maddie, placing Freddie's bum on the island, facing Sarah. She blew a zerbert on his stomach.

Maddie quickly followed suit with Ollie before the eldest twin could squawk about being left out.

I continued scanning an article, waiting for the twins' giggles to cease.

"As I was saying, Meg had dinner with us last night." Sarah avoided my eyes.

Maddie put her hand on Sarah's leg. "I knew she was presenting, but dinner? How'd that happen? I don't know much about Meg, except she's the ex who should never be mentioned."

Exactly. So why was Sarah uttering her name?

"Allen," Sarah said.

Maddie shook her head. "I'm not following. How does Allen know Lizzie's ex?"

"Apparently, he thinks she's the greatest Russian Revolution historian. I couldn't peg if his interest is the direct result of Allen's passion for history or... if he's developing a crush, like Jorie on Lizzie." Sarah was trying to steer clear of her main concern—Meg's connection to me.

Maddie shook her head. "Jorie doesn't have a crush on Lizzie. She's struggling with her sexuality, especially given the latest LGBTQ setbacks."

"How do you know that?" I asked, flipping the paper open to the opinion page.

"I asked her." She looked at me with an incredulous expression as if the answer were obvious.

"You asked my former student if she had a crush on me?" My brain struggled to understand Maddie's gumption.

"Yes, except I used the words *hots for* instead of *crush*." Maddie pretended to gobble Olivia's fingers, which was much appreciated given the happy squeals.

"Because the word *crush* is too formal?" I tapped my fingers on the countertop, making a mental note to file that tidbit in the *talking to millennials* file.

Maddie's eyes darted upward. "Back to Allen and Meg. It's kinda sweet if he does have a *crush*"—she looked at me as she emphasized the word—"although slightly creepy given the sibling connection." Maddie exaggerated a shiver, and Ollie clapped her hands, delighted with her aunt's antics. Maddie did it again.

"It's not sweet. I'm worried—"

I cut Sarah off. "I said I'll take care of it." Plotting how to take care of the situation with Sarah was one thing, but letting Maddie in, even a little, about Meg wasn't something I wanted or could handle.

Maddie's eyes grazed my face and then landed on Sarah. "I'm missing something. Is Meg actually *interested* in Allen? He's cute, but in the younger sibling kind of way."

"No!" I said with too much force.

"Are you jealous? Is that the issue?" Maddie pressed.

"Of course not." I sipped my tea with an angry slurp, turning the page of the paper, nearly ripping it in half. Why in the world would she ask me that and in front of Sarah?

"Are you positive? Dealing with exes can be confusing." Maddie offered a sympathetic nod.

Says the woman who slept with her ex, my brother, in my home. "I'm one hundred and ten percent positive," I said through gritted teeth.

"Are you?" Sarah asked, her voice lacking her usual punch.

I slammed my mug down, sloshing some onto the newspaper. "How could you of all people ask me that? You know—" I gave her the stink eye.

"Oh, the backstory on Meg must be juicy. Tell me." Maddie motioned for me to come out with it.

"There's no backstory," I lamely said.

Maddie tugged on Sarah's arm. "Spill it."

Sarah shook her head. "What do you have planned today?" she said in an effort to repair the damage she'd inflicted.

Unfortunately, this only made Maddie convulse in delight. Perhaps it was easier for her to handle my messed-up situations over Sarah's. More than likely, she was used to dealing with mine since Sarah was usually everyone's rock. "All these years and I didn't know you had a past."

"That's impossible. Everyone has a past." I used my best history teacher tone.

"Not with Meg. Whose name really isn't Meg. She's…" Maddie tapped her fingers against her teeth. "A Russian spy." She shook her head. "Too easy these days." She bolted up. "Another half sibling!"

I stared at her slack-jawed.

"Maddie, please…" Sarah's face buckled with guilt.

Not deterred, she said, "That's why Sarah is so concerned about Allen. Avoiding a *Flowers in the Attic* scenario. You slept with your sister!" She jabbed a finger in my direction, Ollie giggling with all the excitement.

"She's an alcoholic, who tried to ruin Lizzie's career, blackmailed her, and became a prostitute," Sarah blurted out as if she'd literally explode if she kept everything inside.

Maddie laughed. "That's good but not as good as my theory. Incest is way too taboo." Maddie repeated the word *taboo*, emphasizing the second syllable, to Ollie.

I breathed in and out, my shoulders heaving upward with each intake and my eyes boring into Sarah's.

The smile slowly edged off Maddie's face, like the sun

making way for the night. "That wasn't a wild smokescreen to get me off the scent. All that actually happened."

"Thanks for that, Sarah. Heaven forbid you keep that part of my life private." I stormed out of the kitchen for the library.

Much to my surprise, it was Maddie who appeared in the library not too soon after my hasty departure.

"Don't start!" I knifed a hand in the air and slammed it down onto my desk.

Maddie perched on the arm of the chair on the opposite side.

"Seriously, Maddie. I'm not in the mood to be your punching bag. Not now."

She sat quietly, her sympathetic eyes aggravating me further.

She slid off the arm of the chair onto the seat. "I didn't know."

"I didn't want you to know. I don't want anyone to know." I reached for a yellow notepad but ended up tossing it back down onto the desk.

She nodded, clearly not able to think of some snide comment. Or, perhaps, she was waiting for the perfect time.

"Would you leave… please?" I grabbed the notepad again, tempted to shoo Maddie away with it.

Maddie shook her head.

"Don't, Maddie. Just let me be."

"We don't have to talk. I can sit here with you." She yanked the pad out of my hands, laying it back in its place.

"If I wanted company, I would have asked." I snorted, resulting in a spray of snot. Another indignity to suffer from the Meg debacle—one I had thought ended years ago.

She slanted her head. "Sometimes you don't know when to ask for help."

I groaned, burying my face with my hands. "Jesus, you can be infuriating when you put your mind to it!"

The leather chair creaked, and I prayed she opted to leave. Her hand on my shoulder was further proof no one upstairs ever heard my prayers.

"We all have something we're not proud of in our past," she said.

"You've had a blackmailing ex?"

Maddie hopped up on the edge of my desk, her legs dangling. "Nope. But one took all of my belongings that I left at her apartment and burned them on the lawn outside of my dorm. For weeks, my roommates blared the Alanis Morissette song 'You Oughta Know.'"

"Wow."

Maddie sighed. "Life, love..." She circled a finger. "It can suck."

"That was profound. Have you considered becoming a life coach?" I crossed my arms over my chest.

"How come you can make jokes, but I can't?" she asked with a smile.

"You aren't funny," I deadpanned to the best of my abilities.

"Are you okay?" She squeezed my shoulder.

"You must be worried if you resisted going in for the kill."

"Don't tell anyone, but I care about you." Her voice lacked her usual smart-ass vibe. "I know you were kidding about the life coach thing, but maybe it would help you to talk to someone."

"I stopped going to therapy months ago. Everything had been going so well." I tapped my open hand against my forehead, making a slapping sound.

"I know. I was thinking of Courtney."

"*Courtney*, Courtney?"

She nodded.

"Kit's fiancée, who potentially could be Tie's sister-in-law if Kit and Courtney decide to take their sham of an engagement to the next level? That's your idea of the perfect life coach?"

"She's a great listener and has a unique perspective on human behavior. When I was spiraling out of control—"

I pointed a finger at her. "Like when you slept with my married brother in my home?"

She showed her palms, shaking her head to stop me. "I talked to her quite a bit, and Court did a couple of things for me. One,"—Maddie extended her index finger in the air—"she didn't judge me. Two,"—she added her middle finger—"she let me talk to figure things out myself with minimal guidance." Maddie lowered her head to make direct eye contact. "Courtney has a gift. You really should talk to her."

I sucked in a breath, a technique I utilized to keep from saying the first thing that came to my mind, since history, not to mention my therapist, warned me to think before speaking. "I'll... think about it."

Maddie hopped to her feet and did a happy gig accompanied with hand clapping.

"You seem way too excited about my emotional distress."

"Not that part. You're learning. There's hope for you yet, Lizzie Petrie."

I exaggerated an eye roll, knowing she was wrong.

CHAPTER THIRTEEN

*E*than's ranch-style house in Loveland was modest but true to his character. All the surfaces were spotless with minimalist decoration, aside from books overflowing on the shelves and a small pile of paperbacks next to a worn recliner near the fireplace.

Our wives were in the kitchen, supposedly prepping dinner, but Ethan suspected it was their way of retreating to dish the dirt about us since the dinner involved ordering pizza.

In the corner of the family room, Casey sat at a kid-size table with the twins, playing tea-party host. "One lump or two, Freddie?"

Freddie rubbed the errant hairs on top of his head, a crooked grin on his adorable face.

"Two," Casey confirmed with a confident nod.

"Did he rub twice?" I whispered out of the side of my mouth to Ethan.

He hefted a shoulder. "It's hard to tell with Casey. She has a script inside her head and goes with it no matter what. Comes from being an only child I think. Like you."

I laughed. "Seems like I have siblings and family connections coming out of the ying-yang these days."

"Ah, but during your formative years, you were alone, mostly. And that's why you're this way." He tapped a finger against his temple. "Locked away ninety percent of the time."

"Am not!"

"Are too. You try to act nonchalant, but underneath it all, trouble is brewing." He crossed his reedy arms, staring at me with a *confess all* expression.

"Did Maddie call or text?" I asked Ethan, immediately kicking myself for falling into his trap. Lately, I was realizing the perils of being book smart.

Sitting in his recliner, he pressed his hands into his thighs as if trying to curtail his excitement. "I knew something was troubling you."

My eyes darted to the ceiling. "Nope."

"Nope, nothing's troubling you? Or nope, you don't want to talk about it?"

"Both."

He cocked his head, his brow furrowed. "How can it be both?"

"It just is."

He nodded. "Ah, the Casey answer."

"Says the man who doesn't open up much about things. Like your marriage." I whispered the last word so Casey wouldn't hear.

"Oooh, that was a good attempt to get me to shut up." His kind eyes stayed on mine, not overly inquisitive, but with an openness to unload my angst.

Damn him. After all these years, Ethan knew how to work me. And this human need for comfort was confounding me.

I glanced at the stack of books by his chair. "Meg's back."

"I heard." He steepled his fingers and rested his chin on the tips.

"It's weird."

"I imagine." He spread his fingers briefly but returned to the steeple position.

I couldn't have this conversation in Ethan's home, while our children conducted a tea party—well, Casey was doing her best to keep them involved, but Ollie was morphing into a drunken pirate banging her tiny cup against the table, yelling something that sounded like *grrrr*.

Luckily, Sarah and Lisa waltzed into the room, laughing. Both of them gave us a look implying they were making fun of us.

"I do believe one of us is the source of the fun." Ethan rose and kissed Lisa on the cheek.

"Do you think the only thing we can discuss is our spouses?" Lisa shot back with an evil grin that lacked her typical warmth.

Ethan backpedaled. "Of course not."

Lisa seemed somewhat mollified.

Their relationship had always been rocky, and that had helped Ethan and me reconnect while I was still in grad school. Back then, he had claimed no matter how hard things got between them, they had a bond that kept them together. Their closeness was refreshing to witness, making me believe relationships, no matter the obstacles, could survive. Over the last six months, their bond was visibly fraying, and I worried they were cruising for divorce court.

Ethan continued. "I just know that laugh. It's the one implying someone is an idiot, which usually is directed toward a spouse."

Lisa huffed, turning her back to him. "Whatever."

Ethan wheeled about to me. "Dropping it and fast."

Perched on the side of the couch, Sarah ringed her arm around my neck. "Probably for the best. Dinner will be here in ten."

"Casey, it's almost chow time. Put your toys away, and go wash your hands." Ethan gestured chop-chop.

"It's a tea set, not a toy," she grumbled, although she got to work.

Sarah and I wrestled with the twins. Getting Ollie to relinquish her cup involved switching her focus to her stuffed giraffe, which immediately spurred Fred to reach for it. Before Sarah and I could separate the twins, both started crying, Ollie's face turning a deep shade of purplish red. Neighbors three blocks away could probably hear their shrieks.

Wide-eyed, Ethan asked Lisa, "And you want another baby?"

Lisa, unperturbed by the commotion that was already dissipating due to Fred's lack of urgency to take on his sister, said, "Yep."

I smiled at Ethan. "I recommend twins. They're twice the fun."

Sarah kicked me. "Don't get in the middle."

"Says the woman who insisted we use my eggs."

"If we do have another child, rest assured, we won't ask for your eggs," Ethan said.

I clipped Ollie into her car seat. "Your loss—"

Sarah rushed the words out. "Is our gain."

"Wait, are you thinking of using my eggs again?" My insides clenched.

"Would that be so weird?"

"Do we want to risk our perfect family with more of my offspring? You've met my family, right?"

Sarah and Lisa shared a look that didn't sit well with me. Was that what they'd been discussing? How to convince their unwilling spouses to increase the world's population? And with more Petries?

As if in tune with my thoughts, Ethan thrust a finger at them. "No more bonding time for you two."

From their expressions, neither took his words to heart.

With a hand on Ethan's arm, I said, "We've had a good run, but in the interest of our marriages, not to mention the Doomsday clock ticking closer and closer to *kaboom*, for the lack of a better world, we need to stop seeing each other to prevent them from conspiring."

"That's exactly what Lizzie needs. Fewer friends to be there for her," Sarah said to Lisa.

Lisa added, "Ethan would be lost without her. When I'm nagging him, he loves to say, 'Lizzie did this' to distract me."

I jarred Ethan's shoulder with mine. "You throw me under the bus to get out of trouble?"

He bobbed his head. "Every chance I get."

"That's despicable."

"Are we going to watch *Despicable Me?*" Casey had returned from the bathroom and now stood next to Ethan.

"Yes, with the twins." Ethan motioned for me to arrange the twins in front of the television while Lisa and Sarah moved the plastic table for Casey to sit at while she ate her pizza in front of America's number one babysitter.

The kitchen table, where the adults would sit was within view of Casey and the twins but offered a semblance of privacy.

The doorbell rang.

Ethan rubbed his hands together. "Dinner's ready, folks."

While Ethan was at the door, Casey approached Sarah. "If you have another baby, you should do it right this time."

The kid must have heard everything while in the bathroom.

Sarah failed to suppress a smile. "Meaning?"

"You don't ever let Freddie or Ollie wear blue or pink."

"We don't want to force..." She paused, probably trying to think of a way to explain gender politics to a child.

"Boy or girl things." Casey elevated a hand in the air. "I get it. But, you still gave them boy and girl names." Her eyes lit up. "What are their middle names?"

The color leeched out of Sarah's face, so I answered, "Frederick James and Olivia Rose." The look of disapproval on Casey's pinched face compelled me to say more. "James was Sarah's father's name, and you've met Rose, Sarah's mom."

"How come neither is named after one of your parents?" Casey peered upward into my eyes. "You have two kids and two sets of parents."

"Um… that's very logical." Unlike my response. "They have my last name."

"Did you change your last name?" Casey asked Sarah.

"Yes." For some reason, Sarah seemed uncomfortable with this answer. We thought it too cruel to the twinks to hyphenate Petrie-Cavanaugh.

I felt compelled to say, "You'll always be a Cavanaugh to me."

"Casey, time for dinner." Ethan stood behind his daughter with two pizza boxes in his hands. "And, we have chocolate chip cookies for little ones who behave."

Casey made a beeline for the plastic table.

After serving his daughter and cuing up the movie, Ethan took his seat at the grown-ups' table. "I don't know what we're going to do in a few years." He glanced over his shoulder. "She's too smart for her own good. It's like she's an adult trapped in a child's body."

I nodded, while Sarah and Lisa shot him a withering look.

"Her zero tolerance for BS is refreshing," Sarah said, recovering from being schooled by an elementary student about not taking her beliefs to the extreme.

"And intimidating," I added.

"Not surprising, coming from you." Ethan chomped into a slice.

I clamped my hand on his shoulder. "Now I feel pressured to keep screwing up in order to save your marriage."

"Yeah, that's why you do and say things that get you in trouble. For me." Ethan placed a hand over his heart.

"You totally owe me." I swiped one of the pepperonis from his slice.

"How do you live with her?" Ethan asked Sarah.

* * *

IN BED LATER THAT NIGHT, I asked Sarah, "Are you serious about wanting to use my eggs again?"

She opened one eye as if not entirely willing to enter this conversation right when she was about to drift off to sleep. "I've thought about it, but only briefly, so don't get your panties twisted just yet."

"Is this because of Meg?" I supported my head on bent elbow.

"No... not really. I go back and forth. Not just about using your eggs but about having another child. The last two months of pregnancy weren't fun."

I readjusted onto my back and fluffed a pillow behind my head. "When I was a kid, I used to dream about nice parents adopting me."

Sarah rolled over on her side, placing her hand on my chest. "Daydream or *dream* dream?"

"Both."

She nodded as if she'd guessed my feelings before. "Do you still wish for it?"

"I'm a bit old for adoption, I think."

"No one is ever too old to want to be loved."

"Things have changed some. Dad, Peter, and I are adapting. I'm not sure how to put it. We've grown to be there for each other, and now there's Helen."

Sarah remained quiet, but her eyes were wide-awake now. She burrowed against my side, an indication she was willing to chat. "Have you considered adopting a child?"

I ran my fingers through her silky dark hair. "I haven't

thought about it much. Not sure why I brought it up, really. Except maybe, I worry Ollie and Freddie will someday wish they were adopted."

She laughed. "Oh, I imagine when they don't get their way, they'll say stupid things in the midst of a tantrum. Especially Ollie."

"Are we good parents, Sarah?" I asked in all seriousness.

Sarah propped up her head. "Yes, I think we are."

"Failure isn't an option, not when it comes to the twinks. I don't want us to be like Ethan and Lisa. Casey's never mentioned it, but she has to pick up on the fact her parents aren't getting along. Not like they used to."

She planted a tender kiss on my lips. "We'll make mistakes, but we won't outright fail. No one really knows what they're doing as parents. Even when their children are grown and they start dating a boy toy."

"I'm not sure Troy falls into that category." Deciding it was best to dig deeper, I said, "Speaking of tense situations that may affect the kids, how are you dealing with Troy now?" She didn't answer, so I changed tactics. "If he wasn't dating your mom, would you like him as a person? A friend, even?"

She shot me a withering glare. "You need to stop hanging out with Casey."

Unperturbed, I forged ahead. "Does that mean you think Troy's a decent man?"

She sucked in a deep breath.

"What if they got married?"

Sarah lurched up. "Whoa! Where's this coming from? Did my mom say something to you?"

I motioned for her to settle down. "No. I was only asking hypothetically."

Sarah refused to speak, giving me the feeling she'd have issues having a stepfather. Finally, she said, "I thought we were talking about the twinks." She scrambled out of bed and jerked her head for me to follow suit.

"Before I do, can I say one thing?"

She heaved an exasperated sigh but nodded her consent.

"Before we really consider having more children, I think it's important for us to resolve certain family issues."

"Meg and Allen?"

"That's one problem I need to handle. And you need to fix the situation with your mom. Both of you act semi-normal around the twinks, but if either of them is half as cunning as Casey, I think they'll start to pick up on it. I meant it earlier when I said failure isn't an option."

Sarah, once again, didn't speak, but the recognition in her *yes* confirmed she knew I spoke the truth. "Come with me."

I did.

We stood in the nursery doorway, watching our children sleep in their cribs.

"They're happy. That's all we need to accomplish." Sarah rested her head against my shoulder. "Perfection isn't possible, but understand this; they both know how much we love them. And I believe if we used your eggs again it would all work out."

"Same goes if we used yours." I kissed the side of her head. "I love them and you, even if you're being stubborn about things I'm not supposed to mention."

"Look who's talking," she whispered, jouncing her hip into mine.

CHAPTER FOURTEEN

*T*he following week, Sarah and I splurged on a five-star hotel and spa in Boulder for a weekend away. She didn't outright say so, but I think this was the first step of Sarah offering an olive branch to Rose, trusting Troy, who I was certain stayed over every night, with the twinks for an entire weekend. And, miraculously, Sarah had checked on them only twice, granted we'd been away for just a few hours.

On our way back to the hotel, after a romantic dinner followed by drinks at Prohibition, Sarah said, "When we get back, I need you to hang out in the lobby bar for a few minutes. I have a surprise for you."

"Really?" I slipped my hand into hers when we crossed Pearl Street. "Good or bad?"

She laughed nervously. "We'll see."

Intrigued, I turned my head to appraise her profile. "You like to keep me on my toes."

We reached the hotel entrance.

"I'll text you when I'm ready." She kissed my cheek.

I took a seat at the bar, and the bartender in white shirt,

red-checkered tie, and charcoal vest asked, "What can I get you?"

I wasn't sure how long Sarah would be, so I opted for a Coke instead of tea.

"Just a Coke?" He poured a drink into an elegant sapphire-colored glass, adding some orange peel and sprigs of mint. The recipient oohed and aahed as if it was the fanciest drink she'd ever been served.

"Yep."

The bartender mercifully complied, not bothering to try to upsell me.

A man and woman in their sixties took the two seats next to me.

While the bartender took their orders, I whipped out my phone. I'd learned scanning my device prevented people from initiating small talk. As I perused the headlines of the *New York Times*, I sipped my Coke.

My phone chimed, and I read Sarah's text alerting me to come upstairs.

Upon opening the door, Sarah instructed me to close my eyes.

I complied, carefully easing into the room, not wanting to bump into the four-poster bed.

"Okay, you can open them."

"Oh, wow." I blinked.

Sarah wore black suede stiletto boots, which laced in the front and ended right below her knees, lace-topped stockings, garters, and a matching bra. No panties. Her hair was fluffed in the way I've learned to know meant *I want you to fuck me good and hard.*

"You're staring," she said.

"No. Leering. Ogling. Goggling." I made a motion implying my eyes were popping out of my sockets.

"I think there's a bit of drool." She tapped one side of her glossed lips with a newly manicured nail.

I swiped the right corner of my mouth with the back of my hand. "Too much ChapStick," I lamely defended.

"The other side as well," Sarah said in her bedroom voice.

My eyes roamed up her body. Down. Up again. "I don't—"

"Maybe speaking isn't your best option right now."

I nodded.

She tapped a black stick with a paddle-like thing at one end and a fluffy feather at the other against her leg. "Ah, you've noticed my riding crop."

I swallowed.

"It's for spanking, but you've read Fifty Shades series, so you know that." She was clearly enjoying herself.

My eyes widened further, the extra oxygen causing them to water.

"And tickling." She jerked her head to the bed. "And there are some restraints."

I peered around and spied nylon straps snaking from underneath the bed. Four in total. "You want me to tie you down?"

She shook her head.

"Me?" I croaked, placing a hand on my chest.

"You've been bad."

"I—"

Sarah took three massive steps, stopping in front of me. With her hand covering my mouth, she said, "I said no talking. If you do—" She slapped the crop against her leg. "Now, strip!"

I lifted my V-neck sweater and polo over my head somewhat clumsily due to shaky hands. Sarah motioned for me to hurry up. I let my gray chinos drop to the floor and stepped out of my cotton panties, flinging them across the room with my toe.

She smiled. "You forgot your bra. Or did you think I wouldn't notice?"

I started to defend myself, but her crop-wielding hand flickered, silencing my tongue. I slid the bra straps over my arms.

Sarah pointed with the crop. "On your back."

I slowly made my way, wondering what in the hell had gotten into my wife. My mind raced over the details of the day and discovered not one clue that she planned on punishing me —not like this anyhow.

Granted, I'd purchased the Fifty Shades books to breathe life back into Sexy Sarah, but I didn't mean for her to take it to this extreme. A riding crop? Whipping?

Sarah secured my right wrist. Then my ankle. The other one. And, finally, my left wrist. She'd tugged on each to ensure I couldn't escape.

My eyes followed her as she patrolled the perimeter of the bed, slapping the crop against her palm. "Where should I start?"

Fuck, she looked hot as hell.

I took a deep breath, bracing for the pain.

I should have known when I stumbled upon the sequel to *Fifty Shades of Grey* tucked into one of the travel bags. But, the thought of my sweet wife, tying me up to torture me had never crossed my mind. Shouldn't she have at least broached the subject beforehand? Or had my buying her the books been all the permission she needed? Not to mention reading portions aloud to each other?

And when did she have the time to purchase all of this? Had she ordered everything online? Did the mail carrier know my fate before I did? In the past she'd surprised me with a strap on, but BDSM? Was that the clue I missed over a year ago? Were strap ons the gateway drug, so to speak, for *this*? Maybe I was dreaming.

As Sarah edged the right side of the bed, she trailed the feather down that side of my body.

I squirmed.

She tickled the bottoms of my feet, causing me to wiggle even more.

"You like?"

Was I allowed to answer, or was this a trick?

Her hand rose as if preparing to strike.

"Yes!" I blurted.

"Yes, what?"

"Yes, please." My voice sounded weak. I made a mental note to reread the goddamned Fifty Shades books to prep better for the next time my wife went off the rails in the bedroom. No way would I watch the movies, which even Sarah said were subpar.

"That'll work this time, but in the future, please respond with, *Yes, Mistress.*"

I nodded.

The crop went up again.

"Yes, Mistress," I said too loudly.

Sarah glanced over her shoulder as if expecting hotel personnel to barge in. None did, of course.

Her distraction allowed me to take in her outfit, which was smoking hot, and although fear coursed through me, the warm sensation between my legs increased exponentially. Did that make me a freak? Did that matter? What would my students think of me if they knew?

Stop it, Lizzie.

As if in tune with the inner dialogue, Sarah thwacked the sheet next to my left leg.

I flinched.

She did it again, followed by lightly tracing the outside of my leg with the feather. Sarah slinked to the end of the bed, placing one foot on the bench, allowing my eyes access to her glistening pussy.

"Oh, look." She skimmed a finger over her engorged lips.

"I'm getting wet." With lightning speed, she snapped the crop onto the sheets between my legs.

I snapped my eyes shut, waiting for her to achieve her ultimate goal. Which was what, exactly?

"Did I say you could close your eyes?" she asked.

My eyelids flew open.

Sarah placed a finger into her mouth, licking it. "Although, that gives me an idea." She disappeared into the bathroom, where she must have stashed her sex gear.

I yanked on my arm restraints to no avail.

Her head peered around the doorframe. "Don't think about it, or you'll pay."

"I wasn't—"

"Is that how you should respond?" She approached with one hand behind her back. Not the one with the crop, unfortunately.

"No, Mistress."

"That's better. And now for—" In her hand was an eye mask she'd purchased earlier in the spa.

I inhaled a deep breath.

"Now, now. You act like you're afraid of me. I haven't done a thing to hurt you... not yet. So, behave." Sarah motioned for me to lift my head to allow her to tie the black and pink silky fabric. "Trust is key to all relationships," she declared in what could only be described as her BDSM voice. A new thing.

I didn't react.

She spanked the bed close to my side, and the feather brushed me. "Don't you agree?"

"Yes, Mistress."

She shuffled on her feet, but I couldn't make out her next move, unwilling to risk peeking through the sliver of light at the bottom of the mask. The bottom half of the bed lurched. Dear God. Was she on the bed? Between my legs? With the crop? I pinched my eyes shut, bracing for what came next.

As if answering my unspoken concerns, the feather teased between my legs.

"Your tenseness may show fear, but this"—she pressed the crop between my pussy lips—"shows me how turned on you are. Let's see how much you can handle."

Did that mean…?

The feather danced on my lower stomach.

I thrashed about, causing the restraints to pull on my skin.

She continued, tickling my right nipple.

My body responded by trembling.

The bed moved again, and I think her hip was pressed into my crotch. The feather continued its wondrous torture, now focusing under my chin. Sarah's leg slowly gyrated against me down below.

It was maddening not being able to see all of her.

Not being able to touch her.

The feather skimmed my lips, followed by Sarah's mouth.

I moaned into the quick and dirty kiss, instantly wishing it lasted longer. Forever.

Sarah's tongue teased my already hardened right nipple, sucking it into her mouth. Both of her hands trailed up and down the sides of my body.

Up and down.

Did that mean she'd let go of the crop?

Her mouth moved to my other nipple, biting it hard, making me suck in a deep breath, but not too hard to make me cry out in pain.

Oh, Sarah was the master… er, mistress when it came to knowing my body. What I could take. What I wanted. How far to push me.

The bed shifted again, and Sarah straddled my pussy.

Both of her hands were kneading my breasts. "What do you want, Lizzie? This isn't all about me." Her voice was husky.

Words failed me.

"Nothing?" Her breath tickled my nose.

"Everything," I managed to say.

She laughed, deep and sexy. "Care to elaborate."

"You," I croaked.

Her hands gripped my wrists as if the handcuffs needed assistance in preventing me to break free.

I had zero desire to do so, though.

And I sensed Sarah understood. Hell, she'd known before I realized how much I loved her. Needed her. Craved her.

Her tongue traced a straight line from the hollow of my throat, between my breasts, down my stomach, dipping briefly into my belly button, reaching my pubic area, and stopping on my clit.

My back arched.

Sarah's mouth consumed my pussy. Sucking my lips into her mouth. Releasing. Her tongue gliding through them, dipping inside me. Flicking my clit. And repeating the process with slight variations. Sometimes she dove inside and then sucked, returning to my clit.

I lost track of time.

And hell, if time could stop permanently for Sarah's exploration, I'd die happy.

Her ministrations sent my body into a writhing tizzy—as much as the restraints would allow. And the restraints, while physically keeping my hands and legs out of play, made my body more present in the situation. Nerve endings in my skin I'd never noticed before were zapping to life. My nose feasted on the mixture of Sarah's jasmine perfume and our primal desire. Each lap of her tongue mimicked the sound of a wave slamming into the side of a boat.

Sarah drove two of her fingers inside.

My head dug into the pillow. "Yes!" I called out.

She pulled them out but quickly thrust them inside again, deeper.

Her mouth was on mine.

Again and again, she invaded me.

All the while her tongue mouth-fucked me.

It was hot as hell.

And I was close.

So close I could taste it.

Sarah probably could as well.

Once again, her mouth was on my clit, frantically lapping my pulsing sex, her fingers zeroing in on my G spot, pulling upward.

"Come now!" she commanded.

I couldn't have stopped the sexual release if I wanted to. But why would anyone want to refuse this? Wave upon wave flooded my sensory system. Even my toes trembled with excitement.

Sarah stilled her tongue on my bud, pressing it firmly to force out the last and most satisfying crest of orgasm.

My body stilled, with Sarah lying on top of me.

Neither of us spoke for several moments.

Her cheek was pressed against my chest. "Your heart is about to burst," she said.

"Let it. Can't think of a better way to go."

She quietly laughed. "I love you."

"Jesus, Sarah. Not only do I love you, but I give myself to you completely. This. You. Fuck." I couldn't find the words to complete wherever my mind wanted to go, because in that moment, my mind wasn't in control. My heart powered everything.

Her finger nudged the blindfold off, her eyes shimmering. "Shall I set you free?"

"Only so I can hold you in my arms."

It didn't take her long to undo the restraints, and I cradled her body.

"Your arms are shaking. Did I hurt you?"

"Not at all. My body is still feeling everything." I nuzzled my nose against her cheek.

She propped herself up on bent elbow, her other hand resting on the swell of my breasts. "Would you do it again?"

"Being tied up?"

"Yes or trying something else. Something new to us."

I cupped her cheek. "Anything you want."

"Anything?"

"I trust you. I know you won't propose something that will be too much for the stuffy historian inside me." I winked at her.

The smile on her face connected to my soul. "If your students knew what you did behind closed doors, they wouldn't think you stuffy at all. Although, given the Jorie situation"—she boosted her eyebrows playfully—"that might be for the best. Besides, I want this part of you—us all to ourselves. No one should ever know." She leaned down and kissed me sweetly.

I loved that she could torture me one moment and then switch gears and kiss me with such tenderness.

"How come you never actually whipped me?" I asked.

"Did you want me to?"

I shook my head.

"Exactly. Sometimes the fear of something is enough." She pressed her index finger against the tip of my nose. "Besides, I liked tickling you with the feather. The way you twitched. And how it turned you on."

"Can I tie you up and blindfold you?"

"Tonight?" Her voice was excited.

I laughed. "I would if Sexy Sarah hadn't worn me out."

She tipped her head back, laughing. "I haven't heard that nickname in a while."

"Do you like it?"

Sarah waggled her brows.

"What about Administrating Mistress?"

She crinkled her nose. "No! Sounds like menstruating. And is that a word?"

"Are you doubting my vocab skills?" I pulled her back into my arms and kissed the top of her head.

"Never."

"Good. You may be the mistress of the bedroom, but words —that's my wheelhouse."

Her body shook with giggles. "How did you ever get Sexy Sarah to fall madly in love with you?"

"Don't ask how. Just let us be. We're a good team."

CHAPTER FIFTEEN

On Monday, I sat in my office on campus, staring at the email I'd received in the middle of the night but was just now reading.

The subject line: Do you have time to talk?

The sender: Meg.

There was a time, after first meeting her, when the mere thought of Meg made my heart flutter.

The flutter had turned into heart-palpitating dread when dealing first with Drunk Meg, ultimately leading to Blackmailing Meg.

Now, in the confines of my office, I tried putting my finger on the emotion coursing through my body. Fear? Guilt? Shame? Morbid curiosity? A mixture of all four?

My brain tried to work out the time of her email. Did the 1:32 a.m. timestamp mean she'd fallen off the wagon? Did not drinking enflame insomnia? Possibly, her single status allowed her to keep odd hours.

The old Lizzie, the one Sarah had ditched after the Maddie fiasco, would have reacted without consulting anyone. And by that, I meant pretend I'd never received the email. Surely, it didn't have a read receipt.

"And the new Lizzie remains inactive," I said aloud. Clearly, the old and new Lizzie were unnervingly alike.

Taking Maddie's advice, I picked up my desk phone and punched in the numbers.

Courtney's assistant answered the phone. Kicking myself for not prepping for this, and I should have considering Courtney was a bigwig in her family's business, I mumbled, "Sorry, wrong number."

Old Lizzie was coming back to life—not dealing with anything.

My phone rang soon afterward. "Hello?"

"Lizzie?"

"Yes," I said with hesitation.

"It's Courtney."

"How'd you do that?" I asked, glancing around my room as if looking for a recording device.

"Do what?"

"Call me?"

"I'm using newfangled technology. Some call it a cellular device. I prefer mobile." Her tone was lighthearted and not nearly as sarcastic as Maddie's.

I could feel a blush, although Courtney couldn't see me. Or could she? Obviously, Meg's talk about spies lurking everywhere and my guilt for not sharing more with Sarah was getting to me. "I just hung up on your assistant."

She laughed. "Why?"

"I… It's not important."

She laughed some more. "Maddie has you pegged. She said I'd have to hunt you down to talk."

"About?"

"Your brother and Tie."

"Oh," I said in an attempt to stall for time. Did she really need to talk, or was she using the Peter and Tie card to get me in the same room? Possibly, Maddie planted the seed in Courtney's head that I needed to know the details of Peter's marriage, which I'd rather stay blissfully unaware of. My life was overly complicated at the moment, and the games people played were time-consuming.

"Lizzie, you there?"

"Yeah, I'm sorry. A student popped their head in," I said in a lame attempt to explain the awkward silence.

"Why'd you call me?" she asked.

"Maddie mentioned you wanted to talk," I fibbed.

"The six degrees of Maddie. You free for an early dinner on Thursday in Fort Collins? I have to drive up Wednesday night from Denver for two days of meetings. I'm hoping the meeting on Thursday won't take all day."

"That sounds... fun."

"Welcome to my world. At least it gives me a chance to catch up with Maddie."

I wondered if she meant sexually, since the two had had a short fling months ago. I hadn't quite pinned down whether or not Maddie and Gabe were exclusive. Especially considering Maddie had contacted Jorie.

Courtney's voice almost startled me. "Hey, I'm getting a call and have to jump. I'll text you when and where."

"Sure," I said to dead air.

If that was the technique she used with clients, it was pretty effective, although I wondered what lengths she went to when someone declined via text. Given that Maddie was involved, I didn't want to have both conniving women plotting behind the scenes.

There was a knock on the door. "Come in," I said.

Jorie stuck her head inside. "Hey." She looked around as if unsure. "Do your office hours only apply to current students, not former?"

Speak of the devil…

"Huh, I've never given it much thought." I rubbed the top of my head. "But considering there isn't a mad rush to see me,"—I waved her in—"take a seat. What's up?"

"I'm…" She took a seat with her crimson backpack in her lap. Fiddling with one of the front zippers, she said, "I'm having a problem with one of my TAs that oversees my mandatory study session."

"What kind?"

Her cheeks tinged. "He keeps asking me out."

"Oh." I sat up straighter in my chair, taking a red grading pen in my hand.

"I've told him more than once I'm not interested. Not just him, but with the entire male species, but I think it's falling on deaf ears."

Briefly, I considered closing the door, but it was departmental policy to keep the door open when with a student. Did that apply if said student wasn't *my* student? I opted to use caution, leaving the door open.

"Have you told anyone?"

She shook her head. "I think he's of the opinion since I'm the oldest student, and possibly older than he is, the rules don't apply."

"Sexual harassment doesn't have an age requirement." I shifted in my uncomfortable office chair and leaned my forearms on the laminated desk, still clutching the pen in my right hand.

"Right," she said, brightening, making me feel uneasy.

"Do you know if any others in the class are being pestered by him?"

"Just the usual awkward comments and jokes to get a laugh, mostly from the guys in the study sessions. The girls grin and bear it."

I nodded. "Do you get along with the professor?"

She hefted her shoulders. "There are three hundred in the class with five TAs. The TA in question is also a student in one of my other classes, making it even more confusing. Kinda like we're only classmates, but as my TA, he grades my tests and quizzes. I would drop the class, but the date to do so has passed. I could take a W."

All of this info put me somewhat at ease. She'd clearly given some thought to her options. "That is a possibility, but you don't receive a refund and the 'W' will always appear on your transcript, without affecting your GPA, though." I mimed weighing the benefits with two hands. "One, talk to your professor. Two, take a W."

"What's behind door three?" she joked.

"Sarah always says I see things in black and white."

Jorie offered a tiny smile. "What would you do?"

"Ah." I leaned back and scratched my head with the pen. I had to reframe the question in my mind to "What advice would Sarah give?" It didn't take long to come up with, "I think you should make an appointment with the professor. Talk to him—"

"Her," she interjected.

"Her. It's possible the TA doesn't really understand what he's doing is wrong, or it's possible he does. Both scenarios should be addressed."

"What if she doesn't believe me?" Jorie stared at the stack of exam books on my desk.

"Trust me; she'll take action." I rested on my forearms again. "But, if she doesn't, you can always escalate it to the department head or..." I flipped open the university's phone directory, thumbing my way to the needed page. Jotting down the number on a slip of paper, I said, "Here's the number for the Student Resolution office. They can probably offer more insight into your... dilemma."

She took the paper from my hand. "Thanks, Lizzie."

"Anytime. I admire your honesty." Was it wrong of me to

ponder Jorie's motives for seeking me out, especially considering Maddie's observation that the young woman was coming
to terms with her sexuality and I was a role model of sorts? At
least I had Maddie's reassurance that she didn't have the hots
for me. It was weird, though. Being someone Jorie looked up to
all the while I feared people learning about my lack of a back-
bone when it came to Meg.

Jorie rose. "I have class." She held up the paper. "But, I'll
make an appointment with my professor and, if need be, call
this number."

"Yes, don't let it fester hoping it'll go away."

She left without saying another word, letting my own advice
crowd my mind.

* * *

"WHAT DOES she want to talk about?" Sarah asked, her arms
crossed.

I flicked my palms up. "I haven't spoken to Meg yet. I
wanted to talk to you first."

"You said *yet*, meaning you plan to?"

"Should I?"

"Do you want to?"

I readjusted on the library couch to face Sarah, on the other
side, full-on. "I feel like you're trying to trap me into saying
something when I'm asking you what I should do."

Sarah's face acknowledged the accusation by speckling some
with embarrassment. "I'm sorry. This is different—you coming
to me for advice about your ex, whom I hate. Have I mentioned
that in the last few minutes?"

I sucked in a deep breath and rubbed my eyes with my
fingers. "Maybe I should wait until Thursday."

"Did Meg give you a deadline or something?" She made a
checkmark in the air. "Another tick in the *do not like* column."

My error seeped into my brain. "Uh, no."

Sarah wasn't so easily put off and waved for me to come out with it.

I spoke to my folded hands in my lap. "Maddie suggested I speak with Courtney."

Much to my surprise, Sarah nodded. "A friend who isn't tainted with any prior knowledge of Meg. Not a bad suggestion."

"What about the Kit-Tie-Peter connection?"

"Courtney didn't get to where she is in the business world by blabbing. I think you can trust her."

"Over you?" I blinked as if trying to determine if I was having a dream. Nightmare was more like it.

"In this situation, yes. I'm more than biased." Sarah swept a water glass from the end table to her lips.

I rubbed my face. "All these years, you've wanted me to open up more. And now when I'm seeking your advice, you're sending me to Courtney, who is a shameless flirt with you, I might add. And you flirt with her."

"Only because I'm safe to flirt with and vice versa."

"What does that mean?" I wrinkled my forehead.

"She knows I would never act on it. It's one of her ways of dealing with stress."

"She's told you this?"

Sarah rolled her eyes. "She didn't have to. It's like Maddie teasing you mercilessly. She doesn't mean it."

"I'm not following." I shook my head in an attempt to rationalize the words. "Are you saying Maddie's so stressed out she has to tease me or she'll what—explode?"

"Okay." Sarah set her glass down on the table, giving me her complete attention. "You know how you bury yourself in work when you don't want to deal with things?" She plowed on without waiting for a sign of agreement. "Everyone has their coping mechanisms. Courtney flirts with women who'll never take her up on it. Maddie teases you. Both are harmless."

"You might not say that if Maddie was constantly teasing you. Self-esteem, as my therapist liked to point out, are delicate for some. And how come Courtney never flirts with me?" I plucked at a loose string on the velvet midnight blue throw pillow.

"You love Maddie's teasing. You egg her on." Sarah gave me a look that said *Don't try to dispute it.*

I feigned being annoyed but was unsure if Sarah's assumption was true. Deep down, did I enjoy Maddie's relentless ribbing?

"It's one of Maddie's ways of showing you she cares without upsetting your boundaries. Face it; you aren't the easiest person to talk to with all of your walls. Most of the time when uncomfortable situations arise, I can almost see you tucking away into your head, debating weird shit that has no bearing on the matter at hand." She mimicked with one hand chatting mindlessly, followed by the other hand.

I groaned, resting my cheek on the back of the couch. "Why do I share anything with you when you toss it back in my face?"

"Because you need to. A person can only stay locked inside their own head for so long before losing it." With one hand, she motioned a bomb detonating.

"Whatever. You didn't address why Courtney never flirts with me."

"Because you might punch Court in the face if she did."

"I would not."

She quirked an eyebrow.

"Okay. What about Kit? Is he harmless?"

Sarah shook her head. "I wouldn't trust him with chewed up gum on the sidewalk."

I closed my eyes, trying to work out her meaning. Were my secrets unimportant like discarded gum?

"Never say anything to Kit that you want to keep private. Kit will tell you he'll never share a secret, but he'll blab to gain friends. It's a compulsion he probably isn't aware of. There's a reason he's never held a job—no one trusts him. Not even his family."

"But he's engaged to Courtney to keep his gay secret, or so he says."

Sarah laughed out loud. "Please, it's not a secret. People may choose not to see it, but the guy's flaming. He likes to think he's keeping it secret. It's fun for him. I keep telling you everything is a game to him."

Not wanting to spend too much time on the Kit issue, I went back to the other. "Courtney knows she's a shameless but harmless flirt?"

"Exactly."

"And this makes sense to you?" With my index fingers, I traced a circle in the air.

Another head nod. "It doesn't to you?"

I shook my head. "I don't see how all the dots connect, but I'm going to trust you and Maddie on this. Much cheaper than therapy."

"There's always that option."

"Do I need to go back to therapy?" Even to me, my voice sounded worried.

Sarah remained mute.

I readjusted on the couch to allow me to prop my legs up on the coffee table. Slouching down, I said, "I'm glad Meg is getting a hold of her life, but did she have to come back into mine right when everything was going so well?"

"Don't let her get control. Not again."

I let my feet crash to the floor. "Yes, exactly. Since Courtney is like the wizard behind the curtain, maybe we should send

Meg to Courtney. Cut me, the middleman, out and eliminate my contact with Meg." I smiled with satisfaction.

"Not sure it works that way. Meg seems insistent to wiggle her way back in."

"If I controlled the situation, it would work out perfectly." I mimed being a puppeteer. "Do you think Courtney would sleep with her? That would be a huge plus and could potentially distract Meg."

Sarah shot me an amused grin. "Sometimes, I do enjoy watching you extricate your way out of things."

"You should have seen me earlier today with Jorie."

This got her attention and not in a good way, although when did a spouse enjoy hearing about another woman, even when the other wasn't a threat? Human nature always seems to win to a certain extent. "Relax, she wasn't being a Courtney, and by that, I mean a flirt."

Sarah had the decency to look somewhat guilty.

"She's having an issue with a TA asking her out."

"Male or female?"

"Male."

"And she came to you?" Sarah didn't mask her surprise.

"Yeah." My voice squeaked with astonishment. "During my office hours."

"What did you say?" Sarah attempted to control a worried look. It wasn't a secret to those who knew us that I was the one half of the couple people avoided when they needed advice or a shoulder to cry on. Truthfully, I preferred it that way.

I laid out the conversation to the best of my recollection.

Sarah mulled over the info. "That may have been her way of coming out to you. Testing the waters to see how others would react."

"The thought had crossed my mind, although, I'm a lesbian, so it isn't much of a test." I shrugged because it wasn't out of the question either, and it worried me. Would all students who were dealing with their sexual identity seek me out to help them with the process? I wasn't Dr. Ruth. Or Ellen. "What I can't decide is if the TA part was pure fabrication?"

Sarah, looking out the bay window, jostled her head from side to side, again absorbing the situation. "Maddie's friends with Jorie. I'll call her tomorrow to follow up." Her tone implied nothing I said would deter her. I let her think she won, but with everything that was going on, Jorie was at the bottom of the totem pole. "This, I can offer advice on. Not the Meg thing." She flicked her fingers as if the mere mention of the name cursed our home. Was there a Yankee candle that purified negative auras?

"Ah," I said. "You need to feel helpful. That's your thing, in case you're wondering. Courtney flirts. Maddie teases. Kit blabs. You act like Mother Teresa. And I drown myself with research. Who has the most productive coping mechanism?"

Sarah blew out a rush of air. "Maybe you can mention your competitive streak to Courtney. See if she has advice on that."

"Wait. Are you going to defer to Courtney now on all things Lizzie?" I tweaked her side.

"Depends on how well she handles the problem with your ex. Dealing with you can be exhausting." She made her body go limp.

I yanked her legs, pulling her toward me. "I can say the same about you. Infuriating, most of the time." Given the direction we were heading, I opted not to bring up the Troy factor.

"Then why are you trying to get closer to me?" Sarah wore a coquettish expression—the one that drove me mad with desire, which she knew.

She didn't resist when I got on my knees on the couch cushions to get a better hold of her.

"Good call with replacing our couches with extra-long

ones." I widened my eyes. "To answer your question, you happen to have one redeeming quality."

"What's that?" she asked.

"You're a great lay." She was now on her back on the couch, and I hovered over her. "With such soft lips."

We kissed.

"Are you saying I'm only good for bedroom activities?" Her breath hitched.

"Don't limit yourself to the bedroom. Own this couch." I spread my arms out to demonstrate we had plenty of space for what I had in mind.

"You aren't making much sense."

"Oh, I think I am." I cupped her cheek. "Your eyes say so."

"Get on your knees." She shoved me to the ground, repositioned on the couch, and then undid the top of her jeans.

I didn't waste any time and stripped Sarah from the waist down.

"Prove your worth to me," she commanded, tossing her head against the couch and spreading her legs.

"I love it when you're bossy."

"I love it when you show me." She motioned for me to get busy.

I did.

* * *

AFTER, with Sarah's fingers still intertwined in my hair, holding my head between her legs, she said, "Quick and beautiful."

"Can I get up yet?" I mumbled into her pussy.

She let go of my head. "Sorry."

I stood, kicking my legs out and then stretching my back to the right and left. "I'm getting old."

Sarah's expression had a glazed look. "You don't look it."

With my hands on my hips, I leaned back to work out a kink in my lower back. "Is it weird we went from talking about Meg to Jorie's issue to me eating your poontang?"

She laughed, her shoulders shaking. "I saw an opening."

"I'm seeing one now." I offered a hand to help her off the couch. "Put me to bed. I'm exhausted."

Sarah didn't bother putting her jeans back on, leading me upstairs half-naked. "Something tells me you actually want to go to sleep." She scouted over her shoulder, catching me mid-yawn. "Poor baby."

We peeked into the twinks' room to ensure all was well, although I had both baby monitors in my hands.

"They're so cute when asleep." She wore a dreamy expression, her eyes conveying a look I didn't want to address.

"I don't want to talk about maybe adding another nursery. Not tonight."

Sarah jerked her head to our bedroom. "Fine, but we'll have to discuss it soon."

Sitting on the bench at the end of the bed, I asked, "What's the rush?"

"We aren't getting any younger. You said as much not five minutes ago."

"I can't keep up with you tonight." I tugged my sweater and shirt over my head.

Sarah tossed me a T-shirt from the pajama drawer. "Just one more, Lizzie."

"Last time when we got pregnant, we got twins." I placed two fingers in the air.

"And do you regret either one?" She knew she had me there.

"Don't even go that route. It worries me. Not having multiple births, but Freddie's birth wasn't seamless. I don't know if I can go through that. Not again." I closed my eyes on the memory of them slicing Sarah's belly and then the terrifying moments when Fred wasn't able to breathe on his own. "What if something happens to you? Or the baby? Or both?"

Sarah peeled down the comforter, climbing under and patting the bed for me to join her. With her arms around me, she said, "Nothing will happen."

"You can't promise that. Modern medicine only goes so far. The rate of maternal deaths is rising in the US." I let out a puff of air. "America has the worst rate in the modern world."

"What about adoption? You've mentioned it before."

I nuzzled my face into the pillow, unwilling to have this discussion when so exhausted.

"Go to sleep. We can talk later," Sarah relented.

CHAPTER SIXTEEN

Courtney opened the door to her hotel room. "Lizzie, come on in." She air-kissed my right cheek. "I just got off the phone with Sarah."

"It's weird having my wife's blessing to meet you in a hotel room"—I looked around and corrected my word choice—"suite. Nice view." We were only on the fifth floor, the top of this hotel, but the dark clouds added drama to the setting sun.

"This is my favorite time of day." She stood at the bar, a hand on a bottle of wine in a bucket of ice. "Would you like a drink?"

"Water's fine. I'm driving."

"I can arrange a ride for you." She pulled her iPhone out of the pocket of her loose-fitting black slacks.

I smiled. "It's my turn to get up with the twinks tomorrow."

She nodded, replacing the phone in her pocket. "And how are my favorite niece and nephew?"

For some reason, it didn't bother me that she referred to the twinks as family. The older I got, the more I realized what Clinton meant when she said it takes a village. "Full of beans."

"So, they're taking after me, then?" She pitched her eyebrows in a way that made my heart stop.

"Are you trying to make my hair go completely white before I turn forty?"

Courtney handed me an iced water with a lemon wedge. She motioned for me to take a seat in one of the wingback chairs, while she settled on the floral loveseat, her legs under her, a glass of chilled white wine in her left hand. Instead of prompting me to unburden myself, she sipped her drink.

I gulped my water.

Courtney seemed content admiring the final splash of the sunset.

"Why is this your favorite time of day?" I asked.

"Any day I survive is a good day." She took another sip of wine.

"You make your life sound like a battle."

"Yours isn't?"

I crossed my legs, turning my body away from her slightly. "How's Kit?"

"We're going to do this the hard way, I see." She widened her eyes as if saying she had me in her sights. "Kit is Kit."

I folded my arms over my chest. "You two still engaged?"

She nodded. "Before you ask, my job is fine. Business is booming. That pretty much covers all the bases."

I laughed. "Did Maddie warn you? Or Sarah?"

"They didn't have to. You're so tightly wound most times I almost expect your head to shoot off into space." She waved her hand to the way I sat.

I curbed my desire to uncross my legs and arms to prove her wrong. "You mentioned Peter and Tie on the phone."

"I did."

Did Maddie really find Courtney helpful? At the moment, the only thing I felt was a desire to chuck my water in her face. "And?"

"I'm worried."

"About?" Why was she being cagey?

"Tie's no fool. And Peter isn't a saint." She pinned me with a knowing expression, perhaps wondering if I'd rise to Peter's defense. When I didn't, she pressed on. "Now, there's poor Demi in the mix. She deserves better."

I blinked several times. "Wow, you aren't telling me anything I don't already know."

Courtney fixed her gaze on me, an approving smile tugging up the corners of her mouth. "Have a chat with Peter. Give him the heads-up that she's about to declare all-out war."

"What does that involve?"

"With Tie, anything." She paused, quite possibly for dramatic effect. "I wish I could go into details, but I don't know any. I can only say Tie isn't happy with Peter's choices. And, I don't think she even knows about the tryst he had with Maddie in your home. For your sake, I hope she never learns."

"Huh." I glanced out the window, taking in the dark sky. "Sarah said you weren't the type to blurt out secrets."

"That wasn't a secret. Maddie and Peter slept together in your home. Besides, she told me you and Sarah confronted her about it." She resembled a judge who'd just overturned a guilty plea.

"But, you don't plan on telling Tie, who used to be one of your besties."

"Besties? Somehow I think you're mocking me by using a word that doesn't suit you."

It annoyed me that she knew that about me.

"No, I don't plan on telling Tie. Just like I don't plan on telling anyone what's troubling you." She waved her hand for me to get to it.

"Is this your side business? Counseling the inept?"

"You aren't inept." She took a tiny sip of wine.

"Flattery will get you nowhere."

"Not talking won't help you, Bottle Rocket." She tapped her fingernails against her glass.

Was she counting down the seconds for my head to shoot off into the sky?

"What did Maddie tell you?" I asked.

"Not a thing."

I gave her my *level with me* glare.

She didn't take the bait. "You don't intimidate me."

"Does anything?"

"I hate snakes."

"Literally or figuratively?"

She furrowed her brow. "Are you going to yank my chain all night? If so, do you mind if I order Chinese? I'm famished."

"Sounds good to me. I can't remember if I ate lunch."

"Me neither." Courtney offered a genuine smile. "I'm hankering for egg drop soup, sesame chicken, egg rolls, and fried wontons."

"Add crab cheese wontons and orange beef, and I'll spill my guts out to you."

She tapped the screen on her phone. "I would have thought crab too much for you."

"It's a new thing I've added to my limited repertoire. They aren't too crabby."

"Unlike you." Her voice was sultry.

My eyes boggled, I assumed since I felt a rush of air under the lids, and I blurted, "I thought you only flirted with Sarah and Maddie."

"That was until I knew you had a thing for crab cheese wontons. Oh, yes. Delivery." Courtney put a finger up to me as if I was going to stop her from ordering. She rattled off the selections, at the last moment adding chicken with cashews. Ending the call, she spoke to me. "You have another twenty minutes to stall."

"Does that mean I don't get dinner until I spill?"

"You see; you're not inept at all." She raised one eyebrow.

"And you're nothing like my therapist."

Her eyes widened, causing her forehead to crease. "God, I hope not."

"What are you saying about my therapist?"

"It's cute how you get worked up about little things."

"Are you saying the return of my alcoholic ex, who also blackmailed me, became a prostitute, and nearly ruined my relationship with Sarah in the beginning stages, is a little thing?"

Courtney steepled her fingers, resting them against her chin. "Nope, that doesn't sound like a little thing at all. Tell me about her."

"You tricked me."

"That's a possibility. Or it could have been an accident. Does it matter, though? It opened the door." She mimicked this.

I stabbed the air with my finger, about to list the reasons why it mattered.

Courtney's headshake and hand motion for me not to start quieted me. "Your ex. I only want to hear about her."

* * *

WE SAT at the round table by the window. Most of the Chinese food containers were now empty.

"Meg sounds like a piece of work. And to waltz back into your life, acting as if you two could pick up like nothing happened—even Kit, who doesn't have many scruples, would know better. Or he would at least intimate he should know better." Courtney deftly selected a lone slice of chicken with her chopsticks. After chewing, she asked, "How does that make you feel? Her acting like the way she treated you wasn't that awful?"

"Annoyed. Frustrated. And…"

"Yes?" Her eyes were hopeful.

"It makes me question if she really had treated me badly or if I'm blowing things out of proportion. She seems to think everything is water under the bridge and I should get over it. At least, that's how she makes me feel."

"Our minds do love to torture us. Let's run down the big-ticket items. She showed up drunk at a conference. She was verbally abusive. In a drunken rage, she hit you. She black-mailed you for months, threatening to spread malicious rumors to ruin your career." Courtney leaned on her forearms. "Just one of those is bad news. Add them all up and it paints the picture of a monster."

And I let that monster control me—the true source of my shame.

"You want it?" After getting the go-ahead gesture, I munched into the last crab cheese wonton.

"The question is can you forgive her?"

I forced the bite down and covered my mouth. "Meg?"

She bonked my head with her hand. "Who else?"

I studied my image in the gilded mirror behind Courtney's head. "I really don't know. Part of me just wants to ignore her completely. Leave her in the past."

"How many times have you told your students, 'Those who don't learn from their mistakes are doomed to repeat them'?"

"Never," I said with forced conviction.

"You're either a terrible historian or a liar."

"Or both." I shrugged.

She laughed.

"Do you think I should forgive Meg?" Something I didn't think I was capable of. Not completely. Maybe I could accept an apology—a heartfelt one, but that was all.

Courtney set her chopsticks down. Plucking a fortune cookie from the bag, she said, "Let's leave it to fate."

I groaned. "This is why Maddie instructed me to come to you? For you to decide my fate via a fortune cookie? Why not just buy a dartboard? Wad up all the fortunes, and then blind-fold me before tossing the dart?"

"That sounds like the perfect solution, but I don't have a dartboard and the thought of making a Target run makes me want to puke." She placed the cookie on the table and proceeded to smash it with her palm. "Okay, whatever this slip says, you have to abide by it." She fished the paper out of the crumbs and read in a melodramatic voice, *"Today it's up to you to create the peacefulness you long for."*

"You made that up!" I snatched the slip from her. After reading the same words, I crumpled it up and tossed it over my shoulder. "This is bogus."

"Fortune cookies don't lie."

I grabbed another one. "Let's see what this says about your life." I cracked it in half. *"Your shoes will make you happy today."*

We both glanced down at her bare feet, her toenails a lurid red.

"See!" I said in a victorious voice.

Courtney pointed to her discarded heels by the loveseat. "A woman complimented my Jimmy Choos right before giving me her number."

"Oh, please. I'm not buying that."

Courtney fiddled with her phone before tapping the screen. The name associated with the number was Jimmy Choo fan. Of course, this didn't mean it'd happened earlier today.

I grunted, leaning back in my chair and flailing my arms to the side. "I give up."

"Does that mean you'll meet with Meg? Get everything out in the open?"

"I don't know what it means. I had peace before Meg reappeared."

"Maybe you should tell her that. Tell her you wish her the

best, but you have too much to lose letting her back in. End it there."

Courtney was right, as much as I hated to admit that.

"Do you feel better?" She put one foot on the chair cushion and hugged her knee.

"I feel stuffed." I patted my belly.

She looked me up and down. "I think you feel better. Fortune cookie magic has that effect on even those who won't admit they believe."

"You're a charlatan. A total fraud."

She let out a bark of laughter. "I'm in advertising. It's my job to get people to believe in anything. To make them want things they don't need. Of course, I'm a fraud. A very successful one, I might add."

"Then why'd you let me go on and on about Meg?" I circled a useless hand in the air.

"You wanted to," she said in a tone that made it seem like that was plain as day.

"I'm afraid to talk to her."

"Why?"

"She has—had this power over me. Made me feel pathetic. Like my mom used to make me feel. I don't like myself when I'm around her. I don't want to go back to feeling that way."

"Then don't."

I sighed in exasperation. "Like it's that easy."

"It is." She set her foot back down on the floor. Taking both of my hands in hers, she said, "You are not the same person you were back then. You're happily married to a gorgeous woman." She exaggerated the word *gorgeous*. "You have two amazing kids. Great friends. And fortune cookie power."

I dropped her hands. "You had me until—"

She motioned *stop right there*. "In all seriousness, don't let Meg or the old feelings creep back in. Even before Meg walked back into your life, her presence or the damage she inflicted probably never left you. But you're stronger. And you have Sarah and the twins to fight for. All you have to do is believe in yourself. You're right; that slip of paper doesn't hold the power." She took my hand and placed it on my chest, with both of hers on top. "You do. Feel it. Embrace it. Believe it." She leaned in, resting her forehead to mine. "You can do it, Lizzie."

I bobbed my head, pulling away. "I can do it."

"And to remind you." She got to her feet and retrieved the fortune from the floor. Uncrumpling it, she slipped it into my hand. "Take this with you."

At the door, she placed a hand on my shoulders, making a show of kissing each of my cheeks. Then she shoved me into the harsh lighting in the hallway, closing the door with emphasis.

"Was that necessary?" I muttered as I made my way to the elevator.

* * *

THE HOUSE WAS EERILY quiet when I returned at a quarter to ten.

Sarah was sitting up in bed with all the pillows behind her, Maddie's tattered copy of *The Girl on the Train* resting against her face as she sawed logs.

I tiptoed to her side of the bed and carefully eased the paperback off her face. She stirred but didn't wake. I kissed her forehead.

Not ready to go to sleep, I headed for the library to get some work done, but soon enough, my fingers pounded away on the laptop, making progress on my secret project, not university work.

Around midnight, I stretched my arms overhead. Although my mind was racing, I knew I'd better get some sleep. Not only was it my turn to get the twinkies up and going, I had two lectures to give. Back in grad school, I could pull an all-nighter and not pay for it the following day. The closer I inched to forty, the less energy I had. In my younger years, I'd thought losing the ability to steamroll through exhaustion was a myth. Sadly, it was becoming a reality.

CHAPTER SEVENTEEN

a sliver of daylight fell on my face, rousing me from a restful and deep sleep.

Sitting up, I assessed the situation.

I was alone in bed.

The twinks weren't on the video monitors, meaning they weren't in their cribs.

The alarm I'd set had been shut off.

"Shit."

I rushed downstairs and found Sarah feeding Ollie and Fred.

"I'm so sorry." I motioned for her to move so I could take over.

Sarah laughed. "Mommy crashed the party right when we're finishing. Typical." She playfully tsked.

"My alarm—"

She raised the oatmeal spoon to cut me off, some splattering onto Ollie's tray. "I turned it off. You looked like you needed sleep. Of course, I'll have to punish you later." Her suggestive smile magically abolished all traces of guilt.

"Looking forward to it." I wiped Freddie's face and fingers. "How's my little man?" I lifted him out of the high chair into my arms, cuddling him close. Even though he was a year old, it still amazed me that Sarah and I had created two humans whom I loved more every single day.

His smile made me regret missing the early shift with him.

"Good morning!" Rose shouted from the entryway.

"In the kitchen," I responded.

Sarah's eyes were glued to Ollie, who was decimating a slice of banana with her fingers.

"Good morning," Rose repeated.

"Would you like a cup of coffee?" I said after Sarah didn't speak, although her body wasn't completely rigid, which I took as a thawing of her feelings toward Rose and Troy.

"I would love one," she spoke sweetly, and I wondered if she felt like Stalin at the Yalta Conference, wanting to convince FDR to give the Soviets a sphere of political influence in Eastern and Central Europe.

I handed Fred off to Rose. "Sarah?"

"Please."

Rose leaned down and kissed Ollie's head. After sitting on the seat across from Sarah, she locked her eyes onto mine. "What's new here?"

Not used to making small talk with the woman who loved to torture me by miming she wanted to mow me down with her car, I stared for a handful of heartbeats before stating, "All's well on the Western Front. You?"

"No complaints." The way she said it suggested the opposite.

"How's Troy?" I scooped coffee grinds into the filter.

"Looking forward to Thanksgiving break."

I nodded. "I haven't met a teacher yet who didn't have a countdown. Not that we tell our students that, of course."

Rose's laughter was genuine. She turned her attention to Fred, chatting with the observant child who still didn't speak much. Not that Rose minded.

I held both cups of coffee in the air. "Stay seated."

Rose nodded, her expression thankful.

Don't thank me yet. I imagined brokering the Treaty of Versailles would be an easier feat. Of course, that had led to World War II, so probably not the best example, unless my goal was to separate Sarah from Rose in a spectacular way involving the death of millions.

I placed the mugs down, dashed back for my tea, and quickly took my seat.

Sarah fussed with Ollie, who seesawed in her lap.

Fred laid his head against his grandmother's shoulder.

I slurped my tea.

"Anything happen last night?" I posed to Sarah.

She shook her head.

"Did you have History Club?" Rose asked, her face displaying she was grabbing at straws to keep silence from dampening the mood even more.

My brain scrambled for a solution.

"Nah. I had dinner with Courtney." I shrugged as if saying, "Give me something I can use."

Rose's eyes widened. "Really?"

"She has some concerns about Peter and Tie and wanted to hash them out."

"And?"

"Not sure we solved anything. Families, you know, can be difficult waters to navigate at times."

Sarah kicked me under the table, but Rose perked up in her seat as if hoping I'd go further. How, though?

Honesty, perhaps. "Like you two acting like strangers."

The look Sarah shot me would have zapped my courage if I hadn't felt completely in the right.

"This has been going on for weeks, and what has it gotten you?" I asked Sarah. "It's tearing you up inside." I turned my focus to Rose. "While I like it when you're nice to me, the reason behind your kindness is upsetting the balance between you two. Please, work it out. Say sorry. And move forward together. If you can't do it for yourselves, think about the twins."

Sarah swept a few strands of hair out of Ollie's eyes and said, "You're using our twins. That's low."

I extended a finger in the air. "But true. Children need love." I'd gone this far, so I decided to finish it. "Take me for an example. I craved love and attention from those around me but didn't get it. Both of you know how that's played out. My mother. Meg. Not being the greatest partner." I put my hands together. "Talk this out. I'm literally begging you two." I let my hands fall. "I didn't have the reckoning I needed with my mother before her death. I danced around it some but didn't put it to bed. I don't want to make that mistake with others in my life. I don't want you two to have regrets."

"Is that what you're going to do with Meg? Talk things out?" Sarah shot back at me with a look that suggested she would go there to shut me up.

I swatted it away and simply nodded.

"Meg? *The* Meg?" Rose said, concern giving force to her meaning.

"She's back in town and wants Lizzie to forgive her and be friends, apparently," Sarah told her mom.

"Oh, dear. That's a lot for her to ask of you," Rose said to Sarah, making me realize Rose knew a lot more about Meg than I thought.

Sarah continued. "Tell me about it. The woman did everything in her power to control Lizzie, and then when Lizzie broke free, she tried to destroy her. Just like Lizzie's mother."

The two of them fell into conversation, dissecting the Meg/Mom connection as if I weren't in the room.

Halle-fucking-lujah!

I bolted my tea. "My work here is done. Next on my to-do

list: prep Wednesday's evening lecture and shape the young minds of America's future." I tapped my fingers together, mad-scientist like.

I kissed Sarah's cheek and patted each twin on the head on my way out of the kitchen to shower and dress before heading to campus. Not that Sarah noticed. Once she and her mother got going on one of their favorite threads, hours could slip by in a flurry.

* * *

AROUND FIVE, I returned home, exhausted from being up late the previous night.

Voices coming from the dining room sucked me in.

Sarah, Rose, Troy, and Maddie stood around the table like WWII generals plotting excitedly about the next offensive. Papers with drawings were scattered on the table. I wasn't an expert by any means, but from all the times I'd watched *Elf* with Sarah, not to mention reading to the twinks, I'd venture to say the sheets were sketches from a children's book.

Ollie and Freddie sat on the floor, playing with toys that flashed lights and emitted robotic voices.

Talk about sensory overload.

"Hello!" I shouted, giving an embarrassed wave.

Sarah smiled.

The rest continued their hand gestures, talking over each other.

"I'm going to the kitchen. Can I get anyone anything?"

No one acknowledged my offer.

Okeydokey.

Not willing to stay to figure out what in the hell was going on, I retreated to the kitchen.

Sarah approached all smiles. "Thank you." She wrapped me in a hug.

"For what?"

With her arms still around me, she pulled her face back. "For tossing yourself under the bus to bring harmony back into my relationship with Mom."

I jerked my chin to the dining area. "That qualifies as harmony?"

She laughed. "A start at least. We've decided to collaborate on a children's book."

"Ah, I see," I said, not following, but Sarah radiated happiness and it was a relief to see her getting along with her mother again.

"Of course, collaborating by committee hasn't been entirely fruitful yet. Early days." Her laughter tickled my ears. "But, it's better to quibble over storylines and artwork, not"—she leaned in and whispered in my ear—"Troy."

"You're channeling your conflict into the stories? Are they horror stories for kids?"

Sarah shoved my shoulder. "Seriously, Lizzie, thank you. You've been patient with me, all the while making comments and asking questions that helped me see the way. I can't tell Mom not to date Troy, especially if he makes her happy. Given all the things going on in the world, how can I deny the woman who gave me everything for so many years my blessing?"

"Did you say sorry?" I pressed my forehead to hers.

"Yes." Her eyes were big with sincerity.

"Do you still think he's after her money?" I whispered.

She pushed her head into mine as if needing more support. "No. Not unless this entire time he's been angling to propose this publishing venture." She pulled away to reveal a teasing smile, but she still added, "He didn't get involved until after school ended."

I eased onto a barstool and encircled her waist with my arms. "Is everything okay between you two, then?"

"Well on the way."

Laughter from the dining room grabbed my attention. "How did this idea spring up?"

"Earlier, after you left, Mom mentioned Troy had always wanted to write children's stories, and I started talking about ideas I had. Maddie popped by on her lunch break. And voilà!"

Shaking my head, I said, "Whatever makes you happy."

"Does that mean you'll invest?"

"Raising capital already. This must be serious." I hefted my brows, perhaps a little more mockingly than was necessary.

She clobbered my side with her fingers. "It is!"

I pulled her in for a kiss, only receiving a quick peck.

"Dinner will be here in twenty." Sarah stepped back. "I'll wrap up in there. Can you get dinner ready for the twinkies?"

I saluted.

She started to leave but stopped. "How was your day?"

"No business ventures, so not as exciting as yours."

Sarah smiled. "You want to be one of the forces behind T.M. Cavanaugh?"

"What?" I rubbed my chin.

"It's a penname using the initials of Troy and Maddie and Cavanaugh for mom and me." With that, she wheeled about and headed back into the children's book writing battle.

"I honestly don't know what's going to happen next in this family," I said to Hank sitting in the kitchen window watching the blue jays at the feeder. "One minute they're barely speaking to each other, and the next, they're starting a new business. If only the Meg issue were that easy to solve." I stroked his fur, causing him to arch his back. "Careful, they may put you to work."

Hank stilled.

"Or turn you into a character."

Ollie's cries turned my attention from Hank.

* * *

AFTER EVERYONE LEFT, we put the kids to bed.

"Fancy a drink to celebrate?" Sarah asked.

"I'll pour the wine. Why don't you change into some cozy clothes and meet me in the library?" I did my best to sound seductive.

"I won't be long." She ran a finger down my front.

"You should start a business every day," I hollered after her.

Several minutes later, Sarah, in sweats and a T-shirt, waltzed back into the room.

I traced a finger up and down in the air. "Not the outfit I had in mind."

"The whips and chains are at the cleaners." She took the wineglass from my hand. "Nice touch with the fire." She plopped down onto the couch, her back against the arm.

Sitting next to her, I covered us with a blue and purple fleece blanket.

She nudged me with her bare foot. "How'd it go last night?"

I sipped my water. "Okay, I think. It was different."

"Did she flirt with you?"

I held my thumb and forefinger in the air. "A bit."

Sarah hiked up her eyebrows.

"And she placed her hands on my chest when encouraging me to believe in myself."

"Maybe I should go to her with my problems." Her smile was too wide.

"Good thing the Troy issue has eased." I turned on the cushion, resting against the arm of the couch and pressing my feet into her thigh. "Wait? Is this the true reason you wanted me to meet with Courtney? To help you play out some fantasy?"

"Perhaps. Tell me more." She appeared way too eager for my liking.

"Should I be jealous that you're living vicariously through me?"

"No way!"

I pushed my feet more into her. "You have to admit it's kinda odd how excited you are to hear details about a woman you clearly have a crush on. Or should I say *have the hots for?*"

"Why is that odd?" She slanted her head.

"How is it not? I really can't wrap my head around if I should be upset or not?" I joggled my open palms up and down in the air, pondering the choices.

"Don't be silly. If I can't talk to you about this, who can I talk to?"

"Maddie. Your mom. George. The checkout lady at the grocery store. You have options."

Her eyes darted to the ceiling. "But I want to be open and honest with you. All the time."

"It's a dangerous game."

"But necessary for a healthy relationship." She hunkered down into the cushions. "Do you have a secret crush on someone?"

"Your crush isn't secret, *dear*." I stared deeply into her eyes.

She waved the technicality away. "Do you?"

"Why?" I was hesitant to dive in. Had this been her plan from the beginning? To get me relaxed to confess all?

"Because I can seek the person out and get to know them. Help you, like you're helping me."

"Interacting by proxy?"

"Exactly."

I scratched a tenacious itch on the back of my right shoulder. "Nope."

Her eyes narrowed. "None at all?"

"Nope."

"I don't believe you." She tossed a pillow at me.

I pushed the pillow off onto the floor. "You have to, because it's the truth."

"Everyone has crushes. We're married, not dead. What about Jorie?"

I squinted my eyes. "Ewww. She's a student and so much younger."

"Former student," she corrected.

Slowly, I opened my eyes. "Still not okay in my book."

"Lizzie! Tell me!" She dug her nails into my calf, and I pushed harder against her thigh, feeling her muscle tighten.

I applied more pressure to hers. "Clearly, chasing the twinks has done wonders for your legs."

She gave one last shove before relenting. "You're stubborn."

"Because I'm not crushing on someone?"

"Because you won't admit it."

"How can I admit something that isn't happening? You want me to make up a crush? That would be lying. Something I try not to do anymore, at your behest, I might add." I smothered my heart with my hands.

She eyed me curiously. "You really don't have one?"

I tossed up my hands. "That's what I've been saying."

Her face clouded over. "Why not?"

"Seriously?"

She arched an eyebrow.

"Because I'm in love with you. Remember that whole *until death do us part* thing you made me do?"

She rolled her eyes but ignored the wedding comment. "And I love and adore you."

"Obviously not enough," I teased, immediately relenting with upraised palms.

"It's not normal. You're not normal."

I repositioned, now sitting next to her. "You're just figuring this out?"

She placed a hand on each of my cheeks. "Oh, I've known. But, it's important for me to point it out every chance I get."

"I've noticed. Another one of your faults."

"Promise me you'll work on your faults." She implored me with her eyes.

"Duly noted. I'll find a hot woman to crush on, immediately." I kissed her.

"There are plenty to choose from, and there's only one you are absolutely forbidden to crush on."

"Who gave you the power to tell me who's off-limits?" I teased, nuzzling her neck and inhaling her musky scent.

"I did."

"Fine." I pulled away. "Who's on the Do-Not-Crush list?"

"Meg."

I laughed. "I can totally live with that."

"That's better. Now, take me to bed." She yawned.

It was catchy, and I followed suit. "Don't tell my future crush about this. Not being able to stay up to seduce the hottest woman on the planet."

"Your secret is safe with me."

CHAPTER EIGHTEEN

*S*itting at a table near the back window in the coffee shop, I lined up my red, blue, and green liquid ink pens on the table. Not happy, I swapped the red with the green. Then flipped the blue, in the middle, so the tip faced in the opposite direction.

"Ah, the prep work that goes into every research paper."

The voice made me go limp with fear.

Uninvited, Meg slid into the empty chair.

Not wanting to give any indication of the true emotion swirling inside, I said, "It's important to have the proper setup." I tried to sound like I was taking my work seriously and not using this trip to the coffee shop as a way to get some time to myself while Sarah and her writing partners discussed, aka talked loudly and over each other, their new publishing venture.

"You still write out your notes by hand?" She leaned on her forearms to peer at my notebook, which pushed up her breasts. Not that I was looking, but her V-neck shirt made it impossible not to notice.

"Can't seem to break away from the habit." I shrugged one shoulder.

"Would you like something to drink?"

Not wanting to be indebted and possibly have to agree to another meeting or ambush, I asked, "What can I get you?" I rose.

She motioned for me to retake my seat. "Let me. I know what you want." Meg slipped into the back of the Starbucks line, staring at the board as if she didn't know what she wanted.

Given how many times she'd been in rehab for drinking, maybe she didn't know many non-alcoholic beverages. I rearranged my pens once again, with the green pen now breaking ranks from the others.

"A chai, madam." Meg set it down to the left of my notepad and journal articles.

"What brings you here?"

Meg stifled a laugh but didn't offer any explanation as to why. "I was thinking of going to the movies, but none starts for another thirty minutes."

There was a movie theater around the corner, but this still felt like a frame-up job. But how would she have tracked me down considering this wasn't my typical Starbucks? Tracking device?

"What project are you working on?"

"An article about scarcity on the German home front." I sounded more robotic than I'd intended. My goal was not to let Meg in but not come across as a complete social misfit. Although, that might help my cause of pushing her out of my life permanently.

She rested her chin on her interlaced fingers. "Let me know if you want me to read it."

"Uh, thanks." I tapped the green pen on my leg. "How

about you? Any projects in the pipelines?" Maybe if I stuck to work subjects, I'd make it through relatively unscathed.

"Working on a book."

"Already." I whistled, surprised by her motivation. "Considering you just completed your PhD, nice job."

She smiled. "Not really. I'm expanding on my dissertation."

I nodded. "It'd be foolish not to."

"You know me. Never foolish."

The image of her in the hotel lobby, with her hair dyed red, in her prostitute clothes filled my mind. I blinked it away.

"Everyone gets that look around me. At least the people who knew me when…"

"I…" I reached for the pens, but opted not to rearrange them again, kicking myself for not capitalizing on the opening to say, "Hey, speaking of that, I want you out of my life for good." Or, "Really, I don't want to hurt your feelings or threaten your sobriety, but it'd be better for me and my family if you'd leave me alone."

She put her hand on my arm. "No, I get it. I did things that still make my skin crawl."

I started to nod but quickly pretended my scalp itched. Another opportunity lost.

"It's okay. You aren't the one who should be embarrassed. Leave that bit up to me." For someone who was admitting she was a terrible person, her relaxed shoulders and guilt-free expression reminded me of Actress Meg.

I swallowed, still unable to add anything to her line of conversation.

"I really appreciate you talking to me. I don't have many people willing…" She sat up straighter. "I'm sorry. I didn't mean to lay a guilt trip on you." She purposefully looked away. Had she rehearsed this scene and waited for the right opportunity?

I glanced around the pre-movie patrons, wondering if I was

involved in some type of documentary about an addict trying to repair the damage.

She fiddled with my blue pen. "It's just... I miss you."

Did she expect me to follow her script and say I missed her? I didn't. At least not the Meg that popped into my memories. The one who...

"I don't want to complicate your life," Meg said.

Too late.

"Although, I don't know how to avoid that." She shrugged. "You're one of the people I admire. Your dedication. Thirst for knowledge. I need to be around people like you."

Her tactic of buttering me was further proof this was a setup job, reminiscent of the days when we dated, like when I used to grade her students' exams when she was too inebriated.

Meg swigged her drink. "I'm doing a shitty job of putting your mind at ease. Maybe this was a bad idea. Coming here." Her eyes scanned the joint as if looking for the best escape route.

It was hard to argue with her; however, I wasn't sure what she meant. Stopping to chat with me or returning to Colorado after everything?

Or was she giving me an opening to forgive or tell her to buzz off. There was a flicker of loneliness and fear in her eyes that compelled me to do the unthinkable. "I..." I flipped open one of the European history journals. "Do you know anything about this historian? I can't get a grip on his thesis. He seems to argue one thing until the conclusion, when he flips to the other line of thought."

Meg took the journal into her hand. "His name rings a bell. Can I take this and read it?"

I nodded, irked that I was trying to make her feel better when she wasn't my concern anymore. I needed to draw a line in the sand, with my family and me on one side and Meg on the other. That had been my plan since speaking with Courtney. To unequivocally cut Meg off. When I left the house this morning, though, I had no idea the opportunity would present itself.

"Did you hear about Trump's comments at the Boy Scout jamboree?" she asked, clearly pleased her routine had had the effect she wanted.

Dammit!

I could salvage my goal now.

Just say, "Buzz off, Meg!"

I sucked in a deep breath and then said, "How could I not? Everyone considers me the expert."

Clearly wanting to tell Meg to go to hell and actually doing it were two different ballgames, and I was stuck playing T-ball while Meg was a pro at getting what she wanted out of others.

"Even though your focus is on the British Boy Scouts."

"Yes!" I slapped the tabletop, more out of anger at myself. "Not many can get that through their heads."

"Yesterday, at a meeting, a man dropped a fact about ancient Rome and was floored I didn't know a thing about it. You know the look. Mouth forming a disappointed O." She mimicked it. "As if we know every name, date, and event since the—"

"Beginning of time." *No, Lizzie. Do not complete her sentences.*

"No wonder I started drinking with pressure like that."

My jaw dropped.

She laughed, pointing at my face. "Kidding, of course. According to my therapist, I use ill-advised jokes when nervous."

"Has to be better than whiskey." At least that was honest, even if I hadn't intended to say it out loud.

A quirky smile that was difficult to decipher appeared on her face. "Depends on who you ask." She sipped her drink. "Tell me about your article." Meg leaned forward in her chair, eager to delve into the nitty-gritty of my research, probably knowing that was the safest way to handle me.

"Don't you have a movie to catch?"

Meg glanced at her watch. "Oh! How'd that happen?" She downed the rest of her coffee, and part of me hoped it burned.

I leaned back in my seat, relieved at least that tactic worked.

Meg snatched the journal. "I'll read this tonight, and if you want, we can get together in a week or two. That'll give me some time to let the ideas marinate." She tapped the rolled-up pages against her temple.

Well, it didn't take long for my relief to turn into an oozing pool of shit.

"You don't have to." *Seriously, don't.*

She peered down into my eyes. "I want to."

"Maybe." I offered a wary shrug, knowing not only didn't I want to, but Sarah would be adamantly opposed. For good reason. Just like old times, Meg was putting her needs first, and I was letting it happen.

Meg placed a firm hand on my shoulder. "I'd like that. If you can." She dashed out of the joint.

Why couldn't I put the brakes on this impending train crash?

So much for having fortune cookie magic on my side. Somehow, Meg had said a few mollifying things and I'd let her weasel her way back in. I buried my face in my hands.

"Lizzie?"

I parted my hands and saw Bailey holding a textbook. "Hey."

"You okay?"

"Splendid." I straightened in my chair.

Bailey laughed. "Janice warned me about your aversion tactics. Was that Meg?" She hooked her thumb over her shoulder at the door Meg had recently bolted through.

"Yep."

"That explains it."

I had to laugh. "It does?"

"Janice also gave me the heads-up that she might be on the hunt for you. Want to talk?"

I pointed at the book. "What class is that for?"

"I'll take that to mean you don't want to talk. Music theory." She slipped into the chair across from me.

"You're serious, then? About your band and music?"

She pushed her glasses back into place. "I think so. It's hard, though, figuring out how to get noticed and build a brand."

"Sarah's been reading some books about it. Branding, I mean. Not bands. Ask her for some recommendations."

"I will."

I tapped the green pen against the edge of the table. "You know, since the start of school I wondered if you were actually enrolled in classes."

"Why didn't you ask me? Or call my grandmother?"

"Sometimes, I think it's best to wait to see how you can help someone." I leaned over the tabletop and whispered, "And Dottie scares me."

"She means well." She shrugged.

"But...?"

"She has her heart set on me being a doctor or lawyer or something along those lines." She slumped down into her chair.

I chewed on my bottom lip. "I see. Not that you want my advice, but if you were to ask me, I'd recommend following your own path, but don't close the door on other possibilities."

"That's why I'm considering teaching music." She smiled, perking up some. "Fred really loves the drums. I know he's super young, but I see a spark in his eyes when there's music."

"Then it's a good thing his nanny is a music fan, which is not my specialty."

"Understatement of the century!"

"That's harsh."

"Any adult who claims 'The Monster Mash' is their favorite song knows nothing about music. But next semester I'm taking Western Civ, so maybe we can work something out. I'll load up your iPod, and you can tutor me."

"Deal." I stuck out a hand to seal the deal. "Are you studying for a test?"

"Yep. Meeting a classmate. Can I borrow a pen?" She glanced down at my stash.

"Take the blue one." I didn't want to touch the one Meg had fondled.

She gleefully swiped it. "Thanks!"

"Now if you'll excuse me, I think it's time I head home to help Sarah with the twinks." And fill her in on my inability to cut Meg out of my life.

Yet.

CHAPTER NINETEEN

*T*wo days later, Maddie cornered me right when I stepped through the door from the garage into the kitchen. Grabbing my hands, even the one still clutching my workbag, she said, "Say yes."

"Thought you knew, but I'm married." I yanked my left hand from hers and wiggled my ring finger.

"Who'd want to marry you?" Maddie stepped back. "Except for Sarah. Your soul mate. You two are the definition of *happily married*."

"Nice recovery," Sarah chimed in, standing on the other side of the island, holding a coffee cup in both hands.

"Where are the twinks?"

"With Bailey. Can't you hear the racket?" She cupped her ear.

I mirrored her. "Maracas, drums, and..." I strained to hear. "Triangle, perhaps?"

Sarah nodded. "We may have to soundproof the nursery if the music lessons continue."

"Freddie does love the drums."

"Yeah, yeah. They're musical prodigies." Maddie hopped up and down. "Can we get back to the matter at hand and, more importantly, to Lizzie saying yes?"

I slid onto the closest barstool, exhausted from teaching, polishing an article, grading, and the latest department meeting. "Enlighten me."

Maddie rolled her eyes. "There's a weekend retreat for children's authors. Rose, Troy, and I have signed up."

"That's great news!" I reached for her shoulder. In the past, I hadn't always been super supportive of her passing whims, so I really wanted to make a better effort. "I wholeheartedly support you in this."

She flicked off my hand. "Sarah says she can't go."

I swiveled around to my wife, cocking my head. "Why not?"

Sarah strained her eyes to convey her thoughts. "I can think of two reasons. They go by Ollie and Freddie."

I crossed my arms. "You don't trust me with the twinks?"

Her eyes bored further into mine.

"I have been left with them before."

"For a few hours, here and there. Never for an entire weekend. Alone."

"News flash!" I waved my hand in the air, pretending to read a headline. "I am one of their mothers."

Her face wasn't warming to the idea.

I mulled this over. "Let's change gears. Do you want to go to the retreat? We've talked about you starting a hobby or something more."

"It'd be a great opportunity to see if this is something I really want to pursue. Right now, the concept is in its infancy, but I don't know. It could turn into something." It was clear she was trying to mask her excitement.

"Then go."

Maddie clamped a hand on my shoulder. "I told you Lizzie

would be fine with it. There are only a few hours left to register." She set to work on her tablet.

Sarah covered the screen with her hand. "Not so fast."

Maddie pried her fingers away. "I'm signing you up," she said through gritted teeth.

I skirted the island and took Sarah in my arms. "I've got this."

"*This*—we're talking about our children."

"Oh, I'm aware of their connection to us. With insurance, benefits forms, wills, birth certificates—I now know their names, birthdates, identifying marks, and social security numbers by heart. I may be able to sketch out their fingerprints if needed."

"This isn't a joke."

"And it's not life or death, either. One weekend. I can handle one weekend on my own. Throughout history, women have been able to care for their young."

"I don't give a damn about women in history."

"I'll try not to mention that to our daughter or liberal son." I flashed a teasing smile. "You're going. What will make you feel better? See if Bailey will stay with me? Hire a nurse and pediatrician for the weekend?" I grinned. "Recruit the National Guard?"

"Don't put national emergencies into my head," she said, the defiance in her expression lessening.

"The way the current administration is operating, they probably don't have anyone staffing the National Guard phone lines anyway."

Sarah's nostrils flared. "Are you trying to talk me out of going?"

"No. I'm telling you nothing bad will happen while you're gone. I won't let it."

"You'll miss your Sunday morning ride."

I laughed. "Is that your best last-ditch effort?"

Sarah buried her face in the crook of my neck.

Maddie let out a whoop. "Everyone is confirmed. This is going to be so much fun!" She did a happy dance.

CHAPTER TWENTY

*T*he doorbell rang. It'd been one hour since Sarah had cleared out for the retreat. She'd texted at least a dozen times and called on three separate occasions. When I flung the door open, I half expected to see her.

Instead, it was Ethan and Casey.

"Color me not surprised."

Ethan hoisted pizza boxes. "Casey and I thought we'd start a Friday night pizza club. Are you and the twinks in?"

Since I had a twin on each hip, I jerked my head for them to enter. "Did Sarah provide you with the excuse for dropping in unannounced?"

"Not verbatim." Ethan followed his daughter to the kitchen.

I maneuvered Freddie into his high chair and then Ollie. "Where's Lisa?"

"Girls' night out. Do you have paper plates?"

I sighed. "As much as I hate to admit it, considering the planet's days are numbered, yes. It's best to have them for when my best friend decides to pop in with his daughter. I'm blaming you for me partaking in the ruination of the planet."

Ethan flicked his hand for me to get on with it.

"In the cabinet next to the microwave."

He counted out three plates. "At least they're eco-friendly." He held one at eyelevel. "I'm guessing not cheap."

"Not by a long shot." I heated up dinner for the twins. "There's milk and other beverages in the fridge. Go ahead and start. I'm used to having cold meals. I don't think I can remember otherwise."

He gave a knowing smile. After retrieving milk for Casey and a diet soda for himself, he settled at the table. Flipping the lid to the top box, he said, "Here you go, Casey."

She dug in.

I sat between the twins, laying out their finger foods. "Is your luggage in the car?"

"I'm only on the hook for Friday night dinner and a movie."

"We're going to the movies?" I asked, struggling to picture the twins patiently sitting in a dark theater.

Ethan sipped his soda. "No. We're going to watch one here. Meaning we'll put one on for the kids and you and I can talk or read."

"Daddy always reads when I watch movies." She slurped up a piece of cheese dangling from her mouth.

"He's a smart man." I scooted a piece of chicken closer to Freddie's hand.

Casey shook her head as if she'd caught me in a lie. "That's not what Mommy said yesterday."

"Casey, would you like another slice?" Ethan asked.

She nodded but continued. "Mommy called him a word I'm not allowed to repeat."

"I'm sure Aunt Lizzie doesn't want to hear about it." Ethan squirmed in his seat.

"Oh, I do. Go on." I motioned for Casey to continue.

"Once, when I said the word, I was put in a time-out. Not Mommy." Casey gulped her milk, wiping her lips with the back of her hand.

Ethan, much relieved Casey didn't fill me in completely, nodded his sympathy. "The world isn't fair, kiddo."

"I have a boyfriend," Casey blurted. "We have a date tomorrow."

I smiled at Casey. "Is he picking you up? Make him come to the door. Not just honk."

"We're meeting in a park." Her shrug implied that was how kids did it these days.

I had to stifle a laugh.

"I'm looking for a girlfriend." She smacked her lips.

"Casey is determined to keep her options open with all things in life." Ethan placed another slice on Casey's plate.

"Me too," I said. "At least when it comes to finding a girlfriend."

Casey's face twisted into confusion. "What about Sarah?"

"She's my wife." Part of me felt guilty for teasing Casey.

"That means you can't have a girlfriend," she said with conviction, adding a flourish of her neck to push the point home.

"Not according to Sarah." I handed Ollie a piece of steamed broccoli.

Ethan raised an eyebrow but didn't press.

Casey tossed her crust onto Ethan's plate. "Can I watch now?"

"After you take care of your plate."

"Do you recycle or reuse them?" she asked me.

"Unfortunately, grease doesn't recycle all that well. Just toss them into the trash can under the sink."

She skipped to the sink and raced past the table into the family room.

"Do you need help with Netflix?" I asked, starting to get out of my chair.

She showed the universal *stop* sign. "I got it."

"Last weekend, I locked myself out of my cell phone and she

fixed it." Ethan grabbed another slice from the grease-stained box. "What's this about finding a girlfriend?"

I finally selected a slice for myself. "Oh, Sarah's concerned because I don't have a crush on anyone. She thinks it's unhealthy not to lust after someone else."

"Susan Sarandon's character in *Bull Durham*. I hate baseball, but after seeing that film, I briefly considered playing."

"You and baseball? Heck, I didn't even know you watched films about baseball or any sport." I shook my head, unable to put the two together. "I should have tossed out a celebrity's name. Once Sarah gets one of her crackpot ideas into her head…" I circled a finger around my temple, followed by taking a bite of pizza.

Freddie shoved all the food off his tray with both hands.

"I think he's done," Ethan said.

"I don't know how he has so much energy considering he hardly ever eats. The doctor says it's normal." I eyed him with worry.

"Children know when to stop." Ethan licked his fingers. "Unlike adults. Another slice?" He added the final from the first box to his plate, immediately opening the spare pepperoni.

I nodded. "When Lisa called you this name, did you throw me under the bus again?"

"She wouldn't let me." He pouted.

"Poor baby. You must have screwed up big time. Does it relate to why your wife is having girls' night out?"

"Absolutely. If the doorbell rings, don't answer it. I want to finish dinner before being served divorce papers."

I held my slice midair, the tip flopping downward. "You aren't really worried about that, are you?"

His non-reply was damning.

I whistled. "What'd you do?"

"Said no."

"To sex? When have you ever said yes?" I asked in all seriousness.

He glared at me. "To having another child," he whispered.

Ollie started to fuss.

"Grab Fred before she really gets going. We can set them up in the room with Casey."

"We should keep an eye on them, or Sarah will kill me. She was clear with her directive." He rose.

"I can set up the video monitors if you want to talk in the kitchen."

He shook his head and swept Fred into his arms. "Come on, little man. Movie time with Casey and Uncle Ethan."

The fight must have been a doozy, hence his reason for killing any chance of discussing it further by moving into the room with Casey.

With Ollie in my arms, I said, "The one thing I've learned about marriage is every day, no matter what, is a battle and a victory."

"Yes, but for whom?"

"History's written by the winners." I shrugged.

"Does that mean you won't be writing the history of the Petrie-Cavanaugh clan?" he joked, but his eyes gleamed with worry.

Casey paused *The Little Mermaid*, catching the twins up on what they'd missed. Fred, sitting on the carpet, to his credit, looked as if he followed every word. Ollie leafed through a numbers, colors, and shapes chunky board book.

"She takes after you," I said to Ethan.

He smiled proudly. "Uncles can have a mighty effect."

"I'll have to teach her about having the book right side up."

Ethan didn't balk. "She's honing her spy craft skills."

I put a finger to the side of my nose and then pointed it at him. "Got it. Tell me, my favorite spy, who does Sarah have lined up tomorrow to *stop by*." I made quote marks.

"Helen."

I patted the top of my noggin. "I should have been able to figure that out."

"There aren't many options considering most of the people you know are at the retreat. If you had read more books upside down as a child, you'd have better problem-solving skills."

"Where's your book?" I made a show of seeking a hidden text in his deep pockets.

"Funny thing, I didn't bring one. Are you actually going to let me read?"

"What else would we do on a Friday night while the wives are away and the kids are engrossed in quiet activities?"

"I knew there was a reason we got along." He strode into the library.

I cracked the spine of *The Nighingale*, a World War II novel I'd picked up two months ago but hadn't opened until tonight.

* * *

THE PHONE RANG a little after eight on Saturday morning.

"Good morning, sweetheart," I said as cheerily as possible, not bothering to look at the caller ID so I wouldn't clue Sarah into the fit Ollie was having, spurring Fred to cry out of either sympathy or frustration.

"Hi." It was Peter's voice.

"Oh, hey." I squeezed the phone tighter between my ear and shoulder. "I thought you were Sarah."

"What's going on there?"

"Ollie doesn't want to wear pants, apparently."

He laughed. "A conversation I never thought I'd have about your daughter."

"The fun never ends here. What's up with you?"

"I was wondering if you and Sarah could watch Demi later

today. I have golf. Dad's out of town. Helen is in your neck of the woods, and Allen isn't answering his phone."

"Allen's spending the day with my nanny. Which means, I'm the last resort."

"Is Sarah there?" he joked. At least, I think he was kidding.

"Nope. It's just me this weekend, but drop her off. The more the merrier." I cringed when Ollie's screeching reached an impressive eardrum-shattering decibel.

"Are you sure?" Peter's tone lacked his usual confidence.

I wasn't, but I didn't want to leave little Demi in a lurch. "Sure, I'm super mommy this weekend. I'm even wearing a cape." A bathrobe but I could dream. Delusions—the parent's last-ditch effort when pretending everything was on the up-and-up.

* * *

AROUND FIVE, Peter breezed into the kitchen, returning to pick up Demi. "I brought Chinese." He hoisted two white plastic bags in the air.

"You're a lifesaver. The little ones are just finishing up with their dinner." I had Demi in my lap, feeding her the posh baby food Peter had packed. "She loves her Jamaican curried pork."

Peter's smile was genuine, an emotion I was starting to get used to seeing on his face. He peered across the table. "Fred still doesn't eat much?"

I shook my head. "We might have to try this stuff." I motioned to Demi's stash. "Where do you get it?"

"Uh… I'll ask." He placed the bags on the table.

That meant he'd ask the woman in charge of Demi Monday through Friday. Tie was taking to motherhood like the Scotch-lady—not one bit.

I rose. "Can you watch the twinks? I think Demi needs to be changed."

"Sure." He didn't bother looking abashed for not offering to change his own daughter, but I didn't expect him to.

Afterward, I returned with Demi. "Good as new." I handed her to Peter so I could get the twins out of their high chairs. "Shall we eat in the front room, allow the kids free rein with their toys?"

It didn't take long to set up around the coffee table and serve ourselves.

"Where's Tie today?" I ate sesame chicken and rice with a plastic fork.

Peter wolfed down a greasy egg roll, shrugging to let me know he didn't have a clue. I think that was his perpetual state when it came to his marriage. "And Sarah?"

"A writing conference."

He nodded, not pursuing the conversation.

We ate in silence for many moments, but I couldn't, in good conscience, ignore his surly demeanor.

Covering my mouth, I asked, "What's going on?" I motioned to his stiff posture.

He tried to relax but gave up. "Long day, that's all."

"Losing to more potential clients?" I joked. "Although, you aren't in your typical Easter Bunny golf outfit."

"Very funny." His grimace implied the exact opposite. "Just had meetings today."

"International finance never stops, not even on a Saturday."

"Something like that. Be glad you're a teacher." He discarded his plate onto the coffee table.

I laughed. "I don't have to be on campus much, but I have a night of grading to look forward to after putting the twins to bed. That is, if I can muster the energy. Maybe Tie has the right idea. Not work or… anything."

"She's been filling her time reading crap like *The Wizard of Lies, Den of Thieves, Liar's Poker, The Smartest Guys in the Room…*" He waved that the list went on.

"I'm not familiar with those titles." I inhaled my last bite.

His laughter sounded cruel. "I don't think she understands half. Less than half. They're books about corporate greed, white-collar crime, and whatnot. As if she understands what it's like to make a buck in this world."

I hadn't pegged Tie as the crusader type, so it was difficult to see her motivation. "Interesting," I managed to say after swallowing. Was she worried Peter was involved in unsavory business tactics? Worried about their livelihood?

He picked up Demi. "You're smarter than Mommy, aren't you?" Peter glanced over his daughter's head. "Do you ever regret getting married?"

Gobsmacked, I looked at my babies playing on the floor.

"Not about having kids but getting hitched?" he clarified.

"Nope."

"You're lucky. Very lucky."

It was heartfelt and probably the first time he'd said something like that to me. "Are you and Tie okay?" Should I bring up Courtney's warning? I did have experience with conniving women. Then again, Peter was raised by the same mother and he dealt with cut-throat business types.

He looked into Demi's innocent face, tapping her perky nose. "I should get you home."

Apparently, Peter was done confiding. If that was what he was actually trying to do. Did divorce lawyers hold meetings on the weekend? Were Sarah and I the only couple in our circle who'd make it to the end of the year?

CHAPTER TWENTY-ONE

"*H*ere comes the airplane, Freddie." I made buzzing sounds as I steered a bite of oatmeal to Fred's pinched mouth.

The call alert window on Skype flashed.

"Ten bucks, it's Mommy."

Ollie continued smooshing a banana chunk with her fingers and then licking them. Whatever worked.

"Sweetheart, are you okay? I haven't heard from you in at least five minutes," I said to Sarah's image on the tablet, which was propped up since I'd been expecting another call.

Ignoring the jab, Sarah said, "Here comes the airplane, Freddie."

I laughed. "Right on cue. It's like you have the morning routine here memorized."

"I miss you guys."

I looked over my shoulder at her image. "Luckily, you'll be home in a few hours."

"Do they miss me?" There was desperation in her voice.

"Nope. I managed to wipe their memories of you completely. I'm thinking of selling the technology to the highest bidder. North Korea. Russia. College educations don't come cheap, you know."

"Earlier, when I said I missed you guys, I was only referring to the children."

I gave up getting Fred to eat and lifted the tablet. "Are you at the airport?" I squinted at the screen.

"Yes, and good news, I thought we'd miss the flight because Maddie got hammered last night and wouldn't get out of bed, but our plane isn't even here yet." Her broad smile was faker than the propaganda films made during World War II claiming Japanese Americans loved internment camps.

"I'm sorry, sweetheart. At least there's good people-watching at the airport. Keep an eye out for a hottie for me to lust after. I know you're concerned about my *crushless* state."

"There were a few contenders at the retreat." She grinned.

"Huh, I've always pictured the creators of children's stories as pudgy old grandmothers."

"Hey!"

"Excluding you of course."

"Are you going to be okay with the twinks for a few extra hours?"

Like she could do anything about it. "I was thinking of locking them in a closet with power tools so I can go for a bike ride."

"We don't have any power tools." I couldn't see her expression all that well since Sarah was seated next to a window and the brightness was obscuring her face, but I was certain from the tone her jaw was clenched when she spoke.

"Did I forget to mention we went shopping at Home Depot yesterday to prepare for this eventuality?"

Her face got really close to the screen. "I can't tell if you're lying."

"Clearly, my mind sweep program is starting to work

wonders on you. Since when have I ever enjoyed shopping? And power tools? I'm not a DIY dyke."

Ollie lobbed a gooey chunk of banana at my face, which oozed from my hairline on down.

"Good girl!" Sarah cheered. "I'll let you go. See all of you soon!"

I wiped my face with a hand towel. "Learn from your sister. That banana trick worked like a charm. Who wants to finger paint?" I asked in the typical over-exaggerated parent voice I'd once sworn I'd never use around my children.

* * *

RIGHT AFTER LUNCH, which happened every day at eleven, Helen returned for the second time that weekend, with Allen in tow.

"Let me guess, a little bird told you Sarah's flight was late?"

Helen kissed my cheek before taking Freddie from my hip. "I had inventory to check in at the Fort Collins store. How's my favorite little man?"

"I thought *I* was?" Allen asked, and it was hard to tell if he was joking.

To be safe, I said, "You're her favorite *big* man."

Allen blinked as if trying to determine if I was speaking in code. "Where does that leave Dad and Gabe?"

Maybe Sarah was right. Allen couldn't handle the likes of Meg. "You're asking the wrong person. Would either of you mind if I hopped in the shower?"

"Looks like you need it." Helen peered at my hair.

"Is that a boogie?" Allen moved closer to inspect.

I took a massive step back. "I'm praying its banana from breakfast, but it's hard to know for sure around here these days."

Helen bobbled Freddie in her arms. "Take your time. Goodness knows you've earned it."

"You're a godsend." I handed Ollie off to Allen. "My arms are going to be sore from lugging these two from room to room."

Helen laughed. "Rent them out. It may become an exercise trend."

The idea wasn't all that bad and not as crazy as the goat yoga craze I'd read about.

I scampered upstairs.

With the water set to the hottest level I could stand, I let it fall over my head, streaming down my body, wiping away the strain of the weekend. While I'd confidently proclaimed to Sarah I could manage the weekend alone with the twinkies, secretly I'd been terrified something terrible would happen on my watch. Even with the pop-in guests, being the sole parent hadn't been easy. Downright exhausting. And I didn't want to intrude on Bailey's weekend. We'd only hired her for fifteen hours a week, Monday through Friday.

Was Lisa prepared for that if she did divorce Ethan?

Was Ethan?

I made a solemn vow to avoid divorce at all possible costs.

Jesus, what would Peter do if he divorced Tie? Raise Demi or leave her with a woman who couldn't be bothered to water a plant?

The hot water turned a degree or two chillier, an indication it was time to get out.

Quickly, I toweled off and tossed on baggy jeans, a button-up shirt, and a navy sweater.

Laughter from the family room drifted to my ears.

I loved being a family woman.

The twins.

Stepmom.

Stepbrother.

The whole package, including Dad, who wasn't physically present but my thoughts drifted to him more and more. He had checked in via texts and emails the past couple of days.

"Oh man, did that feel—?"

My eyes laser-locked on Meg.

What in the fuck was she doing here? In my home?

My phone vibrated.

A feeling in my bones told me it had to be a message from Sarah letting me know her plane had landed.

How would I explain her presence?

Better yet, how would I prevent Sarah from murdering Meg?

"You don't look like a woman who's just spent seventy-two hours alone with twins." Meg smiled, holding Ollie.

Had Allen handed over my daughter to Meg? This made it abundantly clear I needed to have a chat with Allen about Meg. Was it possible to fill him in about her character without sharing the details I wanted to keep private?

The big picture invaded my mind. If I didn't get her out of my house before Sarah's homecoming, I would be heading for divorce court. Maybe Ethan and I could get the same lawyer. A twofer.

Stop it, Lizzie.

Think.

Act.

"Hope you don't mind, but Allen asked me to come over." Meg appraised my *frozen in time* stance.

"N-no... not at all. Would you like a drink?" I rushed to say as a way to cover my fear. Meg was like a bear wanting to make me her dinner, and I needed to stand tall to show her she wasn't in control. "Tea, coffee, water..." The sickness churning in my stomach spread throughout my body.

"Coffee, please. And then Allen and I need to head out. There's a special lecture this afternoon on campus." She consulted her watch.

Campus? The one where I worked? How did I not know about this special lecture? It wasn't sponsored by the history department or club. Of that, I was certain.

"Yeah, a Russian author will be discussing her latest novel." Allen was as giddy as a child who'd received his very first helium balloon.

Helen handed Freddie to her son. "I'll help you with the coffee, Lizzie."

I nodded a thank-you.

In the kitchen, Helen whispered, "What's wrong?"

I scooped coffee into the filter. "Nothing."

"It's Meg." Helen twisted a tea towel into a knot. "Something about her seems off. Allen adores her. I appreciate her taking an interest, but why is she taking an interest in my nineteen-year-old son?"

I shrugged, unable to voice the same concern. Although, I sensed the underlining reason for Meg's actions I'd conjured in my mind was entirely different than Helen's.

"Is she trying to get back into your life?"

Ding, ding, ding!

"Would you like a cup?" I asked, not waiting for a response and pulling down four mugs.

Helen spun me around, keeping her hands on my shoulders. "Give it to me straight. Will Sarah flip out if she finds Meg here?"

I moved my head upward and then let it crash down.

"Should I ask her to leave?"

Yes!

I closed my eyes, trying to think of a solution. Didn't every problem have a solution? Or was I thinking of Newton's third law of physics: every action has an equal and opposite reaction? My brain couldn't comprehend if that rule helped me in this situation. What would Dwight D. Eisenhower do? But the allies spent months planning the Normandy invasion... Why hadn't I mapped out a response to Meg showing up at my house?

"I—"

The coffee dribbled slowly into the pot. We watched it. I didn't know about Helen, but I was praying to a higher power, any of them, to speed up the process.

As if in tune, Helen proclaimed, "First step, get Meg out of the house. One cup and then I'll shoo them out to the lecture. I'll have a chat with Allen later about his *friendship* with Meg." She glanced at the clock on the microwave. "What time is Sarah expected?"

I fished my phone out of my pocket. "The plane has landed."

Helen looked skyward. "Retrieving luggage—"

"They didn't check any bags."

"O-okay. Less than two hours. Surely, it won't take that long for one cup of coffee. I'll get the milk." She went into action.

It struck me that for so many years I'd wanted a mother like Helen. One who had my back. And the entire time I'd lived with the Scotch-lady, Helen was in the shadows. There for my father. For Allen. I hadn't known she existed.

This line of thinking wasn't going to help me with the situation at hand.

The last gurgling sound of the coffee maker nearly made my heart sing. I splashed coffee into all four cups and transferred them to the serving tray. Helen added the milk pot, sugar bowl, and spoons. I took the tray in my hand, the cups rattling on the saucers. Sucking in a steadying breath, I motioned I was ready for the coffee operation, which would be quickly followed by the *kick Meg out of my house* maneuver.

She gave me a supportive nod.

We entered the room.

"How do you like your coffee, Meg?" Helen used a soothing voice, which I think was meant to calm my nerves.

"Two spoons of sugar."

"Milk? It's one percent. Or would you prefer almond? I can get the almond milk." Helen utilized her best grandmother expression, helpfully holding milk over Meg's cup.

Meg, who usually only had sugar, said, "One percent is fine."

"As Allen's mother, I already know how he takes it. Lots of sugar and extra milk. Extra sweet for my sweet *little* boy." She handed him his cup, while I arranged the twins at the art center in the corner.

"Lizzie?"

"Uh—"

Meg interrupted. "You drink coffee now?"

In my hurry, I'd poured myself a cup. "You know, parenting does things..." Not sure where I was going, I told Helen, "Just like Allen's, with maybe slightly more sugar." Like triple.

Helen smiled as if I were her daughter. "Of course, sweetheart."

Helen was doing her damnedest to make it clear to the interloper that she was the mother hen in the room and Meg had better watch her step. Was this part of her plan to get Allen out of her clutches?

Now that everyone had a cup in their hands, Helen sat on the couch next to Allen. Meg was in the chair on the far side of the room, and I stood by the table, where the twins colored with wax finger crayons that looked massive and unwieldy in their little hands. At least I didn't have to worry about them choking on them. If I could manage to force down my coffee without grimacing or spitting it out, we would be golden.

"Tell me about the lecture," Helen spoke to Allen.

"The author will be discussing her latest novel involving Rasputin and his rise to power. Much of Rasputin's background and such isn't known." Allen spoke with gravitas, taking a sip of his sickly-sweet coffee prepared by his mother.

A desire to break into hysterical laughter nearly overtook me. I drank heavily from the mug, trying not to taste it.

"And this novel tries to fill in the blanks," Helen supplied, setting her cup back onto the saucer she balanced on her knee.

Allen nodded, taking another dignified mouthful.

Meg placed a hand on Allen's arm. "One of my favorite aspects of history is the importance of literature. How many disciplines allow academics to read fiction to root out vital clues to the past? It's almost like detective work."

What game are you playing, Meg? She sat there, smug and righteous, while she was using my brother to wheedle her way back into my life. And every passing minute brought Sarah closer to home.

Was Meg aware of my dilemma? Had Allen mentioned Sarah would be returning today? She'd always loved to cause trouble, making everything about her.

Meg turned to me. "Don't you agree?"

I nodded, adding to give the appearance everything was just dandy, "I assign students two to three novels each semester in addition to their textbooks." I kneeled down to admire Ollie's squiggles on the newsprint, careful to keep my cup out of the twins' reach. "Good job, Ollie Dollie."

Meg took this as an invitation to come over to inspect. "Excellent use of red." She skirted to Fred's side. Looking up at me, she said, "He's a thinker. Takes after you."

Fred's drawing consisted of a lopsided half circle with some dashes inside, to the best of my analysis.

Ollie attacked the paper with the jumbo yellow crayon, an evil grin on her face.

"And this one is going to keep you up nights when she hits her teen years." Meg took a seat at the table with the twinks, setting her cup down on the coaster in the window ledge, where Sarah usually placed her cup. Freddie was overly curious and stopped his drawing to observe Meg. She glanced at me. "It's fascinating to see their personalities at play."

"It really is." Helen said, not taking her eyes off my ex, giving me the impression she was plumbing the depths of Meg's manipulative nature.

I continued to blink at the woman who had tormented me, sitting at the twin's table as if she belonged, which she most assuredly did not. I'd rather she sucker punch me in the gut than interact with my children.

Allen took the opportunity to chat further with his mom about the novel, not bothering to notice Meg had left his side. Even though I abhorred his friendship with Meg, I had to admire his dedication and love of history. How many college kids would stay up most of the night reading a novel to better understand an extracurricular lecture on a Sunday afternoon no less?

Out of the corner of my eye, I noticed Helen whisper something to Allen. He lifted the sleeve of his sweater to consult his watch. With his eyes bulging, he downed the remnants of his coffee.

He stood. "Meg, we should get going."

"Allen, I'll swing by the campus to pick you up after the lecture so you aren't late for dinner with Gabe and your father." Helen's tone implied Allen shouldn't argue.

Considering he was a freshman in college, I was surprised he didn't blush about the fact his mom would be picking him up. Instead, he chirped, "Thanks!"

"That works out well since I have dinner plans of my own tonight." Was Meg detecting Helen's *hands off my son* vibes.

It relieved me some that Meg didn't attempt to inveigle an invite to dinner. Did she consider getting inside my home mission accomplished? At least for today?

"Thanks for letting me hang, you two." Meg patted Ollie and Freddie on their heads.

The twins giggled.

I forced my right hand to unfurl.

"You stay with the twins, Lizzie. I'll walk them to the door." Helen put her hand out to show Meg the way.

Meg wheeled around. "Give me a call about your article."

"Enjoy the lecture." I raised my cup at Allen as a goodbye, purposefully avoiding eye contact with Meg.

I didn't take in a breath until the front door closed with an extra oomph. The more I got to know Helen, the more I admired her gumption.

"It's never boring in the Petrie family." Helen returned and gathered the coffee mugs.

"Let me do that. Spend time with your grandbabies."

Not surprisingly, she took me up on the deal.

After adding the cups and saucers to the dishwasher, I turned it on, relieved to hear the spray of water demolishing Meg's contamination.

"Hello!" Sarah shouted upon entering the front door.

I stepped into the family room in the nick of time to see both twinks yelp with delight, followed by Sarah dashing to them. "Did you miss Mommy?" She wrapped them in her arms.

"Yes," I said.

Sarah, with a twin on each hip, closed the distance between us. "Ditto."

CHAPTER TWENTY-TWO

*W*e put the twins down for their afternoon nap. Helen had left only a few minutes prior to pick up Allen, and secretly I hoped she'd have a private word to Meg about backing off. How old was too old for wanting motherly protection? And did I get extra time since I hadn't had it for the majority of my life?

"I need coffee. Come to the kitchen with me." Sarah threaded her fingers through mine.

"Two nights away and the only thing you can think about is coffee," I teased.

"I'm planning for a stellar night alone with you. Mom missed the twins, and they're staying at her place tonight."

"In that case, let's get caffeine in both of us stat!"

Sarah opened the cabinet. "Where are all the mugs?"

I swallowed. "With all the visitors you arranged, I couldn't keep up with the dishes." I placed my palm on the dishwasher door. "I think we can bust in." Steam gushed out when I lowered it. "Jesus, they're hot." I set two on the counter and then plunged my fingers under a steady stream of cold water from the faucet.

"That desperate for sex?" Sarah wrapped her arms around my stomach, resting her face on my shoulder. "How'd it go?"

"We managed to survive."

"No trips to the ER or any other emergency-type situations?"

Depends on your definition of 'situations.'

I placed my hands on her arms and eased back into her embrace. "No ER, and Ollie only had three, no, four major breakdowns."

"Normal, then."

"Yes," I started but couldn't do it. "We did have one interesting visitor."

"Santa?" she joked.

"Was he expected?" I craned my neck to gauge her expression.

"Sadly, he was booked." Sarah let her arms fall to prep the coffee machine, while I filled the teakettle. "Who came over?"

"Let's finish with this and sit."

"W-why?" she stuttered. "Did something happen with the twins I should know about?"

"They're fine. One hundred percent A-OK. I'm just exhausted."

Sarah abided the temporary stay of execution, waiting for my ass to hit the library couch cushion. "Who came?"

"We ended up babysitting Demi."

"We?"

"The twins and I. Who else? Do you think we have to file taxes for them? Ollie charged Peter top dollar."

Sarah was amused. "I'm sure she did."

"Peter ended up staying for Chinese, which he provided without any prompting." I sipped my tea, grateful for the full-bodied flavor of Earl Grey.

"And, here I thought you'd have too much time on your hands."

"Yeah, that's the complaint of all single mothers."

"Don't say it like that." She glared at me. "Any other unexpected visitors?" I'd seen that expression before. The one that implied she already knew everything.

"Allen invited a friend over for coffee. He's at the campus to hear a Russian author speak."

"It's possible your brother is nerdier than you."

I feigned being hurt.

Sarah swiveled her body on the couch and placed her feet in my lap, snapping her eyes shut. "Can you massage them? Spending a weekend in the same hotel room as Maddie was exhausting."

"Anything I should know about?" I used my best *jealous wife* voice.

Sarah cracked open one eye. "She snores."

I dispensed with my tea and grasped one of her feet.

Sarah let out a moan.

Neither of us spoke, and I'd never welcomed silence as much as I cheered inside for it now. Was it necessary to mention Meg's name? I'd said Allen invited a friend over, which wasn't a lie. Did I have to go the final step by revealing a name? Although, there was Sarah's *I know everything* look earlier.

Was she testing me?

The name of the game was diversion. "Ethan's worried Lisa wants a divorce." Yep, I totally just tossed my best friend under the proverbial bus.

She laughed.

"No, seriously. He's really concerned. When he was here Friday, he joked I shouldn't answer the door so he could avoid getting served with papers."

Sarah opened her eyes. "I hadn't realized Lisa had reached her breaking point."

"Ethan can't be an easy man to be married to... with his quirks."

She nodded. "True. He's an outstanding father, though. Funny, charming, protective—"

I busted in, laughing. "Come on."

"No, I'm serious. Lisa told me about a college incident when Ethan beat the shit out of some dude who wouldn't take no for an answer."

It was difficult to reconcile the image of the lanky man who'd sat in the family room reading my childhood copy of *Little Women* cracking someone's skull. "He's never told me a thing about it."

"His grandfather had to pull some strings to purge his arrest."

"He was arrested?" My voice sounded like a startled chipmunk.

"Cops tend to get involved when you put someone in the hospital."

I stared wide-eyed for a moment. "Wow. I had no idea. And this is one of his selling points?"

"Depends what side you're on. If someone tried to—"

I motioned for her not to say the word. "I don't want to think of it."

"Exactly."

I resumed massaging Sarah's foot. "Do you think she'll leave him?"

Sarah raised one shoulder. "They've been fighting about this issue for months now. Lisa has always wanted a big family. She claims Ethan knew this before getting hitched, but he's conveniently expunged the memory."

"Again, he never mentioned this to me."

"Ethan doesn't really share all that much." She let out a moan, which was surely in response to the foot massage, not Ethan's cageyness.

I thought this over. "No wonder we always got along."

Sarah playfully kicked me. "Look where it's leading Ethan."

"Don't even joke about that. Although, maybe matchmaking can become your hobby. I think Peter and Tie are cruising toward divorce court."

"Your brother's situation doesn't surprise me. I'm pretty sure he never got over Maddie and thought getting married would be the best way to bury his feelings once and for all. If I remember correctly, I bet you Peter would ask her for a divorce sooner rather than later." Her victorious smile faded quickly and she sighed when I dug my fingers into her left foot. "I do hope Ethan and Lisa can work things out."

"Me, too. Now that the weekend is over, I never want to be a single parent again. Ever." I nodded my head with emphasis.

"Luckily you don't have to worry about it." She took a drink of her coffee.

"No matter what?" I asked.

"Are you ready to spill yet?"

"You were testing me?" I squeezed her foot.

"If I keep at it, will you continue?" She wore a look of extreme pleasure.

"If I can avoid getting hand cramps. How'd you know, by the way?"

"Helen mentioned something that wasn't your fault."

I smiled. "I like her style. She didn't bust me but gave you enough to ask, all the while planting the seed of my innocence."

"She cares a lot about you."

"Like put *someone in the hospital* level?"

"You're stalling." She motioned for me to get it over with.

"Allen's friend was Meg."

Sarah blinked as if I'd spoken in Russian.

I opted to get it all out. "She was in our house. Interacted with the twins. Had a cup of coffee."

"And?"

"Helen helped me dispatch Allen and Meg before you

arrived home. She's picking him up and hopefully will have a conversation about not inviting my ex to our house without permission." I sighed, knowing Allen wasn't entirely at fault. If I'd been honest with him before the conference, all of this could have been avoided.

"I see." Ironically, she closed her eyes, blunting me out of her vision. Or was she imagining me interacting with Meg in our house? Meg meeting our children?

"I didn't invite her. I swear!"

"What's the Allen angle she's playing?" Her eyes popped open, and she was much calmer than I'd anticipated.

"Helen is trying to figure that out as well. Are you mad at me? Should I avoid answering the door?"

"Oh, I'm mad. Not at you, though. And not at Allen. He really has no clue when it comes to Meg." She remained stoic, although I was willing to bet thoughts raced through her mind.

"You don't seem like your normal mad self. You're too calm. And that's really scaring me." I sat back.

As if I hadn't spoken, Sarah continued. "Maybe it's time for Meg and I to have a sit-down."

"You want to have her over for dinner or something?" The mere thought made me want to vomit.

Sarah gave me the smile when she thought I was being obtuse. "No. It'll be just the two of us."

"I'm not so sure that's a good idea. Ethan's grandfather isn't around anymore to offer a *get out of jail free* card."

"Trust me; Mom knows all the right people in certain situations." Her continued carefree body language was getting creepier.

"Can I think about this?"

Sarah slanted her head. "Why?"

"Because I don't trust Meg. She's given me a black eye and—"

"It won't come to that." Her fingers wrapped around the coffee cup, python-like.

"You don't know Meg."

"If you truly fear her that much, you need to tell Allen. Or at least Helen."

"I hate this. It's hard enough with you knowing everything, and you've been witness to some of my most embarrassing moments. Aside from you and my therapist, I never wanted to tell another soul about what it was like with Meg. The shit she put me through." I sighed, massaging my eyes with my thumb and forefinger. "Why did she have to come back? And why did she have to complete her PhD? Academia is a cesspool for drama. Who knows what she'll do to get even if spurned?"

Sarah came to me, pulling my head to her chest. "I got you. We'll get through this together."

"Thanks," I mumbled into her sweater.

"For?"

"Not jumping to conclusions. I'm not sure what I would have done in your shoes."

She squeezed me tighter. "Maybe thousands of dollars spent on couple's therapy really does help."

I laughed. "Perhaps. And you only joked about taking Meg out."

"Who said I was joking?"

Neither of us spoke for several seconds.

"Come on," Sarah said. "Let's get dinner ready for the twinks and pack their overnight bags. Tonight is you and me time."

* * *

RELAXING IN A BUBBLE BATH, I rested my head on the lip of the tub. "You know, I never got those *Calgon take me away* commercials when I was younger."

Pressed against me, Sarah said, "I think it takes a parent to realize how tiring life can be." She sat up, plunged the bath sponge into the water, and then squeezed it over her shoulder, down her back.

"Can I help you, my dear?"

She nodded, dropping the natural sea sponge into the water.

I applied a generous amount of mint tea body scrub onto the sponge and cleaned her back with circular motions. "According to the directions, I should repeat the process."

"Yes. And it's ideal for reinvigorating weary legs."

"That's an odd attribute." I picked it up to read more but couldn't make out the tiny print in the dim lighting. Setting it on the ledge, I asked, "What does it do for your boobs?"

"Less talk, more revitalizing."

"Flip around so I can work on your legs."

She managed to change positions, only slopping a small amount of water onto the bath mat. "Oh, that feels good."

I worked the sponge between her toes.

"Jesus, this is almost better than sex."

"Lucky you."

Sarah cracked an eye open. "Why's that?"

"Are you kidding me? After ditching me with the twins for the weekend, you think I'm putting out tonight?" I stopped ministering the sponge. "Shouldn't you be pampering *me*? To show your undying love?"

"After you finish, I promise," she said, the tiredness evident in the way her words slurred.

"It's only seven at night, and we're the walking wounded."

Her eyes lit up. "I have a great idea. Let's put on some relaxing music, climb under the covers, and take a nap."

"I'm pretty sure when you fall asleep two hours before bedtime it's not a nap. It's called throwing in the towel."

"Got a problem with that?" She arched her brow.

"Screw revitalizing my legs." I climbed out of the tub. "Put me to bed."

She laughed, climbing out of the water. "When did we turn into fuddy- duddies?"

"When you decided to have twins." I flattened the tip of her perky nose with my finger.

"Why do I always get blamed for that?" She wrapped a towel around her body.

"I don't remember asking you if I could suck eggs out of your body. Pajamas or au naturel?"

"You had the easy part. I gave birth to them. PJs—the flannels. It's a bit chilly but not cold enough to flip on the heat."

I bobbed my head enthusiastically. "Perfect, we might as well go all the way, Grandma."

We dressed in our cozy pajamas, got under the covers, and snuggled in each other's arms.

"If anyone asks, we had wild and passionate sex on our free night after being apart all weekend," Sarah said, her eyes already shut, and from the limpness in her body, she was on the express train to Sleepville.

"Who's going to ask that?" I nuzzled my nose in her hair. "I missed your scent. Sleeping with your pillow is not the same thing."

"Shush. It's sleepy time."

While Sarah drifted off to sleep, I held her. Even though my body screamed for rest, my brain decided to switch into hyperdrive. There was one surefire way to short-circuit my thoughts, but Sarah was sound asleep and it seemed rude to masturbate with her in the bed.

I waited until I was absolutely certain she wouldn't wake even if a tornado ripped through the room. Then I got up and headed for my office. The second, albeit less satisfying, way to stifle my swirling thoughts was work.

The library was shrouded in darkness, and I opted not to

flip the lights on. It might sound a little too history nerdish, but I liked to write in the dark, like so many night owls in bygone eras. Although, they had used candles, while I got by with the glow of my laptop. Once, I lit a candle to help channel the ambiance, but I fell asleep at my desk, and the thought of burning the house down put an end to that.

I had a stack of blue books that needed grading. If I chained myself to my desk for three hours, I could return the tests to my students on Tuesday instead of Thursday, beating my typical seven-day turnaround.

"This is the life, Lizzie." I grabbed the first exam and my bright blue markup pencil.

* * *

AROUND NINE THE FOLLOWING MORNING, Rose arrived with the twins. "Did you two have a nice night?"

The three of us sat at the kitchen table. Freddie sat on my lap, and with the way Ollie jiggled up and down in her bouncy chair, I wondered if she was attempting to launch herself into space.

"The best," Sarah practically purred, looking refreshed.

I got up to make another cup of tea. Handing Fred to Rose, I asked, "More coffee?"

Rose nodded, while Sarah indicated she was good.

"Have you two made plans for Thanksgiving yet?" Rose asked.

Since reconciling with my family and having twins, planning holidays had become drastically more difficult.

"I'm thinking of having everyone here," Sarah said.

This was news to me. "Who's everyone?"

"Mom and Troy, of course. Maddie and Gabe. Your dad and Helen. Allen." She tapped a fingernail against her front tooth. "Peter and Tie. Hopefully, they won't bicker the entire time." It was clear she was making everything up on the fly, which wasn't her usual MO when it came to planning.

I eyed our double oven, which hadn't been used much unless you counted storing baking dishes.

Before I could point out the obvious, Sarah had already started the text invites.

"Maybe we can hire Miranda to cook," I said more to myself.

"You don't think I can manage a turkey?" Sarah's tone was playful with a pinch of a challenge. "Maddie and Gabe are in. So are Peter and Tie," she continued reading her phone before asking, "Is Bailey going home?"

I refilled Rose's coffee, shrugging.

"Maddie wants to invite Jorie." Sarah looked at me. "Sounds like she has a difficult family situation."

"Okay."

Thanksgiving was quickly slipping into the *family and friend* quicksand I'd avoided for so many years.

"What about Troy's mom?" Sarah asked.

Rose shook her head. "Still not talking to Troy or me."

Sarah retrieved a notepad from the desk drawer along the kitchen wall. "That's twelve, not counting the twinks and Demi. What size turkey feeds a dozen adults?" Her phone vibrated. "Oh." She looked at me, and then her eyes dropped to her empty coffee mug. "Actually, I'll have another cup." She got to her feet, sweeping her phone and mug into her hand.

Rose raised a quizzical brow but didn't press.

"Charles and Helen are coming," Sarah hollered, although she was only ten feet away. "And Allen and guest, which I think is Bailey. That gives us an odd number. Now, I need to track down one more." Sarah stood at the counter, furiously drafting her Thanksgiving battle plan on the notepad, looking more comfortable by the second. Sarah and her plans.

"Do you ever miss living like an orphan?" Rose whispered, quickly followed with a sneeze.

I stifled a laugh.

Sarah glanced in our direction. "Neither of you think I can manage this?"

"Not true." I guzzled my tea. "I need to head to campus. Staff meeting."

"I'll have you know our Christmas shindig last year was a big success. Huge. And everyone is still talking about the twins' birthday." Sarah placed a hand on her hip.

"I'm still paying the bills. Please, no bouncy castle. The twins hated it." She started to complain, but I swooped in with a timely kiss. "Love you, Martha."

"Martha Stewart will be jealous of my Thanksgiving!" Sarah shouted after me. "Maddie, I need to call Maddie."

I mouthed "Help me" to Rose on my way out, but she wore a look of defeat. When Sarah put her mind to these matters, it was either get in line or... I didn't know what.

The last thing I heard before the door shut was, "We need to go hiking for pinecones!"

Because buying pinecones would ruin the authenticity. Heaven forbid. I hoped hiking for pinecones didn't morph into hunting for turkey.

CHAPTER TWENTY-THREE

Sarah slammed her laptop closed and tossed it to the side of the bed. "Where's your laptop?"

"In the library. Why?" I asked.

"Mine isn't cooperating." She started to lift the bedcovers.

I laid my book on top of the comforter. "I don't think slamming it shut helps." I flipped hers open to see if I could coax some life back into it.

"Does that mean you don't want me to use your laptop?" Her tone could slice through one-inch thick metal.

"By all means, but I'm secretly pleased with my routine of backing everything up if you plan to destroy mine like this poor thing. Ah, the Blue Screen of Death."

"So funny." Sarah gave me the hairy eyeball.

She'd only started planning Thanksgiving this morning, and already, she was impossible to be around. Was it too much to ask to read a novel for twenty minutes before bed? At this rate, it'll take me a year to read all four hundred plus pages.

I tried keying in a few commands. "Maybe it's time for a new one, after all," I said to myself since Sarah had zipped downstairs. I closed it and picked my book back up.

"What's this?" Sarah stood in the doorway, holding a slip of paper in the air.

"Where's my laptop?"

"Downstairs." She marched to the foot of the bed, balled up the paper, and chucked it at my face. "Explain."

I flattened the paper and saw a note I'd jotted down. "It's for something I'm working on," I said, my eyes avoiding hers.

"For a journal article?"

"More like a book," I hedged.

"You're writing a book that will include the line, 'When I saw her across the field, I knew I wanted her, but giving in would be a grave mistake'? Tell me, Lizzie, what figure in World War Two said those words? Hitler? Goring? Churchill?"

"It's not a direct quote."

"It has quote marks." She tapped the paper. "Give it to me straight. Is this about Meg? You said that day she found you on the quad. Did you replace that with field to sound more historical?"

I swallowed, not wanting to clear the air but also aghast she'd jumped straight to Meg.

"Is our"—she waved her hand around the room and to the nursery—"family life too much for you?"

"You have the wrong idea." I tossed her laptop to the side so I could go to her, but Sarah stomped down the hallway on a rampage. The only thing I could do was follow her.

We ended up in the library, the supposed scene of the crime, where Sarah envisioned I stayed up late pining for Meg.

"Show me!" She jabbed a finger in the direction of my laptop. "Show me the *book* you're working on." She made quote marks.

"It's—"

"Not in a book. Why in the world would you jot this down and then leave it out for me to find? Are you too chicken shit to admit it to me? Is that it? All this talk about drawing a line in the sand." Her words came out quickly, and her nostrils flared. "Did Allen invite Meg over to our house? Or did you? Did you ask Allen to extend an invitation?"

"Remember last night when you said couples' therapy had really helped us? I think it's safe to say that's a crock of shit. You find one note, and now all of a sudden, I don't want to be married or have kids. All so I can be with the one person I can't stand being around. And, I'm using my brother to reach this goal."

"Allen says she's helping you with a journal article."

"When she bumped into me at Starbucks, she offered to read it."

"And you accepted, in spite of the fact you *can't stand being around* her?" She made quote marks. "Isn't that what you just said?"

"I'm not going to take her up on it!" My brain was spinning, trying to figure out how her mind pinballed from one scenario to the next. "I can't do this now. There's no talking sense into you—"

"Oh, am I being a woman? Irrational?" Angry tears threatened to spill. "How long have you felt this way about Meg? Since she came back or the whole fucking time?"

"I can't believe you're saying this… crap!" I paced from the desk to the bay window and back again.

"You'll be happy to know Meg's coming to Thanksgiving. She's Allen's plus one. Not Bailey."

I stopped in midstride and pivoted around. "What are you talking about?"

"Allen asked if he could invite a friend. I said yes, assuming he meant Bailey. Turns out he invited Meg, and she jumped at the chance. Apparently, she's pining after you as well."

"Disinvite her!" I sliced my right hand in a downward motion, slamming into my open palm, guillotine-like.

"Why? You clearly still love her. Maybe she can move in. We can be lesbian Mormons."

"You're not making any sense!" I covered my eyes with my palms. "Please, sit."

"Don't tell me what to do," she said through clenched teeth.

I took a deep breath and then released it slowly. I opened my laptop. "The line from the note isn't in the book yet. I had the idea in the car on my way home from campus, and I haven't had time to include it. But I plan to add it to this." I opened the Word doc. "It's a first draft, so... I'm not sold on the title."

Sarah didn't budge, and from the fleeting looks of anger and guilt, I imagined she was already regretting her flip-out session.

I turned the laptop around for her to see.

"'Torn, A Novel by Lizzie Petrie,'" she whispered.

I hit the page down key until landing on the dedication: *For my loving wife, Sarah.*

She spoke through the cracks of her fingers. "You're writing a novel?"

"Not sure I'd go that far. An idea struck me and..." I shrugged for her to fill in the blank. "It's about two nurses in World War Two who fall in love, but the war and society, not to mention the fear of being killed, tear them apart. They meet up again by chance twenty years later."

"Oh," Sarah said, her voice matching the shock on her face.

"No one's read it yet. If you must, have at it." I went to leave the room, but Sarah reached for my hand. I shook her off. "I don't think it's wise for me to be around you right now." I stared at her, breathing heavily. "How could you even think those things? Let alone fling them at me at first chance as if you've been waiting ever since you heard Meg was back in town? What do I need to do to prove to you I'm worthy of your love and trust?"

Sarah collapsed on the arm of the couch. "I'm sorry. So sorry."

"Me, too."

"What are you sorry about?"

"How can I forget your accusations?" I tapped the side of my head as a way of saying the words still rang loud and clear.

"What do you mean?" Panic seized her eyes.

"You accused me of not wanting to be here with you and the twinks." I took a step back. "I don't know what to say or think right now, but I can't be here." With that, I left the room and headed for the garage.

She chased after me. "You're in your pajamas and socks."

I stabbed my hand in the air, indicating she shouldn't try to stop me.

"At least put on a jacket."

I grabbed one from the hook by the door. "Better?"

"Where are you going?"

"To talk to someone who wants me in their life. Use your imagination."

CHAPTER TWENTY-FOUR

I didn't go to Meg's as I'd insinuated, which I regretted as soon as the words flew out of my mouth. Actually, when I backed out of the garage, I had zero idea of where I was going. It wasn't until I turned on the highway that I realized I was driving to Dad and Helen's place.

I needed a parent.

And the one I sought was Helen.

Outside their home, I texted Helen, not really expecting a reply considering the late hour. It was well after eleven. When my phone lit up, my gut said it was an urgent text from Sarah, but it was a reply from Helen. Soon after, the entryway light switched on.

In the door was my father.

I climbed out of the SUV.

"Helen's getting dressed."

My father had on a bathrobe and sunshine yellow slippers with two googly eyeballs on each. His gaze followed mine, "Oh, these are Helen's." His tone gave me the impression he was lying. Was this how my father dealt with stress? Silly slippers?

"They're colorful."

"Where are your shoes?" He pointed a chubby finger at my feet.

"I left in a hurry. Is it illegal to drive in socks?" Talking about my feet made me realize how cold the cement was. Snow hadn't arrived yet, but it still wasn't *thin sock sans shoes* temperature.

My father pondered the question as if it were perfectly natural to show up in the middle of the night to discuss the legality of driving without shoes. "I'll have to ask Matthew."

Yes, his chauffeur would know. That was the perfect Petrie response.

"You must be half frozen." Helen stepped off the staircase and wrapped an arm around my shoulders, steering us to the kitchen. "Let's get some hot chocolate going."

It was the first time a motherly figure had offered to make me hot chocolate in the middle of a crisis.

Much to my surprise, Dad followed. I hadn't expected this turn of events.

The two busied themselves heating the milk and locating the cocoa powder. Soon, the three of us sat at the small table in the nook.

No one seemed anxious to prod me to speak.

"We're looking forward to Thanksgiving," Dad said, clearly doing his best to come up with small talk.

"Does Sarah need any help?" Helen offered a helpless smile.

"It's almost your first wedding anniversary," I blurted.

"Cap, why don't you get the fire going in the family room?" Helen tightened her robe.

Dad shuffled out, still wearing the ridiculous slippers.

"Did you and Sarah have a fight?"

"She picked a fight with me." I took a sip, not caring that it was *rip several layers off* temperature.

"What happened?"

Flickering light from the fireplace in the next room beckoned, and we sought the warmth.

I filled them in on the events that had transpired.

"I never liked Meg," Dad tossed out.

This was the first time he'd said anything of the sort.

"I don't trust her," Helen said.

Even they were focusing on the Meg aspect.

"But, that doesn't excuse Sarah leaping to conclusions," Helen added, looking thoughtfully at her husband.

"No, it doesn't," he said gruffly, but there was a trace of humor in his eyes. "Although, I seem to remember you saying some harsh words to me in the past."

"And you tossing back ugly ones yourself."

They smiled fondly at each other. I didn't get it. How could memories of fights elicit this closeness?

"I know you're angry, Lizzie, and you have every right to be. But ask yourself something. Were Sarah's words so hurtful you're willing to chuck everything you two have built up?" Helen asked.

"I'm not asking her for a divorce or anything. I-I... just needed space," I said a little defensively.

"But you're here. Not there. I imagine Sarah is worried sick. Did you let her know you're here with us?"

I shook my head.

Helen slipped her phone out of the pocket of her bathrobe, making me laugh. She was more connected to the outside world than I was. That, though, wasn't saying much.

"Take it from a couple of old geezers who made things a lot harder on themselves than they needed to but still found a way to make everything work. Running doesn't help. Relationships are tough. I'm willing to bet this isn't the first time you two have exchanged harsh words. And it won't be the last." Helen let that sink in before continuing, "Love is complicated, and it can drive even the most rational to say and do things that are out of character. Add in the stress of parenthood and Sarah may feel isolated staying at home. I can see why she saw Meg, who just finished her PhD, as a threat."

I stared at Helen, wanting to accept her advice while simultaneously not willing to budge.

"It would be a terrible world if we couldn't forgive the ones we love when they're careless," she said.

Dad nodded his agreement.

"Stay the night. Get some sleep." Helen rose as if everything were settled.

"There's more to… it."

Helen retook her seat.

I looked at her and then Dad. "There's more to the Meg situation." I sniffed, glancing upward. "I never wanted people to find out, but we don't always get what we want." I made eye contact with Helen. "I've been feeling so guilty for not telling you since Allen has latched onto her and vice versa."

It wasn't easy, but I told them everything about Meg.

* * *

I ARRIVED home before anyone was up.

When I entered the nursery, Freddie, wide-eyed, quietly writhed, grabbing his feet with both hands.

"Good morning, little man. Did you have sweet dreams?"

He gave me a quizzical grimace.

"How about you, Ollie Dollie?"

She was unusually quiet, giving me pause.

Had the twins overheard the argument? Sarah had texted that they were sleeping peacefully when I inquired last night after my heart-to-heart.

"Morning." Sarah stood in the doorway, her voice gravelly from lack of sleep.

"Hey," I said. "You okay?"

"Am I?"

I had to smile. "I think so."

She studied me for several seconds. "I'm glad you're home."

"Me, too. Shall we start a new day in the Petrie-Cavanaugh home?"

That was met with a round of giggles from the twinks.

"I love that sound," I said, keeping my eyes on Sarah. "I'm sorry about last night."

She let out a puff of air. "I'm pretty sure I was in the wrong."

I cupped my ear. "Did you hear that, Twinks? Mommy said she was wrong. Go ahead; repeat it." I gestured to Sarah.

She shook her head, but her laughter showed her relief. "Other mommy shouldn't be so cocky." She lifted Ollie into her arms.

"I'm on a roll these days." I hoisted Freddie up. "Let's get you changed and ready for breakfast."

"Helen texted me this morning telling me I should do this." She wrapped me and Freddie in a tight hug.

"I told them," I said into her ear.

Sarah pulled away, her arms still on my shoulders. "About the fight?"

"Yes. And the ugly truth about Meg. Allen is the next stop on my confessions tour. If I'd come clean earlier, all of this could have been avoided. I'm so... ashamed. About everything."

Sarah held me with the twins in the middle.

* * *

I SAT AT THE TABLE, watching Sarah feed the twins.

She eyed me. "What?"

"Do you really think Lisa will divorce Ethan?"

"Time will tell."

"I can't imagine that. Not being with all of you each day. Last night, after I'd been driving for an hour, I thought to myself, 'What are you doing, Lizzie?' And waking alone in a strange bed—I hated it."

"Why didn't you turn around last night?"

"Stupid pride." I added, "And, I was still angry."

"I read your novel." Her voice held no emotion.

"Writing it is just something I do to help me relax." I shifted in my seat, staring at my feet, remembering my dad's slippers. "I don't intend for it to go anywhere."

Sarah set the spoon down. "It's good, Lizzie. Surprisingly good."

"Truly?" I perked up. "You aren't just saying that?"

She smiled. "You might have a shot at making the *New York Times* bestsellers list for non-fiction *and* fiction."

I waved for her to stop. "Now you're teasing me."

"Remember this day, Twinks. I was the first to predict Mommy's book will shoot up the charts. All she needs to do is finish it."

"Ah, famous last words. *Finish it*."

"F-finish," Freddie said. "Fff-finish." He kept saying it.

Sarah and I looked at each other and then at Fred.

Sarah smiled victoriously. "If that's not a sign, I don't know what is." She turned to our son. "You believe in Mommy?"

He reached for Sarah's cheeks, pinching them.

CHAPTER TWENTY-FIVE

"Did you pick up the turkey?" Sarah tucked a pen behind her ear.

"It's in the fridge in the basement." I stuffed student essays into my briefcase. While the students were off for the week, I had grading, two final lectures to prep, edits to make to a journal article, and emails to answer. Thanksgiving couldn't have come at a more inconvenient time, although I did have the week off, so to speak, because of the national holiday. "I won't be on campus too long." I hoped, at least.

"Can you pick up some stuff from the store on your way home?" She shoved a list into my hand.

I scanned it. "What's a sugar pumpkin, and why does it have to be exactly three pounds?"

She took the list back. "On second thought, I'll order everything online. Can you pick it up?"

"Of course, Martha." I kissed her cheek. "Bye, Twinks!" I waved, but they were too busy painting paper plate turkeys Bailey had prepped for them.

"Don't forget the store," Sarah warned. "Or it's off with your head."

I laughed.

Sarah's glare zapped my laughter.

"Tough crowd." I slipped through the door, suddenly relieved to be heading to the office with a to-do list a mile long the day before Thanksgiving.

* * *

AROUND THREE, there was a knock on the office door.

"Come in," I said, not looking up, expecting a fellow professor.

"I've always admired your dedication."

I glanced up from the essay I was grading, red pen clenched between my teeth. "Hey, there. Wasn't expecting you," I mumbled with the pen in my mouth.

Meg sat down. "I had a feeling I'd find you here. You haven't been answering my texts."

I yanked the pen out of my mouth, afraid I'd bite through it, staining my lips and face. "What's up?"

Meg took one of the essays off the completed stack and flipped it to the back. "C minus." She whistled. "Are you in a bad mood?"

"I should have given him a D minus." I flicked my hands up. "I'm feeling generous. Holiday spirit, I guess."

She nodded, tossing it back onto the pile.

I lined it up exactly with the others. "Something tells me you didn't stop by to discuss my grading style."

Meg crossed one leg over her other, fiddling with the shoe-string on her snow boot. "You ready for Thanksgiving?"

I leaned back into the desk chair, my arms overhead, and straightened out my legs. "Is anyone ever really ready?"

"I was surprised when Allen texted it wouldn't be convenient for me to come." She arched a questioning brow.

I sucked my lips into my mouth.

"Was that your doing?"

I hadn't talked to him yet, but Helen had been adamant Meg wasn't allowed and she thought it important for Allen to send the text so Meg would hear loud and clear to stay away.

"Do you really have to ask?" I leveled my eyes on hers, unable to determine what thoughts went on under her stony expression. "Setting aside all the shit you put me through when we were together, followed by the months of blackmail, you nearly wrecked my chances with Sarah after your performance in the hotel. Did you really think you could swoop back into town, say sorry, and we could pick up where we left off?"

"And this has to interfere with my friendship with Allen?" She innocently batted her eyelashes.

I shook my head, whistling. "You have cojones. I'll give you that. I know you, and I remember what it was like to be around you, when you made me feel like I was your entire world. You can be intoxicating. You need people to adore you, and Allen is sweet. Vulnerable, even."

"*Intoxicating.* Interesting word choice and"—she looked to the ceiling—"intentional. Never thought you'd throw my addiction in my face."

There wasn't a need to confirm or to get into a battle.

Meg met my eyes. "I like Allen. His excitement about history is infectious. He's helped me fall in love with it again. For that, I'm truly thankful."

I suppressed a groan. "He's not the only person on the planet who has passion."

"You don't get it. How alone I feel. Holidays are killer for people like me." She avoided my eyes. "I... had a minor slipup." There was overwhelming sadness in her voice, which came across as real.

"When?"

"After being disinvited from Thanksgiving. Not that I blame

Allen or you." She was halfway convincing. "I worked through it with my sponsor."

"I don't know how this works, what constitutes a minor slipup, or if it'll lead to…" I shrugged helplessly, unsure how much I believed and peeved she was playing the victim.

"Me neither. But I do know I can't afford to majorly fuck up, Lizzie. I won't come back from it if I do. I feel it in my bones." Actual tears spilled from her eyes. "I need help. I'm terrified."

"Shall I call your sponsor? Would rehab help?"

"I'm tired of rehab!" Her anger dissipated quickly. She interlaced her fingers, moving them about as if trying to break all the bones. "I thought you'd help me."

"You're putting me in a terrible position. Part of me believes you. The other… Jesus, how do you expect me to rush in and help you after everything? Because you said you were sorry?"

She stared at me for several tense moments. Then, she started to rise.

I gestured for her to sit back down. "No, please, hear what I have to say. This may not be the best timing, but I've been working up the nerve to say it since you came back."

Meg slumped into the seat, pulling one knee to her chest.

"When we were together, after one of your benders that ended with you saying or doing terrible things, you'd brush it off by apologizing, followed by you being on your best behavior until the next time. Each time I believed you… or wanted to. And, each time you let me down." I looked her in the eyes. "Now, you're back and even if you aren't aware of it, you're acting the same way. You've apologized and been on semi-decent behavior. You've even offered to help me with my research, which is another thing you used to do back then." I fiddled with the red pen. "I want the best for you. I always have. But you can't expect me to blindly believe you because you say I should. You also can't expect me to bend over backward to be your rock. I have a wife, children, and… a grocery order I need to pick up for Thanksgiving." Probably shouldn't have said the last part, like I was rubbing in the fact she was disinvited. I steadied my thoughts with a deep breath. What would Sarah do? Although, when it came to Meg, Sarah wasn't the best source of advice. Thank God, Sarah never had a *come to Jesus* chat with Meg, or my wife may be behind bars for the holiday. I made my decision. "Having said that, right now, I'll do what I can to help." I typed *nearest AA meetings* into my phone. "There's an AA meeting starting in twenty minutes right off campus. I'll drive you over."

* * *

I ARRIVED home a little after six. I'd texted Sarah, giving her enough details to clue her in to the Meg dilemma so she wouldn't rip my head off for not being able to pick up the grocery order.

Maddie, Bailey, and Jorie were at the kitchen table, decorating sugar cookies.

"Jorie, how nice of you to help out," I said. "I see Max and Casey are here as well. It's a full house."

The kids were watching *It's the Great Pumpkin, Charlie Brown.*

The phone rang, and Sarah answered it before the second ring.

Rose and Troy traipsed in, their hands full with baking dishes.

Sarah, already off the phone, laughed, taking the pan from Troy's hands. "It's not usually this crazy here. Can I get you anything before I put you to work?"

"I recommend the hot chocolate with cinnamon." Maddie motioned to her empty cup. "I'll have another."

"That's my cue, isn't it?" I shed my jacket and pushed my sweater sleeves up. "How many hot chocolates?"

Everyone's hand went in the air, including Casey's.

"I'll help you," Sarah said.

"Where's Ethan?" I asked Sarah when we were out of earshot.

"With Lisa having a chat. Casey is staying the night." Sarah inched closer. "Are you okay?"

I rattled the box of Red Hots. "Do we have more?"

Sarah didn't push me. She ransacked through the bags that hadn't been unpacked yet. "Here." She handed over a new box. "I'll collect the mugs."

She returned, setting up an assembly line.

"Do you know whose is whose?" I started to pour hot milk into the mugs.

"Their names are on them."

Sure enough, each of the cheap mugs had permanent marker on it. "Are those boobs on Maddie's?"

"Sometimes, it's best not to ask questions." Sarah shrugged. "I think that's the motto for the next twenty-four hours."

That was Sarah's way of telling me she would go with the flow.

"What's taking so long?" Maddie shouted. "The working conditions in this household are inhumane!"

Allen arrived, brushing snow off the hood of his CU sweatshirt.

"Hot chocolate?" Sarah asked.

"Please." He blew into his hands.

"Tell you what. Why don't you take mine into the library?" I gave him my mug. "I'll join you in a second to have a chat about Meg."

* * *

AROUND MIDNIGHT, Sarah and I finally retired to the bedroom.

"What a day." Sarah fell onto the bed, tossing an arm over her face.

"Why did you think it was a good idea to invite everyone over for Thanksgiving?" I yawned.

"Don't start with me."

I climbed onto the bed next to her. "Thanks."

She peeked under her arm. "For?"

"Not pushing me earlier."

Sarah propped herself on bent elbows. "Do you trust her?"

I placed my hand on Sarah's stomach. "No. But, I'd hate myself if I turned my back when she really needed me. Besides, taking her to an AA meeting…" I closed my eyes. Meg had asked me to attend with her and the stories I heard tore at my insides, but I'd never share them with anyone. "This way I won't feel like the world's worst ex-girlfriend."

"Because she was the best when you dated?"

"I know what you're saying, and I get your frustration. I need you to believe me when I say I don't trust Meg. I told her that. But, just because she wasn't nice to me, doesn't mean I have to treat her the same way."

"Are you positive she won't show up tomorrow?"

"I made it clear she wasn't wanted. She was invited to a potluck tomorrow, and I think she'll go. The people were really supportive. It's good to know she has groups like that she can go to… when she needs it." I swallowed. "And, if she does show up, I'll refuse entry."

"I'm proud of you." Sarah pulled me into her arms. "Let's get some rest. I have a feeling tomorrow won't be easy. Oh, Demi is staying with us for the weekend."

"Let me get this straight. Casey and Demi are our new wards?"

"Don't forget Jorie and Max." Sarah yawned. "God help us."

* * *

SARAH, at the head of the table, tapped her wineglass with her knife. When everyone quieted down, after Maddie let rip a deafening whistle, followed by a threat for everyone to be quiet, Sarah rose.

"I wanted to thank all of you for coming to Thanksgiving. It's days like this that remind us how lucky we are to have so many in our lives to help us celebrate not only holidays and birthdays but every day. I'd like to go around the table and have each one of you say what you're thankful for. Helen, you're on my right, so you get to start us off."

Helen beamed at Sarah. "I'm truly thankful for all of you allowing me and my boys into the family fold. We haven't been an official family for that long, but the way all of you act makes it seem like we always have been. For better or worse." She laughed.

Dad said, "Ditto and thanks for not making me carve the turkey or grill steaks."

"No need for a trip to the ER." Helen patted his cheek.

Gabe laughed. "Can't let you massacre another steak, and I love carving a turkey." He looked to Maddie. "I'm thankful for this one." He raised Maddie's hand to his lips and kissed her fingertips softly.

I noticed Peter suppress a shudder.

Maddie, not usually at a loss for words, said, "Ditto."

Rose glanced at Sarah and then Troy. "I'm thankful to have the love and support of my daughters." Her eyes landed on me.

I smiled, willing away the wetness in the corner of my eyes. The one bonus to the Troy issue was Rose finally forgiving me.

Tie was next, and I gripped the edge of the table.

She cleared her throat. "Well, where do I begin?" Tie glanced at her husband, who stared defiantly at her. "I'm thankful to be able to spend the day with Peter, who works… so many hours… and golfs even more."

Before she could go into attack mode, I said, "Jorie?"

Tie shot me a withering look, and I grinned broadly.

"I'm thankful to be included in the Petrie festivities and for you allowing Max to hang with the kids." Jorie bobbed her head toward the kids' table tucked into the corner, with Casey as the de facto adult.

Ethan and Lisa laughed when Casey instructed Freddie to eat some turkey or he wouldn't get any pie, which Fred ignored.

Everyone else spoke, leaving Allen last.

He stood with his water glass in his right hand. "There's not much I can add to the list since most stole my reasons for why I'm grateful to have all of you in my life. But, I would like to offer a toast to Lizzie, who is a kindred spirit, brave, and the best big sister I could ask for."

"Here, here." Maddie banged her fist on the table.

"Don't you dare spill the red wine on the tablecloth." Sarah reached for her glass before it could topple.

After dinner, while most of the guests were in the living room, I found Allen and Bailey snuggling on the couch in the family room, watching *It's A Wonderful Life*. "Hey, you two."

"I need… something." Bailey got to her feet, patting my shoulder as she fled.

I sat down next to Allen, the leather couch creaking. "I may have eaten too much today."

He laughed, patting his Rudolph sweater. "Me too."

I rubbed my chin. "Thanks for saying those words earlier. I wasn't sure how you'd feel after our chat last night."

"I meant what I said." His eyes fell to the newly purchased soft blue afghan on his lap. "I had no idea she put you through all that. I'm sorry for inviting her to that dinner and bringing her to your home."

"Hey now. You have nothing to be sorry for. I should have been upfront right from the start. It's not easy for me to admit… weaknesses."

He nodded as if he understood. "For the record, I don't think you're weak."

"I… thanks." I ruffled the top of his head. "Oh, before I forget." I yanked a business card from my back pocket. "I asked around, and here's a Russian tutor so you can continue your lessons. He's located in Boulder, and your first ten lessons are paid for. Call him."

"Wow!" He tossed his arms around my neck. "Thanks."

"Man, when did you two get so sappy?" Maddie laughed, leading Gabe into the room by the hand.

"Says the woman who actually dittoed earlier because she was verklempt." I got off the couch.

"Whatevs." Maddie threaded an arm around Gabe, resting her head against his chest. "We're heading out."

"Don't let the door hit you on the way out." Allen stood and gave me a high five.

Maddie circled a finger in the air. "I'm not liking this turn of events. You two being the funny ones."

"Get used to it," Allen and I said in unison.

Sarah entered with Freddie on her hip. "Get used to what?"

"Nothing," Allen and I spoke at the same time again.

"A sea change, Sarah. A sea change." Maddie hugged Sarah goodbye, kissed Fred's head, and then wrapped her arms around me briefly.

When Maddie and Gabe left, Sarah asked, "Can you get Ollie? It's way past their bedtimes."

"Of course." I turned to Allen, "Tell Bailey it's safe to come back."

In the nursery, Sarah placed Freddie in his crib. I followed suit with the already sleeping Ollie. After kissing each one on the head, she switched off the light.

In the hallway, she whispered, "Is everything okay between you and Allen?"

"All quiet on the Western—"

She kissed me. "We need to get you a different phrase. One that doesn't involve war."

"How about, I absolutely adore you?"

"I think I can live with that one." She kissed me again. "Let's kick out the guests who aren't staying and retreat to the bedroom."

"How come you can say retreat, but I can't—?"

Her lips were on mine in a second.

ACKNOWLEDGMENTS

AUTHOR'S NOTE

Thank you for reading *A Conflicted Woman*. If you enjoyed the novel, please consider leaving a review on Goodreads or Amazon. No matter how long or short, I would very much appreciate your feedback. You can follow me, T. B. Markinson, on Twitter at @IHeartLesfic or email me at tbm@tbmarkinson.com. I would love to know your thoughts.

ABOUT THE AUTHOR

TB Markinson is an American who's recently returned to the US after a seven-year stint in the UK and Ireland. When she isn't writing, she's traveling the world, watching sports on the telly, visiting pubs in New England, or reading. Not necessarily in that order.

Her novels have hit Amazon bestseller lists for lesbian fiction and lesbian romance.

Feel free to visit TB's website (lesbianromancesbytbm.com) to say hello. On the *Lesbians Who Write* weekly podcast, she and Clare Lydon dish about the good, the bad, and the ugly of writing. TB also runs I Heart Lesfic, a place for authors and fans of lesfic to come together to celebrate and chat about lesbian fiction.

Want to learn more about TB. Hop over to her *About* page on her website for the juicy bits. Okay, it won't be all that titillating, but you'll find out more.

Printed in Great Britain
by Amazon